Shade noticed the tins on the doors. All six were the same design.

"As if it needed anything to make it more perfect, check out the design on the doors, Sue Ann. Six stars and a moon surrounded by holes I think represent more stars, or lights in the sky. I'm thinking it's the Aurora. How perfect is that?"

He left the pie safe and returned to Sue Ann.

"See, I can kiss you under the Northern Lights whether we're in my cabin or yours. Yep, it's a sign, all right." Shade mocked Betsy, who was always looking for a sign, a good omen for her mom and her, and now for Shade, too. He kissed Sue Ann as Northern Voices began pouring messages over the waves to and from people living in the bush: people keen on living a subsistence lifestyle, providing for self and/or family through living off the natural resources of the wild; people isolated from society by choice just to live on their own terms; and people isolated out of fear of their past creeping up on them. Most were normal honest folks experiencing the best part of Alaska, freedom to be one's self and enjoy the surreal beauty and natural resources of the Last Frontier. Some were loners escaping from hell. And a few were the hell from which others escaped.

Praise for Dr. Sue Clifton

In addition to her novels published at The Wild Rose Press, Inc. and elsewhere, Dr. Sue Clifton has won four first-place awards at the Arkansas Writers' Conference for poems in *THE GULLY PATH*, her first novel.

Under Northern Lights

by

Dr. Sue Clifton

Daughters of Parrish Oaks, Book 2

This is a work of fiction. Names, characters, places, and incidents are either the product of the author's imagination or are used fictitiously, and any resemblance to actual persons living or dead, business establishments, events, or locales, is entirely coincidental.

Under Northern Lights

COPYRIGHT © 2015 by Dr. Sue Clifton

All rights reserved. No part of this book may be used or reproduced in any manner whatsoever without written permission of the author or The Wild Rose Press, Inc. except in the case of brief quotations embodied in critical articles or reviews.
Contact Information: info@thewildrosepress.com

Cover Art by *Kim Mendoza*

The Wild Rose Press, Inc.
PO Box 708
Adams Basin, NY 14410-0708
Visit us at www.thewildrosepress.com

Publishing History
First Mainstream Historical Rose Edition, 2015
Print ISBN 978-1-62830-844-0
Digital ISBN 978-1-62830-845-7

Daughters of Parrish Oaks, Book 2
Published in the United States of America

Dedication

This book is dedicated to the heroes in our lives
who promise to cherish, honor, and protect us,
and to
"Love us forever—and then some."

Acknowledgements

As an author, I encourage my readers to express their own creativity by giving me suggestions to use in whatever book I am writing, through contests announced on my Facebook page. For *UNDER NORTHERN LIGHTS*, I would like to thank Iris Stuart, who named the trapline radio station "Northern Voices." To contest winners Patrice O'Brien and DeAnna Graves, thank you for your wonderful descriptions of the Aurora Borealis, "a giant stage curtain swaying in radiant colors"..."dancing in the night like the most beautiful ballet ever seen."

Dr. Sue

The Heavenly Regions

The ends of the land and sea are bounded by an immense abyss, over which a narrow and dangerous pathway leads to the heavenly regions. The sky is a great dome of hard material arched over the earth. There is a hole in it through which the spirits pass to the true heavens. Only the spirits of those who have died a voluntary or violent death, and the raven, have been over this pathway. The spirits who live there light torches to guide the feet of new arrivals. This is the light of the aurora. They can be seen there feasting and playing football with a walrus skull.

The whistling crackling noise which sometimes accompanies the aurora is the voices of these spirits trying to communicate with the people of the earth. They should always be answered in a whispering voice. Youths and small boys dance to the aurora. The heavenly spirits are called sélamiut, "sky-dwellers," those who live in the sky.

Ernest W. Hawkes, *The Labrador Eskimo*, 1916

Prologue

Alaska
Spring 1983

He shot the pregnant girl first, one deadly shot with a low-caliber bullet between the eyes as she sat on a log looking toward the river. Her head was held back laughing, a good belly laugh shared with her unborn child.

Spring breakup was almost over, but the townspeople still came every day to the landing on the Tekooni River. Children came to play on the mountains of ice pushed to shore by the river torrent breaking free after months of captivity in the frozen north. But this day, the outing turned deadly. Four more would follow the girl; enough to spread terror and trepidation throughout bush Alaska for decades to come.

"A mad man, a drifter who leaves macabre scenes of death and brutality hanging in his wake!"

"A demented marksman who thrives on watching blood and life flow from his victims, especially women, the younger the better."

"A demon hell bent on destroying anyone, or everyone, who crosses his path."

And his all-time favorite:

"A masochistic monster, a huntsman of human beings for thrill kills, getting his kicks through

spreading pandemonium and terror among locals."

The shooter chuckled thinking of the names and descriptions he had been given by the media. In reality, none fit.

Mad man, drifter, demented marksman, monster, demon; all kill for the sake of killing without any aspiration or purpose.

He had laughed loudest when he heard the news commentator refer to him as a "drifter," implying someone of low intelligence, perhaps insane, down on his luck, wandering from place to place, with thoughts of comforts and luxuries overshadowed by his attempt just to survive.

"If only they knew how many degrees from prestigious universities I have; and if they could see my beach house in the Caymans or my villa in Tuscany! All is not as it seems." He had talked to the television set that day while in his hotel room in Billings, one of the many cities where he left his mark.

No. Drifter was certainly not what he was, but it was his favorite disguise.

In his "exercises," as he chose to call them, he was purposeful, driven, and passionate, with one main objective. Fourteen years had been wasted, time checked off while morphing from hired executioner to "model prisoner," all to secure his transfer to a low-security prison. The deal was he was to turn informant for the CIA, an agreement he made without hesitation but with no intention of keeping.

His escape was easily maneuvered while en route to his new prison home; he killed the two guards who escorted him. And now, two years later, he was still free to move from place to place, even state to state or

country to country, always incognito, and always leaving his warning signs for the one man he would trap using the two teenage girls he had just seen in the roadhouse. He had done his homework and knew both girls were important to his target. He would succeed in accomplishing his main purpose for living:
"Retribution!"

Chapter One
Moose Tracks to the Outhouse

Alaska
August 1982

"I know you said 'no more,' but I've got to ask. How much further, Mom?"

"Well, let's see." Sue Ann looked at the mileage gauge. "We've come four thousand miles, give or take a few hundred or so, from Mississippi to Fairbanks; it's one hundred sixty-five miles from Fairbanks to Moose Springs; and we've come forty-five miles since we left Fairbanks, so that would be..." Sue Ann rolled her hand expecting Betsy to do the math.

"Does everything have to be an educational experience?" Betsy straightened in her seat, giving her best teenage smirk. "Okay, forget the miles. Just tell me in minutes how far it is."

"Since I've never been on this road, I have no idea." Sue Ann jerked the steering wheel to the left trying to miss a pothole and hit an even bigger one. "Now I know why the man at the truck stop asked if I had plenty of spare tires when I told him we were headed to Moose Springs. This road is an obstacle course!"

"I'm thinking you should have hit the one directly in your path. It only went to France. The hole you hit ended in Siberia." Betsy leaned up and tried to get a station on the radio, but all she got was static. She twisted the radio dial to off and folded her arms. "I told you we should have gotten a newer truck, at least one in the 1980s and one with a cassette player. How will I hear my music with no radio? And please don't tell me you threw in your eight-track player. How embarrassing!"

Sue Ann looked at her daughter and smiled, knowing Betsy had a severe case of butt fatigue after six long days of riding. She had been excited when they finally loaded up the truck and left Mississippi, but after the first two days, she became moody and restless, a normal teenager. Seeing the Rocky Mountains for the first time put her on another high, and they ended up staying a day and two nights in Red Lodge, Montana and fishing Rock Creek, high up a valley in the beautiful Beartooth Mountains. It was the first time Betsy had caught rainbow trout, and it had proved to be the highlight of the trip even with the magnificent scenery ahead.

But as soon as they hit the prairies of Alberta, Canada, the glum and fidgets set in again. Betsy's mood was off and on until she got her first look at the Canadian Rockies. Sue Ann went out of her way choosing the Rockies route to whet their appetites for mountains, mountains, and more mountains, and they were not disappointed. From Mile 0 at Dawson Creek to Fairbanks, Alaska at Milepost 1422, Betsy alternated between hand-clapping excitement and sullen-lipped impatience.

"You know, Mom, I might be disappointed if the mountains aren't as pretty as Montana or Canada."

Betsy looked at her mother, waiting for a reaction.

"Betsy, Moose Springs is surrounded by a distant mountain range, but the town isn't located in the mountains *per se*. You know what I always tell you."

"The beauty without must start within." Mother and daughter chimed in sync.

"You really should try your hand at writing, Mom. You have an awesome way with words."

"Yes, I probably should. I've been writing since I was a child, but I just keep putting off writing my first novel. Maybe Alaska will inspire me, and those awesome words will seep out of my mind and onto the page."

Both grew quiet as they rode along the last leg of their journey, both looking at the scenery. Sue Ann could only take quick glances for fear of dropping off the edge of the next hole in the Last Frontier's nearly nonexistent infrastructure and ending up back in Mississippi. She finally broke the silence.

"We will be going over a mountain pass on our way, or so Superintendent Walker told me at the job fair. This highway turns left and becomes a treacherous gravel road for the last eighty miles to Moose Springs. From what I heard when I accepted the job, the best scenery and the danger begin at that point." Sue Ann reached for Betsy's hand and squeezed it, getting the smile she was seeking. "Be patient, Betsy. It's an adventure. Remember?"

"And you won't break your promise to get me a sled dog. Right?"

"You know I never break a promise."

A good while after turning left onto the last eighty miles of mostly narrow gravel road, mother and daughter began the climb, and Betsy sat up on the edge of her seat waiting for her first view of the distant mountains.

"There they are!" Betsy yelled and pointed.

"And somewhere beyond those peaks is Mount McKinley, or Denali, as the natives call it, but its peak is usually hidden in the clouds. The best way to see it is like I did when I came to Job Fair in Fairbanks—by airplane."

The truck ground its way to the top of the pass, and Sue Ann pulled over at a lookout point. As soon as Betsy was out of the truck, she pulled out her Kodak and began snapping pictures.

"After I get a paycheck or two and we're settled in, we'll get a really good 35-millimeter camera with a zoom lens. I'm afraid your little camera won't do those beauties justice from here." Sue Ann let Betsy mountain-gaze for a few more minutes and then told her it was time to get back on the road.

"What we really need is a video recorder. Now, that would be awesome!" Betsy added as she pulled herself up into the tall truck.

"Stop!" Betsy yelled a few miles away from the pass.

Sue Ann hit the brakes in a panic and put her hand to her chest.

"What's wrong, Betsy? You scared me to death." Before Sue Ann got an answer, Betsy was out of the truck and running back along the road they had just covered.

Sue Ann hurried to see what had caused Betsy's excitement and found her standing over a dead porcupine on the side of the road.

"You have got to stop yelling, Betsy. It's just a porcupine—a dead one, at that."

"No, Mom, it's not! You see dead porcupine; I see the best crappie floats ever." Betsy began pulling quills off the carcass while holding her nose with the other hand. "I think he's been here a while, but we can't let these quills go to waste. Don't you remember that guy we saw fishing for crappie at Enid Lake with porcupine quill bobbers? He caught one after another, and all because of his quills. With these, you can detect the lightest bite from a fish."

"Betsy, there are no crappie in Alaska." Sue Ann realized her words were having no effect on her daughter and bent over to help get the biggest of the quills. "Okay, but just remember we are fly fishers and not bait bobbers."

"That has to be enough." Sue Ann had her hand full of quills, holding them by the tip, not the end that had been next to the decaying flesh. "Let's get moving. We're burnin' daylight." Sue Ann used her best cowboy accent to get Betsy's attention. "And put those in the back of the truck, please. I don't want that smell in the cab."

Soon the mountain pass turned to hills, and they hit pavement. Sue Ann knew they were coming into Moose Springs.

"I think we're here, daughter." A smile covered Sue Ann's face.

Betsy put one foot under her so she could see better, and the first log cabin appeared.

"Look, Mom! That cabin is so quaint—just like what I imagined we would live in. A true Alaskan cabin, just like I read about in *White Fang*!"

More log cabins appeared, and Betsy waved at everyone she saw in the yards. Every person stopped and stared, but they gave only meager waves, if any.

"Not the friendliest place I've ever been." Betsy sat back and rested her hand in her lap.

In less than a half mile, the trading post/post office came into view.

"I'll stop here. The man who runs the store should have a key to the school and one to our house. His name is Don McElroy." Sue Ann parked the truck, and Betsy beat her to the door that jingled when she opened it.

One person stood at the counter, talking to someone who was out of view, but the man became silent when Sue Ann and Betsy walked in, as if they were the topic of his conversation.

"Hi, I'm Sue Ann Parish, the new principal, and this is my daughter Betsy. I'm looking for Mr. McElroy."

"That would be me." The voice came from the post office that was separated from the store by a wall completely enclosing it. A tall man with short gray hair appeared at the store counter, holding a package. "Here you go, Randall. Will that be all for you?"

"Yep." Randall stood with his package under his arm but did not leave. He continued staring at Sue Ann and Betsy as if sizing them up, his curiosity, or nosiness, obvious.

"The superintendent told me you would have the key to the school and to our housing?" Sue Ann asked, giving both men a smile. Don leaned on the counter. Neither he nor Randall returned the smile, and Sue Ann looked at Betsy, who raised her eyebrows. Several seconds passed without either man saying anything—too much time for sixteen-year-old Betsy.

"Well?" Betsy looked at the men and put her hands on her hips.

"It's okay, Betsy. I'll take it from here." Sue Ann turned back and faced the two men, and this time she was not smiling. "We've come over four thousand miles; we're tired and hungry, and I want the keys I was promised by Superintendent Walker, with directions to the school and my house." Sue Ann held out her hand.

With a little hesitation, Don McElroy reached in the drawer and pulled out a ring with two keys and threw them on the counter. "Straight down the road on the right. Your house is beside the school." With that, both men turned and walked to the woodstove, a coffee-drinking area for locals, although the golden embers were out for a few more weeks, awaiting the return of fall and winter. Sue Ann watched as the men turned their backs on her, and she wondered if she would ever be allowed to sit in the conversation pit. She was doubtful and didn't know if this was something she cared about doing anyway.

"Thank you," Sue Ann offered in the least sincere tone she could muster.

"I hope everybody is not like those two. The challenge to living in Alaska might be getting people to acknowledge you." Sue Ann started the truck and threw it in gear. "I guess the welcome wagon went out of business."

Betsy rolled her window down and looked back at the trading post. "Look, Mom. They're peeking out the window at us." Betsy rolled down her window, hung her head out, and threw up her hand giving a huge sarcastic wave and grin. The curtain dropped, and the two hard heads disappeared.

"Must have a problem with strangers." Sue Ann shifted gears as she left the store but never made it through all the gears before Betsy gave a yell.

"There it is!"

The school was large for a one-room school and sat high off the ground. The sign out front, held up by a carved moose, read "Moose Springs School."

"Cute." Sue Ann and Betsy responded in sync and did a pinky wish before getting out of the truck.

Betsy beat her mom out and rushed to the other side of the school.

"Oh, no! Say it ain't so!"

"What is it, Betsy?" Sue Ann hurried to see what Betsy had found, and they both stood with mouths gaping.

A dilapidated brown trailer stared back at them. One shutter hung off the front window, and the other shutter had fallen off completely and was propped against the trailer. Several windows were broken. The faded brown rectangle looked as if it had sunk into the permafrost on one corner, or perhaps it was because of the weight of the old tires that covered the front end of the roof like anchors trying to keep the mobile home from going "mobile."

"So much for my log cabin in Alaska." Betsy left her mother and headed to the trailer door on the side. As she started up the wobbly steps, her right foot went through one of the boards. After pulling her foot out and balancing on the somewhat good side, she reached up to open the door.

"Wait, Betsy, here's the…" Sue Ann watched as

Betsy disappeared inside the trailer. "Key."

Before Sue Ann could get to the steps, Betsy was out and stomping back toward the truck with both arms swinging in dramatic annoyance.

"Where are you going, Betsy?" Sue Ann stared as her daughter opened the truck door.

"Mississippi!" Betsy hurled herself into the truck and slammed the door, propping her elbow on the open window.

Sue Ann was careful not to step in the hole Betsy had left and was even more careful opening the door. Balancing on the good side of the top step, she took a deep breath, preparing for the worst before stepping inside. The worst was what she got.

The trailer looked like generations of rats had taken over, and the smell almost knocked Sue Ann off the step where she stood surveying the disaster from a distance. Gingerly, she placed one foot inside, and then another, but went only a few feet before pulling her collar over her nose. Walking to the refrigerator, she pulled open the door and jumped back half expecting a rat to jump out. The refrigerator was empty except for black mold big enough and dark enough to eat the trailer if left unfettered. Judging from that and the condition of the bare light bulb hanging from the ceiling, the electricity had been off for a long time. As she pondered the refrigerator, Sue Ann heard a vehicle pull up out front and a door slam.

"Hi, young lady. You must be Betsy." The man's voice was loud but raspy.

Before Sue Ann could get back outside, Betsy and the visitor came through the door of the trailer.

"Hello, Dr. Parish. I'm Jake Masterson."

Jake held out his hand to Sue Ann. The visitor had a scruffy gray beard and hair that hung to his collar under a worn cap. His light eyes twinkled as he smiled at her, and Sue Ann immediately liked this man. She took Jake's hand and gave it a hearty shake.

"Pleased to meet you. It's nice to see a friendly face." Sue Ann emphasized the word "friendly."

"Don called me and told me you were here, but I'm sure you did not get the greeting you expected. The store is not the best place for a first stop if you want a proper welcome, but you'll find people open up to you the longer you stay. Folks from the lower forty-eight don't usually stay long, so the locals sit back, watch, and wait. No need hurrying to make ties until you see if they're worth the binding." Jake looked around and let his eyes rest on the open refrigerator door.

"I guess you're a bit overwhelmed with your new accommodations, huh?" Jake grinned and shook his head. "This trailer should be hauled to the dump, and that's saying something for the bush, where we don't throw anything away. In fact, if you need anything for your house, other than a new house, check out the Moose Springs Mall first." Jake looked at Betsy, knowing this would get a reaction.

"Did you say mall?" Betsy perked up, but it was short-lived.

"The dump. If anybody takes something to the dump like furniture or appliances, they set it in the mall part so others can take it if they need it. You passed the dump on your way in. You'll see what I mean after you stay a while."

"The dump? Mom, you are *not* hearing this!" Shaking her head, Betsy overemphasized the word "not" and folded her arms.

"I've been telling the local school board for years better housing is needed, but every once in a while we actually get a principal who tries to clean it up a little and live in it, since it's free, and the board puts new housing on hold. Of course, those principals are usually the ones who don't stay, or more likely get run off for not giving a damn." Jake looked at Betsy, who was holding her nose. "I'd say, from the look on this pretty young lady's face, that will not be the case this time."

"What other options do I have, Mr. Masterson?"

"Please. Call me Jake."

"Thank you, Jake, and call me Sue Ann." Sue Ann looked at Betsy, whose face had taken on dismal disbelief. Placing her hopes in Jake, Sue Ann said, "Now, back to those options."

"If you don't mind riding in a truck that smells like sled dogs, I can show you some places that are for rent. They might be more to your liking." Jake glanced at Betsy, who was nodding her head in agreement to the ride while harboring a definite twinkle in her eyes at the mention of sled dogs.

"Will we all fit?" Sue Ann peered out the door at the truck with its bed stacked high with dog boxes on top of dog boxes.

"Sure. We can all squeeze in the cab. Neither of you are big as a minute."

The real adventure began as Jake showed them the available options.

"I hope you know there's no indoor plumbing in any of the cabins I'm showing you, but each one does have an outhouse. The locals fill up water buckets from the community well for household use."

"Yes, we were prepared for that. I was told the school has showers we can use," Sue Ann offered.

"That's right." Jake looked at Betsy, who was sitting in the middle. "Are you okay with washing those pretty long blonde curls in the school showers, Betsy?"

"Yes, sir. Just so I have access to a shower, I'm good."

"Yes, sir? You really are from the South, aren't you?" Jake asked without looking at Betsy as he dodged a pothole in the road.

"Yes, sir," Betsy repeated, her extra emphasis on "sir" making Jake laugh.

"Don't worry, Jake. It's not a requirement I'll be making for students." Sue Ann cut her eyes at Jake to see his reaction. "When in Rome…"

"Learning a little respect for their elders wouldn't hurt any kids, but that's your decision."

Most of the cabins Jake showed them needed a lot of work and were tiny. Betsy showed no signs of interest in the first two.

Jake turned into a wooded area with cabins spread all through. Betsy sat up on the edge of her seat and smiled her approval.

"I'll warn you. This area is pretty, but they don't call it Mosquito Acres for nothing. But then, the whole state could have been named Mosquito Acres."

"I feel like I'm really in Alaska now." Betsy's gaze devoured each log cabin as they passed. "Oh, Mom, look!" Jake stopped so Betsy and Sue Ann could get a good look at the little rustic two-story cabin with a For Sale sign out front. "This is the one, Mom! Our Alaskan cabin!" Betsy began pushing on her mom to get out.

"It won't hurt to look, Sue Ann. It's old and needs

some work, especially a little roof patching, but it beats the heck out of the trailer."

Jake parked and led the two down the path to the cabin. The door was not locked and had an old timey, rustic wooden latch that had to be lifted to open the door.

Inside, the cabin's real charm could still be detected through years of neglect, dirt, and lack of appreciation. With each step they took, mother and daughter smiled, reading each other's mind. Even with all the work needed, especially a good cleaning, Sue Ann and Betsy could see the potential. Beautiful natural wood cabinets greeted them in the small kitchen, and Sue Ann was surprised to see a sink with a faucet. She gave Jake a questioning look, and he opened the doors under the sink to disclose a plastic bucket ready to be used for a drain.

"Just in case you want to pretend you have running water," Jake explained with a big grin.

A fairly new—as in fifteen years old—stove looked sufficient, as did the ancient refrigerator, the "icebox" from Sue Ann's childhood.

"My mother had an icebox just like this when I was a kid." Sue Ann opened the door and was surprised to see it fairly clean and without mold.

"You mean you have to put ice in it for it to cool?" Betsy asked, peeking her head in the refrigerator.

"No. It's electric. That's just what the older generation called a refrigerator back then."

Sue Ann walked to the eating area, which was raised on a platform by a few inches, like a separate dining nook. The table and benches were also handmade out of the same wood as the kitchen cabinets, with their natural patina calling to Sue Ann's love of primitive furniture. She ran her hand over the table and noticed a set of initials carved in one spot. Jake led the way to the sitting area in the large main room with a big black woodstove for heat. Old, dirty carpet that looked to be from the same era as the icebox covered the floors other than the eating nook.

"The walls are nice," Sue Ann added. "I'm glad they're wood. Goes well with the log exterior walls.

Betsy headed for the stairs, and Sue Ann and Jake followed. Upstairs held two bedrooms. A small vestibule with a closet separated the two rooms. The bed in the master bedroom had log bedposts, with planed wood used for the rest, including drawers underneath the bed. A small window with a window seat looked out through spruce, aspen, and birch trees.

"Mom, come here! You have to see my bedroom."

Sue Ann turned her head and smiled at Jake.

In the other bedroom stood bunk beds also made out of logs, and under the large window was a long rustic window seat with storage beneath.

"Can't you just see this with bright, fluffy cushions where I can sit and read, or write? And look at these beds!" Betsy picked up one corner of a mattress to peek under it, and a mouse jumped out. She screamed and ran behind her mom, while Jake bent double laughing.

"Don't worry, Betsy." Sue Ann spoke through her laughter. "We brought new mattresses. Remember?"

When they got back downstairs, Betsy gazed out the big windows on the back into the forest that could be her back yard.

"Wow! I think this is the one, Mom. We can buy a cabin instead of renting, and it will be all ours and we can stay forever."

"Hold on, business manager. I think we better hear the price first." Sue Ann looked at Jake. "Do you think the owner would consider renting, maybe rent with the option to buy?"

"I have no doubt about it. The owner is a good friend of mine but doesn't live here anymore, and it's been for sale for a couple of years. The longer it's empty, the more it's going down in value and the less he'll get for it." Jake smiled at Betsy. "You want to see the bathroom?"

"I thought you said it didn't have plumbing?" Betsy gave Jake a puzzled look.

"Well, just follow me." Jake beckoned with his hand as he led them out the door.

Jake headed down a path to the side of the cabin with Sue Ann right beside him while Betsy walked slowly, taking in every aspect of the yard, cabin, and woods. Just before they reached the woods surrounding the property, Betsy squealed.

Sue Ann and Jake turned to see Betsy on her knees and hands looking under the porch attached to the end of the cabin.

"You are not going to believe what I see under the cabin!"

Before Sue Ann could stop her adventurous daughter, Betsy disappeared under the porch. Sue Ann and Jake hurried to see where Betsy had gone and saw her butt backing out. She reappeared inch-by-inch, coming out much more slowly than she had crawled under, and when she did reemerge, she had something tucked under her left arm, something she was being very careful not to damage.

Betsy held the object up for her mother to take so she could stand.

"Isn't it beautiful, Mom?" Betsy stood wiping the dirt off her jeans knees. It's just like the three others you bought on our way up, but this one is in a little worse shape."

Sue Ann turned the fishing basket over in her hands and raised the lid wrapped in hard, worn leather trim.

"Oh, my! It is beautiful and looks like it was used by someone who loved fly fishing as much as you and I do, Betsy." Sue Ann gave it to Jake since it belonged to the owner of the cabin. Jake took it and scrutinized it like Sue Ann had done.

"Yep. It's old, all right, and I know who owned it originally. Old Sawyer built this cabin, oh, must have been seventy or eighty years ago, so he'd have a place in town to come to when he wasn't working his gold mine, or when he needed to come to town for supplies..." Jake cocked his head toward Betsy. "Or his monthly bath. He was an avid fly fisher but mostly to add to his diet along with moose and bear. He liked the little stream trout he could catch, preferring them to the salmon and northern pike from the Tekooni River. When I was just a boy, I'd see him walking through town with this creel full of trout slung across his chest and over one shoulder."

Jake tucked the creel under his arm and smiled.

"Yep, it's a sign!" Betsy hooked her arm through her mother's as they headed down the path.

A tall tower-like structure stood to one side of the path, and an outhouse sat farther back.

"What's that tall thing?" Betsy asked, moving

ahead of Jake and her mother.

"It's a cache, where the old sourdough kept his game meat in the winter since he didn't have a freezer. You know—Old Sawyer. Actually, he didn't have electricity back then." Jake continued down the path.

"Old sourdough? I take it you're not talking about bread?" Betsy asked.

"Nope. A sourdough is someone who's been in Alaska for a long time, kind of like me. Now you, Miss Betsy, would be a *cheechako*, a newcomer." Jake continued down the path and stopped in front of a small, rustic shed with a slanted tin roof.

"And back here is that bathroom I promised you." Jake smiled and pushed the door open. "And it's been updated."

Betsy walked to the outhouse but did not look inside. Her eyes were glued to the ground as she circled in front of the outhouse. With eyes still lowered, she continued a little ways into the woods before retracing her steps to the front of the outhouse.

"Now this is something!" Sue Ann stood peering into the outhouse. "Look, Betsy, it's a two-seater! And it even has a little shelf filled with books." Sue Ann held up a chewed copy of *Tisha* by Robert Specht. "And look, my favorite Alaskan book about Anne Hobbs, a young teacher who came to Alaska to teach in the 1920s. Good thing I've got my own copy, since the mice have done a number on this one." Sue Anne placed the book back on the shelf.

"One question, Jake, and be very truthful, because this could be the deal breaker." Betsy squatted down in front of the outhouse, still staring at the ground.

"I'm always truthful. Shoot." Jake grinned as if he

already knew the question Betsy would ask.

"What kind of really big animal, or animals, made all these tracks? The ground is covered in them."

Sue Ann and Jake walked over to get a closer look at the myriad of footprints.

"Well, there could be a bear track or two mixed in, but for the most part, those are moose tracks, Betsy."

"Moose tracks? For real?" Betsy looked up at Jake but did not leave her position close to the ground.

"For real," Jake answered.

Betsy stood up and walked to her mom with a grin the size of the forty-ninth state and put her arm around her mom's shoulder.

"We'll take it." Mother and daughter responded in synchrony.

Jake handed the creel to Sue Ann.

"Welcome to Alaska!"

Chapter Two
Moose Springs Mall

Sue Ann and Betsy got to know the school well in the next three days, since they chose to bunk there with sleeping bags while they got the cabin cleaned and ready to occupy. The price of the cabin, a mere $12,000 after a little bargaining by Sue Ann, cinched the decision to buy. After an affordable down payment, the balance would be paid in monthly installments like rent, interest free. Jake said he knew someone who could patch the roof, and as soon as he came into town, he'd send him over.

The school was only eight years old and had replaced a one-room log structure that became too small once the road to Moose Springs was improved and a few new families moved to town. Also, some of the gold mining operations had reopened for a couple of years. It was not clear how the fifty-six year-round residents made a living since gold mining had shut down now, but the school was one source of employment for several people. On the second day in town, people began dropping by the cabin to introduce themselves, and Sue Ann felt sorry she had misjudged the townspeople. Some seemed a little aloof but still made the effort to come by. She didn't care if they came out of curiosity or for what reason, just so they came.

"Well, not everybody is like Don and Randall, but it is not Mississippi, the hospitality state, and that's not a bad thing. A teacher new to Bartonville once told me that everyone in Mississippi is friendly but no one is your friend. I tried to make sure I was a 'friend' after that."

"That's because everybody in Mississippi works long hours, goes home, eats supper, and watches television until they go to bed at the first sign of dark, getting ready to do it all over again the next morning. You and Elizabeth are best friends, Mom, and that's different. You two actually talk and do things, go places, or just sit on your porches and talk about things you want to do." Betsy smiled. "But my mom took a leap of faith, and here we are in Alaska." Betsy spread her hands as if to encircle the cabin. "But I do miss Annie. She will always be my best friend, no matter how far apart we are."

Sue Ann became contemplative, remembering her conversation with Elizabeth not so long ago. They had been sitting on the front porch of Parrish Oaks, Sue Ann's parents' home left in their youngest daughter's care when they moved to southern Mississippi. Sue Ann and Elizabeth watched their girls cheerlead under the historic old oaks that day and were in a good mood until Sue Ann broke the news she had been harboring for days. She and Betsy were moving to Alaska when school was out, and Sue Ann knew this would upset her dear friend. Elizabeth was shocked and tried her best to change her friend's mind. In her mind, Sue Ann could hear Elizabeth's words:

Think this through, Sue Ann. What about Betsy? Do you think she'll be willing to give up Annie and

Parrish Oaks? And all she and Annie have talked about is being cheerleaders together in high school. To think, they have always gone to school together even though they were in different grades, something history did not allow us to do, being from so-called different races. Annie will be devastated to lose her best friend. I don't want you to chase ghosts, but I don't want you to run away from them, either, especially not to the end of the world—the frozen end, at that.

Sue Ann had not heeded her best friend's warning and hoped she would not regret it. She needed a complete new start now that Betsy was old enough for a challenge. All Betsy's life, Sue Ann had mourned the loss of her child's father through his abandonment and had wallowed in guilt for being an unwed mother living a lie. She had lived with the fabricated name Parish so long she often caught herself believing the story of her pretend marriage. Alaska was to be her promised land, but sometimes she wasn't sure she'd made the right decision, taking Betsy away from the comforts of home, friends, and their rich southern culture. As Sue Ann sat on the side porch of her cabin, going over again in her mind why she was here, she prayed. *Lord, please let this be the right move for Betsy and me. I want this to be a good experience for my daughter, one she will cherish and one that will make her a strong, independent person as an adult. If you can find it in your heart, please let us both find happiness and contentment, even if it's just for a short time.*

Sue Ann and Betsy spent the next few days tearing up carpet, scrubbing the thick wood floors they had found underneath, and unloading the truck holding the few household pieces they had brought. Not having running water proved to be a hassle but was something she and Betsy accepted and chose not to consider a burden.

After purchasing two large aluminum garbage cans at the Trading Post and four five-gallon water cans, the Alaskan water system was in place. Every few days, she and Betsy would go to the community water well and fill the cans as full as they could carry them—or "tote" them as Betsy liked to say, trying to stay with her southern roots. Then they would empty the water into the new sanitized garbage cans. The water supply lasted several days, with rationing.

"You know, Mom, Alaska is a good thing," Betsy mumbled through a mouthful of toothpaste. "Think of the water we're conserving." Betsy took the toothbrush out of her mouth. "Did you know I brush my teeth with only a half glass of water? Used to, I'd leave the water running in the sink."

"Yes, and I am so proud of you for dealing with all of this and staying positive. And if we decide to leave Alaska, we will take what we've learned about conservation with us."

Betsy and Sue Ann walked from room to room admiring their little piece of Alaska. The wood floors, protected by layers of raunchy carpet, turned out to be beautiful with the help of bleach, strong scrub brushes, gallons of water, and a can of varnish bought at the store. Sue Ann had even sneaked in some late-night work to make cushions for Betsy's reading window.

"This cabin is bigger than it appears from the outside. The downstairs looks pretty empty with just the two chairs we brought and the TV and table, but we did the best we could with the space in the truck." Sue Ann had collapsed in one of the easy chairs and was wishing for the comfortable sofa she had left in Parish Oaks.

"But the beds are really nice—well, now that the dump has the old mattresses and our new ones are on the beds. I think we will have the cabin looking spiffy in no time, and I love my bedroom. I can't believe you stayed up the other night and made the cushions for the window seat, Mom."

"You've taken this move like a trooper and deserved a surprise. I'm just glad I brought that box full of fabric, extra pillows, and Mama's old sewing machine that I stuffed in at the last minute."

Betsy moved to the big window and stared into the woods. "I hope some of the high school students will come by before we start school. You said there are six students in grades seven through twelve. How exactly will that work, Mom, having so many different grades in the same room?"

"I'm not sure, but Helen, the other teacher, will be coming back into town in a week, and she'll tell me how they've done it in the past. We'll have everything set up before school starts. I know there's a part-time teacher's assistant who helps with the elementary students. You know, this school, even though it's small, is considered one of the best in the state academically, and did you see all those new Apple computers?" Sue Ann noticed Betsy had become quiet. "Are you missing your old friends, Betsy?"

"Annie, mostly, but I'll be okay. Besides, I'll have my sled dog soon."

"I talked to Jake about one of his malamute puppies. He runs one of the best kennels in the state. People come from all over to buy his dogs, but they are very expensive, Betsy."

"Mom, you promised!" Betsy plopped down in the other chair and crossed her arms.

"I know, sweetie, and some way, some how, you will have your sled dog, but it might not be one of Jake's, and it probably won't be right away, after making the down payment on the cabin. Jake and his wife Bernice invited us out for dinner one night this week. Jake wants to show you the kennels. He has a litter of pups that will be ready to leave their mom soon. They're already sold, but he says plenty more are on their way. You'll have to be patient, Betsy. I can only do what I can do." Sue Ann changed the subject. "I tell you what. Let's run the last of the old carpet out to the dump, come back and get all cleaned up and dressed up, meaning our best jeans, and go to dinner at the Roadhouse. I've wanted to go there ever since I read it's one of the oldest in Alaska. It was built at the turn of the century." Sue Ann was surprised when Betsy jumped up and pulled her out of her chair.

"And do our hair. Wear your hair down, Mama, instead of in a braid." Betsy put her arm around her mother. "I think we should let our curls go wild and be lookalikes again."

"That's a deal." Sue Ann smiled, loving when Betsy regressed to her southern upbringing and called her "Mama." She thought about how everyone said she and Betsy looked like sisters instead of mother and daughter. Betsy was born when Sue Ann was barely twenty-one; Sue Ann did not feel like she was in her late thirties and certainly did not want to look it.

"Okay, let's load that old carpet, so we can make ourselves beautiful. I just might even put a little makeup on tonight—or not." Sue Ann grabbed the truck keys and headed out the door with Betsy right behind her.

As they bounced their way over the rough dirt road leading to the garbage dump, Betsy started making a loud, one-note humming sound with her mouth open, so she could hear her voice "yodel" with each bump. Sue Ann smiled at how childlike her teenage daughter could be, something Sue Ann hoped she would always be at times.

When they reached the huge pit where they would unload the old carpet, something caught Sue Ann's eye over by the old appliances at the "Mall" as Jake called it. Betsy turned to see what her mother was staring at and began shaking her head.

"No way are you taking that old green recliner to our cabin, Mom! It's a dump, not a mall."

"Actually, I'm not looking at the recliner. Well, I am looking at the recliner, but I'm looking more at that brown couch behind it."

"No way! Get it out of your head, Mom. No telling where that came from. It probably has a mouse nest in it." Betsy shivered all over, giving her most disgusted drama act.

After throwing the old carpet in the pit, Sue Ann got in and started the truck but did not head out. Before she could change her mind, or give in to Betsy's pleading, Sue Ann headed for the mall.

"Not bad, actually. Being vinyl, even with all the tears, the cushion stuffing seems okay." Sue Ann put her nose to it and sniffed. "And it doesn't smell. Get in and back the truck over here so we can load it, Betsy. I don't want you forgetting how to drive. You and I both have to get our Alaska driver's licenses, you know."

Betsy did as her mother directed, and just as she knew would happen, the old broken-down brown couch and the green recliner got loaded into the truck.

"How about you driving us home, Betsy? You might as well get used to driving the truck even though you've not quite perfected shifting gears. You won't be smooth with it until you practice."

Betsy got behind the wheel before her mom changed her mind. As they jumped and bounced their way back down the rough dirt road, Betsy offered a comment without looking at her mom.

"Dang, Mom! I hope we don't jostle your new living room suite around too much. I'd hate to scratch it."

Sue Ann glanced at her daughter and noticed the twitch in the corner of her mouth as she tried to hold back her laughter while staring straight ahead. Within seconds, the truck was filled with raucous hooting.

"Dumpster diving! Who'd a thunk it?" Betsy teased.

As they passed the cabins on their way back through Moose Springs, Betsy and her mother waved to everybody outside their cabins, but this time the residents all waved first.

"Guess we're finally home, Betsy." Sue Ann waved to a group of elementary students riding their bikes.

"Yep. Guess so." Betsy replied, keeping her eyes on the lookout for potholes within the "city limits."

Chapter Three
James Dean, Paul Newman, and Sam Elliott

As Sue Ann pulled into the Roadhouse parking lot later, she noticed a motorcycle, a vintage Harley, pulling out and heading down the road. The motorcycle was black and polished to perfection, its chrome reflecting the sun. The driver wore sunglasses and a black leather jacket with the collar turned up, but no helmet, allowing his long hair—as dark and shiny as his motorcycle—to blow in the breeze. Sue Ann was reminded of James Dean, the young movie star she remembered from her childhood, who had died at just twenty-six years of age. She remembered her mother actually crying when she heard the news, something the austere Irene Taylor simply did not do.

While they were enjoying their first meal at the Roadhouse, a woman and her daughter came in and took a seat at a table nearby. The girl looked about Betsy's age. Betsy glanced up from her hamburger and fries and smiled, and was pleased when the girl's face lit into a big grin. Within seconds, the two stood by their table.

"You must be Dr. Parish. I heard you were already in town and had moved into Old Sawyer's cabin. My name is Rose, and I'm your teacher assistant for the younger kids." Rose held out her hand.

"Oh, Rose, I am so pleased to meet you. I have so

many questions about how the school operates. Multi-graded classrooms are new to me." Sue Ann stood, took Rose's hand, and then pulled out a chair for her. "We'd love for you and your daughter to join us, if you'd like."

Rose took off her jacket and sat down by Sue Ann.

"Hi. I'm Betsy." Betsy motioned to the chair beside her, inviting the girl to sit down.

"I'm Lena." Lena pulled her long hair away from her face and threw it behind her as she took her seat. "What grade are you in, Betsy?"

"I'll be starting my junior year. I'm sixteen." Betsy answered. "What about you?"

"This is my last year. I'll turn eighteen in January. I planned to go to Mt. Edgecumbe for my last year, but I changed my mind at the last minute. It's just Mom and me, and I'm just not ready to leave her. Next year will be soon enough, when I'm off to college."

"Yeah, I know what you mean. It's just Mom and me, too."

"What happened to your dad?" Lena asked clasping her hands in front of her. "Oh, I'm sorry. That's getting too personal."

"No, it's fine. He was killed in the Vietnam War before I was born. I never met him." Betsy contemplated asking Lena the same question but decided if she wanted to share this information, she would.

"Mine just left us when I was little. I barely remember him, but what I remember is not good." Lena looked at Betsy's hamburger as the waitress came to the table. "I'll have a burger and fries and a Coke, please."

"Your hair is beautiful, Lena. It's so thick and

shiny, like black velvet."

"I was just about to tell you the same thing. I'm envious of blonde curly hair, but that is not something I could ever have, being Athabascan. You and your mom look just alike with those blonde curls."

"We get that a lot. Thank you. I take it as a compliment," Betsy said. "You're the first Native American I've ever met, Lena. I hope we can be friends."

"If we can't, we're both up a creek. We're the only two girls in the high school this year. That was one of the reasons I wanted to go to Edgecumbe. Couldn't stand being the only girl. You have no idea how happy I am you're here."

Sue Ann and Rose talked through dinner, dessert, and coffee—school talk, and Lena suggested she and Betsy take a walk around the village.

"Don't be gone long, Lena. Thirty minutes at the most, and don't go to the slough. I heard there was a sow and two cubs there yesterday."

Lena rolled her eyes as she and Betsy headed out the door.

"A bear with cubs? Oh, my. That's disconcerting." Sue Ann, with elbows propped on the now empty table clasped her hands and put them under her chin. "And I thought I only had to worry about the moose in my backyard."

"Oh, you should be worried, Sue Ann. Moose are more dangerous than bears, especially if they have a calf."

"Really? I'll be sure and warn Betsy. She is so intrigued with all the moose tracks; I just know she'll go crazy if she actually sees a moose or a bear. I just hope we don't run into either one when we make our treks to the outhouse in the dark, when the short daylight starts."

"Oh, you don't need to do that. Get you a honey bucket."

"A honey bucket?" Sue Ann asked. "Is that some kind of contraption to keep bears away?"

Rose choked on her sip of coffee because she was laughing so hard at Sue Ann's remark. "No one told you about Alaskan honey buckets, huh?"

"Nope. That's a new one. And I thought I'd read everything about Alaska."

"It's just a plastic bucket, usually a five-gallon one, that you use for your toilet so you don't have to go to the outhouse in the dark. You take it out and empty it in the outhouse during daylight. They sell them at the trading post."

Sue Ann stopped by the trading post on the way home and left Betsy in the truck. When she came out, she placed the plastic bucket in the backseat.

"What's that for?" Betsy asked.

"You'll see—later." Sue Ann smiled but offered no more explanation. Her mind was plotting, and the plot involved her dad's old jigsaw, one of the tools in his toolbox that she had brought to Alaska as both a keepsake and for emergency use. Along with the tools came a complete lack of knowledge of how to use them and the determination to learn how if needed.

If I can drive 4000 miles of desolate highway, pull up decades of old carpet and redo the floor underneath, not to mention starting over in a cabin with no running water, all with a sixteen-year-old daughter, I can learn to use a jigsaw.

Sue Ann pulled up in front of her cabin and noticed a man walking around in her yard looking up. The stranger took a few steps backwards toward the truck but kept his eyes focused on the roof. His hair hung to his collar and was dark with a few premature gray streaks that glistened when the late-day sun reflected off it. He wore no cap, which Sue Ann found odd since every other Alaskan man she'd seen had on either a baseball cap or a furry one with ear flaps turned up like they were expecting snow in August. The whole demeanor of this man was different. His jeans were faded but not worn to a frazzle like many she'd seen, and hiking boots replaced the usual work boots, looking somewhat out of place. The only thing about him that looked Alaskan was his red-and-black flannel shirt.

"I wonder what he's doing here," Sue Ann said to Betsy, leaving the truck door open as she walked toward the man. He still did not turn around.

"May I help you with something?" Sue Ann's voice was loud, as if speaking to a deaf person, and she was a little unnerved with the man's continued inspection of her house without acknowledging her presence.

"Yep," he said, without adding context and without looking at Sue Ann. "Bad."

Sue Ann walked up beside the man and stared up at the roof.

"I guess you're here about the roof, huh?"

"Yep," the man repeated as he walked to the back of the cabin, leaving Sue Ann where she stood.

"Now that's a strange one. I better stay with you 'til he leaves." Betsy had joined her mother and watched as the man walked out of sight.

"Nah! Go on in and get back into that book you were reading. I'll be in shortly, as soon as 'Yep' tells me how 'bad' the roof is."

Sue Ann followed the man to the back of the cabin and cupped her hand over her eyes looking up, trying to see what he was seeing.

"How bad is it?" She was hoping for more than two words. She got one.

"Bad."

"Can you be a little more specific? Perhaps more than 'yep' and 'bad'?" Sue Ann realized she sounded rude and began apologizing. "I'm sorry. It's been a long, tiring day, and..." She stopped in mid sentence as the man took a few steps closer, much closer, and turned his face to hers. He was Zeus, tall and muscular but clean-shaven, and his eyes did all the talking, whether in two words or reciting the Declaration of Independence—her independence declared as his thunderbolts hit dead center, radiating through her body and jolting her back to a world of sensing not experienced in seventeen years. Handsome was far too casual as a description for Zeus; this man might have a small vocabulary, but he was beautiful.

"You were saying?" His bedroom eyes, Paul Newman eyes, peered down into her face, cutting through her, making her shiver as if she were inside an iceberg, a pale blue iceberg. His voice was deep, resonant, and sounded as if his words should be spoken through the thick handlebar mustache of Sam Elliott, the sexiest voice in Hollywood. Mesmerized, Sue Ann stood like an ice carving, mouth gaping, unable to look away as he moved even closer, standing inches from her with his gaze fixed on hers.

"You were saying?" He spoke louder and deeper without moving his eyes or offering a smile to ease the effect he had to know he was having on her. Sue Ann shook her head, trying to rejoin the world. Putting one hand to her head and the other on her hip, she looked away, giving herself time to regain control.

"When, how much, and how long will it take?" Her eyes dug into the ground, following the toe of her boot, not wanting to risk looking at him and getting frozen tongue again. She glanced up, wondering why he did not answer, after too many seconds of silence, and met his eyes again.

"What?" he asked, cocking his head and arching his perfect thick brows as if she were asking him when they could go to bed, how much love they could make, and what amount of time she was allowed.

"How much?" Sue Ann repeated more loudly, crossing her arms, but she rephrased it when he still didn't answer. "When can you start, how much will you charge me, and how long will it take to repair the roof?" She gave him her full attention, keeping her eyes on his, needing her questions answered even though her body was screaming, "Lightning CAN strike twice in the same place!"

"Whoa! Don't get your cart before your horse." He turned his head away from her and shook his head. "Damn, I hate clichés. Can't believe I said that." And with that he headed back around the cabin, taking advantage of his height and long stride. He did not stop in the front but headed at a fast gait down the road.

"Wait! Don't leave! I'm sorry if I offended you." Sue Ann had no idea why she was running after a complete stranger and apologizing for something although she didn't know what, but she was sure it had nothing to do with her roof. She stopped behind her truck, trying to catch her breath, and watched as he turned the curve and disappeared behind a clump of bushes. Within seconds, a motorcycle rounded the curve onto the paved part of the road, and Sam Elliott, with Paul Newman eyes never looking back, shapeshifted into James Dean with his leather collar turned up—a "rebel without a cause." As she watched him go, she noticed his personalized tag.

"Raven!" she announced aloud as he roared out of sight.

Chapter Four
Shade Dubois

School was about to begin, and after several days with Helen the elementary teacher/counselor, Hank the custodian/maintenance man, Jean the secretary/bus driver, and Rose the teacher assistant/cook, Sue Ann had everything ready for school. Betsy and Lena helped organize the library and computer lab, and when they set up the twelve computers between the elementary section and the secondary section, the school became a two-room schoolhouse, almost.

Sue Ann was pleased to learn of Helen's expertise in math and science, and the two divided up the high school with Helen teaching those subjects and Sue Ann teaching language arts and social studies for the half day when she was not acting as principal. Rose was hired full time rather than part time to help out with the elementary students, while Helen helped in the high school. Community experts, as they were called, would teach the extracurricular activities such as culture, music, drama, and art.

Sue Ann arrived at school early each morning and stayed late in the afternoons trying to juggle all the different levels and preparations, but she felt good about what she was doing. Betsy, with Lena as her best friend, was thriving and had more time to study and write about the things of particular interest to her.

Everything was self-paced, and Betsy was challenged to excel.

Sue Ann was anxious to get home that Friday after her first week of school and was looking forward to a night alone, to read all night if she wanted, or do anything that suited her, since Betsy was staying at Lena's. But when the tired principal/teacher arrived home, she was shocked to find building materials covering her front yard. Lumber and tin were stacked high on one side, lumber and tin that she had not purchased.

Confused and a little angry, she left the truck door open and hurried over to survey the materials. A thunderous sound of something large coming down startled her, forcing her to step back quickly just before several huge pieces of rotted boards crashed to the ground only inches away. Sue Ann took another step back, her hand on her heart, and tripped over a stump sticking up a few inches, twisting her ankle as she fell. She yelled as a sharp pain cut through her foot and shot up her leg. She held her ankle and rocked as tears filled her eyes.

"My God!" A man's deep voice echoed off the rooftop, and in seconds Zeus was by her side.

"What the hell are you doing here? Of all the stupid things! Didn't you see me throwing those boards off the roof?" He bent down beside Sue Ann, but the damage he had done was far more than physical. He reached to help her up, and she shot him daggers and knocked his hand aside.

"I don't know who you think you are, but you do not have per...permission to be on my cabin roof thr...throwing anything...o...off!" Sue Ann snubbed through pain as she yelled at him. She tried to pull herself up on her good foot but fell back to the ground when another sharp pain hit her.

"Ouch! Damn it to hell!" Getting an adrenaline rush from the pain, she let out a repertoire of swear words. Trying to stand again, she held on to a small tree close by and pulled herself upright this time. Wiping her runny nose on her sleeve, she faced the would-be carpenter and lit into him like a small tornado.

"Who the hell are you? First you try to kill me, and then you have the audacity to curse me in my own yard like...like it's my fault! Get off my property before I call the...the...whoever the hell you call in the Alaska bush!" Doubling her fists and giving a loud "grrrrr," she clenched her jaw and took a step toward him, her face emblazoned and her eyes casting spears of fury. But before she got close enough to actually punch him, the pain hit, and she fell flat on her face. Holding her leg and ankle, she rolled on the ground in a fit of swearing, crying, and yelping. As she lay doubled up on the ground, she felt herself being swooped up by the demon carpenter, who carried her to the cabin.

"Put me down!" she yelled, and beat at the man's chest—his bare chest—but it did no good. Finally, knowing he was not heeding her orders, she laid her head against his sweaty skin and succumbed to crying.

He carried Sue Ann like she was a small child, balancing her on one knee as he opened the cabin door and let himself in. Placing her gently in the recliner that had been cleaned and patched until it looked like it came from a thrift shop instead of the dump, he knelt before her and began untying her bootlaces. Sue Ann, trying to stop her tears, pushed his hands away, but the pain was too sharp. She let her head fall back on the chair and winced as he continued taking her boot and sock off.

"Needs ice."

Leaving Sue Ann, he went into the kitchen and came out with a tray of ice and a dishtowel. He beat the aluminum tray on the floor to loosen the ice and dumped the contents into the dishtowel. After tying the ends, he rolled up her jeans leg and held the ice to her ankle, with the ankle propped on his knee, all the time keeping his eyes down. As he held the ice with one hand, the other hand massaged her foot and leg.

The wrap was freezing but helped the pain to subside. Sue Ann was at a loss as to what to do or say. Her eyes were closed, and she did not want to open them, feeling embarrassed, confused, and still angry.

Eventually Sue Ann opened her eyes in tiny slits and peeked at the man who was sitting on the floor holding the towel and massaging her ankle. His shirt was still off, and she found the cure-all for rage. His chest and arms looked unnatural, a good unnatural, as his muscles flexed with the tiniest movement in his upper body. Even though his dark hair hung in his face, he did not push it back as he continued holding the ice in place and rubbing her ankle. Sue Ann's eyes widened. Before she could close her eyes again so he wouldn't see her looking at him, he shot a glance up at her. Glacial blue peered through raven's wings, chilling her, and she shivered from a discomfort not caused by physical pain.

"I'm sorry." His voice was low, deep, and sounded sincere. He was all three—an older James Dean but with the handsome ruggedness and voice of Sam

Elliott, and he definitely had Paul Newman eyes. His words were not forced, but the brevity of them indicated he was uneasy with the scenario and the need to apologize. As soon as he made the remark, he cast his eyes back to Sue Ann's ankle and continued to hold the ice pack tight against her foot.

"You can let go of the towel. The pain is almost gone. I'm sure it's just a bruise." Sue Ann reached for her ankle, ready to take over holding the ice pack, and her hand touched his. He stopped massaging but did not release the towel. Again, he turned his eyes to hers. Her hand lingered on his for a few seconds until she sat back, keeping her eyes fixed on his.

The silence was longer than daylight on the North Slope in summer and lasted until he took the towel away from her ankle and pushed himself back away from her chair. Leaning against the couch, he pulled one knee up, propping a hand on it. Ice blue met emerald green as their matched gazes dove deep without recognized purpose or intent.

"Shade Dubois."

"What?" Sue Ann asked.

"Shade Dubois," he repeated, his voice so rich, deep, and melodramatic it sounded unearthly.

Sue Ann stared at him and cocked her head to one side, unsure as to what should be said next.

"It's who the hell I am." Shade mocked Sue Ann's earlier question and fought to suppress the grin forming at the corners of his mouth. However, it was not possible to contain the twinkle of sapphire blue.

Again silence took over.

"I'm Sue Ann Parish." She, too, answered in a low voice. "And this is my cabin." She spread her hands out as if marking her territory.

"What?" Shade cocked his head to one side as if asking why she was telling him what he already knew.

"It's what the hell I'm doing here." She mocked his earlier question with only a hint of a smile.

"I know." He dropped his head as he moved his side of the conversation back to two words.

"How do you know who I am, Shade Dubois?" Sue Ann rested her foot on the edge of her chair and pulled her sock back on.

"Jake Masterson." Shade watched Sue Ann's every move.

"And you were on my roof because...?" Sue Ann rolled her hand out.

"Jake ordered the lumber and tin and asked me to repair your roof."

"Well, I'll be a monkey's uncle!" Sue Ann looked at the ceiling and mouthed what he had just said, counting on her fingers.

"What?" Shade asked again.

"You said thirteen words without so much as a pause. It's a record for you, isn't it—not counting the way you cursed me, blaming me for...for...this?" Sue Ann pointed to her ankle and waited for Shade's answer, which did not come quickly.

"I'm sorry about that. I was mad at myself for not looking before I threw the boards down, and I guess I took it out on you. I was making so much noise I didn't hear your truck pull in." He paused for a few seconds, casting his eyes down at her foot. "I guess I'm not much of a talker."

"And why is that, Shade Dubois?" Sue Ann asked.

"It's a long story. I don't do well with women,

least not beautiful women, and I don't give much attention to the other kind." Again, his eyes cut through hers.

"Well, hot damn!" Sue Ann startled him as she belted out her reply. "Let me ball my hair up on top of my head and wash this little bit of makeup off. You're a dangerous man to be around, Shade Dubois. It would behoove me to do everything possible to keep your attention off me." As hard as she tried, Sue Ann could not help smiling.

"Wouldn't do any good." Shade stood and headed for the door.

"What?" The one-word question seemed to be a game they were playing, and it was Sue Ann's turn.

"Wouldn't do any good." He paused, cocking his head to one side. "I've already seen you with your hair down, madder than hell, and I've even been hit by you, although your punch needs work. And I've taken off your toy boot and massaged your sexy little foot." He paused again, looking off to the side for a few seconds before turning his gaze back to Sue Ann. He took a few steps back toward her. She stood holding her hurt foot up while balancing on the other, hands on hips, looking up at him. With his face a few inches from hers, he continued.

"What woman in the bush paints her toenails bright red, especially with winter coming on, unless she's purposely trying to kill a man who's been alone way too long?" He headed toward the door again but stopped. "And…" He did not finish what he was about to say but reached for the cabin door latch.

"And what?" Sue Ann acted intrigued by Shade's sudden outpouring of words and just as quickly with his seeming loss of words.

"And it's been a damn long time since I wanted to kiss any woman, not that the opportunities haven't been thrown at me, but I'm wanting to right now—whether you have lipstick on or not." With those words, he left the cabin.

Sue Ann limped to the window and watched as he picked up his shirt and headed down the road. He put his shirt on but did not button it and, just like before, retrieved his Harley from behind the clump of trees and roared away with his shirt and his thick black hair keeping time with each other as they flapped in the breeze.

Chapter Five
Old Green and the Inside Outhouse

Every day, Sue Ann expected to see Shade working on her roof when she got home from school, but she was unrewarded. The evidence of his work was there, but the mysterious Shade Dubois was not. For the life of her, she could not get him out of her head: the way he looked with his shirt off; his hair blowing as he sped away on his Harley; the hypnotizing, deep sexy voice and uncanny good looks; and those cold blue eyes that could cast a spell on any woman, especially one whose last "roll" was with the man who abandoned her a daughter's lifetime ago.

Jake Masterson had proven to be a godsend for Sue Ann. With some finagling and by sending the school board on a good old-fashioned guilt trip, he managed to get them to pay for the materials for Sue Ann's cabin roof since the housing promised was not livable. Jake had said he'd get someone to repair the roof, and Shade was that someone.

Days and nights were cool, and the leaves were doing their fast fall color metamorphosis, making many tourists hurry up from Fairbanks before they missed the show. The hardwoods from the South were absent in the far north, but were not missed as birch and aspen brightened the surrounding landscape in yellow and orange hues. The low tundra bushes looked like miles and miles of mystical Biblical burning bushes.

With the days growing shorter by the minute, Sue Ann knew it was time to get out her dad's old toolbox and see if she could manage the honey bucket project. She chose a three-day weekend, when Betsy had gone to Fairbanks with Lena and Rose, to get her surprise project underway. First thing Friday morning, she set to work. With scraps of lumber salvaged from the roof project, Sue Ann put the jigsaw to the test. She had spent Thursday night memorizing the old manual still in the box and practicing with the jigsaw.

By the end of the day, she had turned the upstairs closet in the vestibule into an inside outhouse complete with three boards forming a "Z" for the outside door and further enhanced with a half moon patterned after the one on the door on the outside outhouse. Inside, she made a box-type seat with a lid that would open for easy removal of the plastic bucket to be emptied each day.

But the best part of the inside outhouse was another "bargain" from Moose Springs Mall, a proper commode seat with lid intact. Sue Ann knew the toilet was one that had been replaced in the Roadhouse. With a thick set of rubber gloves, a cleansing solution that the school janitor swore "could kill any germs plus your eyesight if you weren't careful," and the conviction she could do this without throwing up her guts, Sue Ann scoured the old seat until it sparkled. It was perfect except for two small cracks. With two screws, she attached the seat to the bench top where she had cut an almost perfect hole, and *Voila*—all the comforts of home! With the addition of Pine Sol and water, the honey bucket was the perfect answer for never having to go to the outhouse again, except to empty the honey bucket.

By late Friday afternoon, several from the school and community had come by to see how the project was coming along and were surprised to see it finished. Jake was first, and not only did he admire the concept and the project, but he was thrilled at the bargains Sue Ann had found at Moose Springs Mall, especially one piece he recognized.

"I told Bernice that was a perfectly good recliner, but she insisted on getting me a leather one that is cold and hard. But that was two years ago. Wonder where my old chair has been since we took it to the Mall."

By the end of the day, Jake's question was answered.

One of the parents, Delaney Scott, said her husband got it as soon as Jake put it out at the Mall, but she'd always draped a cover over it so Jake wouldn't recognize it when he visited.

"Jake loved that old chair, and we didn't have the heart to tell him how much Jack was enjoying it. Our oldest daughter gave her daddy a bigger one she was getting rid of in Fairbanks, so we took Old Green back to the Mall." Delaney rubbed the arms on the recliner as she sat in it and couldn't wait to get home and tell her husband where Old Green was now.

Next came Hank, who said he'd used it for a while but decided he liked his old one better even if it did have a few more holes in it. When he told Rose he was taking it back to the dump, Rose retrieved it for a neighbor of hers who was old and didn't leave the house anymore. When he passed away, his kids returned Old Green to the Mall, where it promptly disappeared for a few months, probably with a trapper who lived far out in the bush.

The last person to comment on Old Green was Don McElroy, who came by not to visit but to bring a package Sue Ann had ordered, or so he said. When he saw Old Green sitting in Sue Ann's living room, his real reason for coming was disclosed.

"So you're the one who beat me to Old Green." Then he offered Sue Ann twenty dollars for it. She declined.

Sue Ann had thought about making a slipcover for Old Green out of a floral fabric found in her fabric box from Mississippi, but after hearing of all the adventures the chair had been on, she decided it should remain Old Green. The chair was so comfortable she and Betsy fought over it every night, with Sue Ann constantly saying, "Remember, dear daughter, you didn't want anything that came from the dump."

It seemed the parade of curious and interested persons was over, and Sue Ann headed to the school for a much-needed shower. A few minutes later, with her hair tied in a towel like a turban and in her oldest, most faded but softest sweats, she left the school and headed home.

And there he was, sitting on her porch at the end of the cabin. It was almost dark, and the moonlight played off the few but pronounced silver streaks in his hair, reminding her of the sparklers she always got in her Christmas stocking as a kid. But it was a different kind of fireworks that took over her mind when she saw Shade Dubois. All she could think about was the last thing he had said to her the day he tried to kill her.

"It's been a damn long time since I wanted to kiss any woman, not that the opportunities haven't been

thrown at me, but I'm wanting to right now—whether you have lipstick on or not."

Sue Ann wondered if he'd still want to kiss her looking like Lawrence of Arabia, but there was only one way to find out.

Shade left the porch and headed toward the truck. The closer he got to Sue Ann, the bigger his grin spread. When he got only a few feet away, he stopped and bowed with his hands clasped under his chin.

"You are the most beautiful guru I know, Maharishi Parish."

"Thank you, Sir Charming." Sue Ann nodded in similar fashion. "Come into my home, and I will teach you a better way." Sue Ann headed to the cabin door with Shade laughing behind her.

"And you chose a cold Saturday night, almost a month after trying to kill me, to visit because…?" Sue Ann stopped and added a stick of wood to the stove and then led the way to the sitting area. She took a seat on the couch now completely redone by adding stuffing to the cushions and a bright slipcover made from more of her surplus fabric.

"You have the honor of sitting on Old Green." Sue Ann rolled her hand out toward the Mall find.

"I know this chair. Has Jake seen it?" Shade smiled, admiring the cleaned-up recliner. He picked up the throw pillow made from fabric matching the couch.

"And the hole is so cleverly concealed." Shade complimented.

"Jake was just here this afternoon checking out my carpentry skills. He noticed Old Green right off and had to sit in it."

"Carpentry skills?" Shade frowned. "Surely the

roof isn't leaking?"

"No, my careless carpenter did a fine job on the roof, and my ankle healed quite nicely. Thank you for asking." Sue Ann ran her sentences together in sarcasm and annoyance for his not checking on her.

"I'm sorry, Sue Ann."

"Yes, so you told me the day you walked out and never came back after trying to kill me. I've never even paid you for fixing the roof." Sue Ann folded her arms, her annoyed stance he had seen before.

"Jake didn't tell you?" Shade turned his head sideways, casting a frown up at her. "I had work to finish after I completed your roof and told Jake I would be out of commission for a few weeks."

"No, he didn't tell me, but then I don't talk to Jake about you. As a matter of fact, I haven't discussed you or the accident with anyone, not even my daughter." Sue Ann noticed the astonished look on Shade's face, or perhaps it was disappointment. "I'm fine, Shade. There was really no need." Sue Ann sat still and turned her eyes away from him, discomfited by his stare.

"Do you think you could lose the turban, Sue Ann?" Shade sat on the edge of his chair with his hands clasped. "I was kind of hoping I'd get to see Goldilocks again."

"In a few minutes." Sue Ann ignored the request and tightened the towel, tucking in the end in front, showing a little defiance. "In a few minutes, I'm going up to change into something a little more appropriate for entertaining company—that is, unless you're going to pull another disappearing act on me." Sue Ann watched Shade to see what his reaction would be.

"No. Not this time." Shade continued to stare at the

turban. "So what do you do with all that thick curly hair when it's wet? Doesn't it tangle in that towel?" Shade seemed to be obsessed with Sue Ann's hair and kept his eyes on her, waiting for an answer. "I bet it hurts like hell trying to brush it out."

Sue Ann reached to undo the towel.

"Wait!" Shade held his hands up. "You're not going to ball it up on top of your head, are you?"

"Why? Aren't you afraid you might be tempted to kiss me if I don't look like a schoolmarm?" Sue Ann tilted her head, giving Shade a shy-girl expression over one shoulder. With her knees together and her legs angled in a ladylike pose, she placed her fingertips on her knees, tipped her toes, and batted her eyelids. "But then, I don't have on any makeup this time."

Sue Ann slipped one foot out of her Birkenstocks, pulled her sock off, and held her foot up. "Bashful pink." She wiggled her toes at him, hoping for a reaction. By the look on his face, it worked. With that, she unwrapped the towel, turned her head upside down and began towel-drying her hair. In only seconds, she threw her hair back and then brought it forward in front of her on each side, running her fingers through it, crimping sections with her fingers. A mass of gold curls encircled her head like a halo and fell to her waist.

"Now, if you'll excuse me, I'll go up and change into something less comfortable."

Chapter Six
The Thirty-Seven-Year-Old Virgin

Sue Ann headed for the stairs in her most provocative walk, leaving Shade sitting on Old Green. She could feel his eyes following her.

As she entered her bedroom, she gave a quick glance in the mirror and crimped her hair with her fingers. She started to put on bright red lipstick just for fun but changed her mind. As she headed to her closet, she pulled her sweatshirt over her head and stepped out of her loose sweatpants. Standing in nothing but her bikini panties, she was reaching into the closet for a pair of jeans and a shirt when her bedroom door creaked open.

Shade stood at the half-open door staring at her. His eyes shone like a beacon in the dim light of her bedroom. Sue Ann dropped her eyes and started to cover herself with the shirt she had in her hands but stopped. As he walked toward her, emeralds met sapphires again in a brief flash, and when he stopped directly in front of her, he forced her chin up with his finger so they could look into each other's eyes. He took the shirt from her hand and dropped it on the floor. Placing a hand on either side of her face, his lips played with hers, pulling each one with his, giving her a hint of the slow, romantic foreplay he had in mind. She parted her lips a little and waited. Soon, his mouth covered hers, moving over it in circles, parting her lips with his tongue, and swallowing her mouth with his.

Sue Ann trembled but did not resist. She felt like a thirty-seven-year-old virgin, even though she had a sixteen-year-old daughter. Seventeen lonely years had passed without so much as one heavy petting session at a drive-in movie.

Seventeen years! Heck fire! To think of it, I've not even had a serious dinner date since Betsy's father left me pregnant and unwed at the impressionable and unforgettable age of twenty-one. I am way overdue, and maybe, just maybe, this is it—the culmination of all I've been waiting for!

Sue Ann's thoughts were interrupted as Shade's kiss deepened, and her trembling gave way to a full-fledged quake. When he thrust his tongue in, searching for hers, she thought she would collapse in a pile on top of her sweats—and would have, if he had not had his hands anchored in her hair, holding her mouth steady as he ravaged it. She stood still, her arms straight beside her like she was marching in a band instead of preparing to have sex with the likeness of three movie stars rolled into one beautiful package. She stood waiting, not remembering what to do with her hands.

Shade knew what to do with his hands. First he curled his fingers deeper into her still damp hair and pulled strands full length, letting them sift through his fingers like gold dust. He draped her hair across her breasts, letting the back of his hand linger over each of her small breasts, with each nipple giving notice of his presence.

Shade sat on the edge of her bed and pulled her to him as he cupped her breasts in his hands, caressing each nipple between his fingertips, teasing, until she wrapped her hands around his face and pulled it to hers. Surprising herself, Sue Ann kissed him with a depth almost equal to his kiss. When she pulled her mouth away from his lips, he pulled his sweater over his head, exposing the muscular chest she had never gotten out of her mind after their first physical encounter. Her hands touched his chest, rubbing her fingers over the ridges of his muscles, allowing her fingertips to linger on his nipples. Her body was on fire, and he knew it. Sue Ann, feeling herself growing weak, removed her hands from him and stood with her eyes closed as he gently squeezed her nipples, stretching each one, watching her enjoy his touch.

Mouth soon replaced fingers as he moved down, consuming each breast, teasing, sucking, until her knees almost buckled. He pulled her panties down, letting them drop to the floor, and grabbed her cheeks, gently pulling her to him. He continued caressing her nipples with his lips, covering each one with his mouth as he marked his territory.

She buried her face and hands in his hair, her fingers pulling tight as his lips extended each nipple, getting the last bit of sexual nourishment offered until it wasn't enough. Sue Ann shivered again, and he released her breasts and pulled her onto the bed. He kissed her gently, and she knew, and hoped, he had another tool hidden, waiting for the perfect moment to appear and blow away the years of nothingness.

Shade stared at her.

"God, you're beautiful!" He stood, added his clothes to the pile, and smiled, enjoying her stare as he stroked himself to maximize his manhood for her.

Sue Ann kept her eyes on him, covering his body from the top of his thick dark hair to his glacial eyes peering at her through collar-length hair that almost covered them. His chest had a patch of dark man fur, and his penis protruded from a thick forest of rich, dark pubic curls.

She rolled to her side as he lay beside her on his back, still stroking himself. Placing her hands on his chest, she allowed her hands to explore his magnificent body. Then she moved her face to his and parted his lips with her own while still caressing him, begging for him as she moved against his thigh.

When she stopped, she stretched out on the bed on her back, moving her hips sensually. As Shade took control of foreplay, she feared she would climax too early. Sometimes he stopped and looked down at her, pulling her curls over her breasts and caressing each one as he wrapped it in golden ringlets, as a stay from finishing too soon.

Sue Ann could not take her eyes off his body. He could pose as a live model for sculptors and artists—but, more important, his was the kind of body to take away seventeen years of a woman's longing and loneliness. Sue Ann was eager for whatever Shade would give her and hoped she had not forgotten how to do her part.

He held his weight off with his hands but lay on top of her, rubbing his erection against every inch of her body as she moved beneath him, her breath becoming heavier.

"I thought…you wanted…to kiss me." Sue Ann whispered between breaths.

"Is that what you want?" His mouth devoured hers

but quickly moved down to her breasts and below, stopping to kiss and caress her belly button with his tongue while his fingers worked more magic. Threading her hands through his hair, she stopped him as his mouth replaced fingertips.

"Have to go slow—been a lo…long time."

"How long?" He continued exploring, kissing every part of her body as her hands tightened in his hair. Moving her hands to his face, she pulled his mouth back to her breasts.

"A…very…long…time," she gasped.

Shade entered her gently, knowing he would take her over the edge prematurely, but he didn't care. His would come later. He wanted Sue Ann to enjoy the ecstasy of the moment. He wanted her to enjoy him and never to forget.

"I can't…stop," she whispered, as spasms of pleasure rippled through her body like a tidal wave. She moaned and arched her body upward, meeting his final intense push. He held taut until she crumpled against the pillow.

Shade rolled off her, propped on one elbow, and smiled down, running his fingers over her face. "Was it good, Baby?"

"Good! Such an inadequate word for something so…" She wheezed out the words, still breathless. "Amazing!" Sue Ann sat up and pulled the sheet up over her breasts and was silent for a few long seconds. She turned her head to face him, and he was still smiling at her.

"I'm sorry, Shade. I tried to warn you. In fact, I can't believe how easily I gave in to you. I've become a bit of a prude in my old age and really didn't think I had it in me—the will to actually be a sexual partner, that is. I was afraid I had forgotten what to do. I'm embarrassed and feel more like a sixteen-year-old virgin than a real woman." She turned her face away from his, hoping he couldn't see the moisture filling her eyes.

Shade pulled her back beside him and put his arm around her. He took her face and pulled it to his chest, caressing her cheek with his free hand.

"Sue Ann Parish, I've never made love to a more real woman than you. If you have forgotten, please forget the next time—the one coming up in a few minutes. I'm not going anywhere—unless you want me to, that is. We've got all night." Shade lowered his lips to hers and kissed her with the same passion of a few minutes earlier. She pulled away and stared into his eyes, her hand on his cheek.

"What if I told you Betsy would be home in a little while?"

"I'd call you a liar. I know she's in town with Rose and Lena." He rolled onto his back and pulled Sue Ann's head to his chest, rubbing her back with his hand.

"You checked up on me before coming over here?" She raised her head up and stared, not smiling. "You planned this, didn't you?"

"No, I didn't plan it," he answered in a defensive tone. "Well, maybe I did. But I didn't ask where you were. I saw Betsy with Rose and Lena in Fairbanks before I left this morning. We were eating breakfast at the same little café where we all eat when in town. In fact, I stopped and said 'hello' and asked Betsy how she liked going to school in a one-room schoolhouse."

Shade smiled down at Sue Ann. "She's quite a

young lady—a chip off the..." He paused, not wanting to use the old cliché. "Off her gorgeous principal mother—same blonde curls, eyes the color of the rarest emeralds in any crown jewels, attitudes bigger than the Last Frontier. Wonder where that combination comes from?"

"Attitude? Really? What makes you say that?"

"She asked me how old I am." Shade smiled.

"What?" Sue Ann sat up, forgetting about the cover.

"Let's not start the 'what' game again, Sue Ann. We just had amazing sex—well, you did, but you had some pretty awesome surprises for me, as well. As you said, you 'showed me a better way.' We are well past the 'what' by now. In fact, in just a minute or two, I get mine." He arched his eyebrows and gave her a wink.

"Why did Betsy ask you how old you are?" She ignored his suggestion.

"Your daughter is matchmaking." Shade chuckled through his answer.

"What?" Sue Ann stopped. "Oh, sorry. I just can't believe Betsy asked you that! What did she say was her reason for wanting to know?"

"You want her exact words?" His grin grew bigger.

"I'm afraid to answer, but yes, I do."

"She said, 'Mom looked for you every day while you were working on the roof and was all sad-eyed when you weren't there when she got home from school. She thinks you're a looker, and she's always watching for your Harley, but she doesn't know I know. I can read her.'"

Sue Ann opened her mouth in her best, most shocked expression and laid her head back on the pillow, not bothering to pull the covers up.

"That's not all she said." Shade knew he was getting a rise out of her, and loved it. "Your daughter told me you were all alone this weekend and needed company."

"Well, I don't think she meant in my bed." Sue Ann was not amused and stared at the ceiling as she put her arms behind her head on her pillow.

"I'm forty-two."

"What?"

"There you go again. I said I'm forty-two. Are you okay with an older man? Betsy told me you're thirty-seven, not exactly what I'd call an older woman, especially not after seeing and feeling you in action. I'd say you have retained your youth."

He straddled her, holding his weight off with his knees. He leaned down and covered one of her breasts with his lips and moved his hands up to hold her arms in place over her head. Then he moved his attention to her other breast, twirling his tongue around it, pulling her nipple with his lips.

She felt the warmth coming back in all the right places. This time he could finish business—or not. The night was young, and she felt twenty-one again and very much alive. She'd be embarrassed later, but for now, she wanted to play.

"Yes," Sue Ann wheezed out with no explanation.

"Yes, what?" Shade left her breasts and moved down, letting his mouth find her most sensual spot. She did not stop him this time.

In one quick surprising move, she pushed him over on his back and straddled him, letting her hair fall across his chest as she let her hand guide him inside her. She put her mouth to his breasts, mimicking his earlier moves of kissing, sucking, and stretching each with her lips. Where this came from, she had no clue, but she was either a fast learner or an old lady left behind and trying to make up for lost time in one fell swoop. Moving her face to his, she kissed him, a long, untimed kiss with no beginning and no end as her hips circled with him inside. She felt his erection growing, but he lingered as if afraid he would cause her to climax too early again. Releasing his lips, she looked down into his eyes, her face inches from his as her hips made loops, taking him with her.

"I'm exceedingly okay with an older man." She paused and smiled down, her eyes twinkling. "But only on one condition, Shade."

"Anything, Baby. Just don't stop what you're doing." His eyes took on a dreamy look as if she were the best he'd ever had.

"Don't be gentle this time." She smiled as his eyes changed from dreamy to excited. "I'm way overdue."

He tumbled her onto her back. The man Shade took over as he drove into her, watching her face as if he thought she might change her mind, yet showing there was no backing out for him now.

She wrapped her legs around his hips, pulling him tighter into her as she gasped, moving her hips in synchrony with his thrusts. Her fingernails dug into his back, drawing blood in a rush of crazed passion, adding painful pleasure for him.

"Later" had arrived for Shade. Together, with each holding tight to the other, they reveled in the rapture of newfound pleasure and moaned, each with overdue release.

****

The next morning, Sue Ann awoke to an empty bed.

"No!" She exclaimed under her breath as she grabbed a robe from her closet. As she rushed down the stairs, her heart pumped with apprehension.

"Not again! He can't be doing this to me again!" She spoke aloud as she hit the living room, searching, only to find it like the rest of the cabin—empty. Her heart fell. He was gone, and she felt trashy and used as she headed back upstairs to get into bed alone. Maybe she'd stay there all day, or for the rest of her life.

Before she reached the bedroom, she heard the door open.

"Shade?" She called but did not get an answer. "Shade?"

He came around the corner in full grin, but his grin softened as he recognized the look of anguish on her face. Her eyes glistened with sadness as they peeked through the unwieldy curls tumbling down the front of her robe. She sniffed but did not smile as she descended a few steps, her bare feet patting on wood, like a small child distraught over losing a favorite toy.

"You thought I left?" Shade stood at the bottom of the steps looking up at her.

Sue Ann had stopped midway the stairs and plopped down as if overcome with worried exhaustion.

"Well, you are good at disappearing." She kept her eyes fixed on his.

Shade placed the paper bag he was carrying on the table and headed up to Sue Ann. He stopped two steps below, took her hands, and lifted her to her feet. She stood eye to eye with him, a feeling she liked. He put his arms around her waist and pulled her tight to him, covering her mouth with a deep, sensual kiss as he lowered her body against his.

"What does this tell you?" he asked as he untied her robe and pulled it off her shoulders, letting it drop to the step. His lips met hers again as he grabbed her hips and lifted her. She wrapped her legs around him as he carried her up the steps to the bed.

****

"What's this?" Sue Ann opened the bag on the table and found three sausage biscuits from the Roadhouse. "You didn't tell them where you spent the night, did you?" She cocked her head and frowned.

"Didn't have to. They already knew." Shade took the bag and turned away, heading to the kitchen.

"How would they know?"

"I left the Harley at the Roadhouse. Got a room, just in case Betsy misled me, but never slept in it."

"That still doesn't explain why they thought you were here." She moved to the counter to set up the coffeepot.

"Because—you're the most beautiful woman in Moose Springs, probably ever, and I'm the most eligible bachelor. Ask any single woman in town—and a couple of married ones." He gave her a side-glance to see what her reaction was. "Small town, Sue Ann. Get used to it."

"I'm the principal of the school, Shade. What if the kids find out?"

"Well, you can ask the Woodson twins during show-and-tell on Monday. They just rode by on their bikes and waved to me as I was coming in."

Sue Ann gave Shade a disgruntled gasp and turned

away from him. He grabbed her, twirled her around, and kissed her.

"I better get out of here before your daughter comes home. You might need to get a shower and try to get that hair under control, or Betsy will figure out you and I had a rumble in your bed. That's a lot more sex than just a tumble, in case you're not familiar with the term."

He headed for the door but stopped before opening it and looked at Sue Ann, giving her a serious look.

"I've got work to do, so I won't be in town for a couple of weeks." He opened the door and then shut it and walked back to her and kissed her again. "Just wanted you to know."

She watched through the kitchen window as he headed back toward the trees where he always left the motorcycle, not wanting to risk damaging it in the pothole-filled dirt road where her cabin was located. Within minutes, "Raven" sped down the road and out of sight.

Chapter Seven
Silence

Shade stopped by the trading post, bought a Fairbanks newspaper, and asked for his mail. When he entered, Don grinned behind his best smirk. Shade figured he'd have to punch him before leaving, knowing Sue Ann's name was about to be brought up. *There are some things you just don't tease a man about, and a woman, one who is important to you, is just such a thing.*

"Here's your Billings paper, your Seattle paper, your Philadelphia paper, and a letter with no return address, as always postmarked Fairbanks. You got a girlfriend that writes you these letters with this fancy handwriting? And what the hell do you want with so many outside newspapers? You a man with a few secrets, Dubois?" Don propped on the counter and grinned again, knowing he was getting Shade riled up.

"None of your damn business, Don. Like I've told you the two hundred or so times before when you've asked, I've got my reasons." Shade took the bundle of newspapers and the letter and headed for the door.

"I got family in Billings myself. Couldn't help but notice that headline on the front page. Some guy got murdered execution style. Right down to cutting off a finger, not to mention a more important part. Ouch! That had to hurt. Reckon he was tortured, Shade?"

Shade held up the newspaper covered in plastic. "I'll let you know, Don, as soon as *I* get a chance to read my mail. I don't get RAT Net out where I live, so these newspapers are my only way to keep in touch with the outside world." Shade turned toward the door and spoke with his back to Don. "Keep your nose out of my mail—and out of my business, McElroy. That's the last time I'm telling you."

Shade stuck the newspapers under his arm and turned the doorknob.

"Hear the principal has been hosting a little extracurricular activity on the side and bringing you along as a chaperone, or more likely as an instructor." Don snickered, waiting for a comeback, but none came as Shade slammed the door on his way out.

Shade stopped at the community well on his way out of town, took the *Billings Gazette* out of the plastic, and read the newspaper article on the cover.

"Damn!" Shade beat the motorcycle handlebars with the newspaper, which ended up on the ground. Realizing he needed to read it several times to make sure he had absorbed all the information, he picked it up and glanced back over it.

One piece of information caught his eye: "Barbiturates were found in the body of bank president William Donovan during the autopsy. Police have not released the type of barbiturates found; nor was any reasonable explanation given by co-workers at the bank for the supposed torture of Mr. Donovan or the presence of barbiturates in his body."

The old truth serum myth.

Shade thought about barbiturates like sodium pentothal but knew they did not cause all people to babble off prime information and hidden secrets, especially people trained like he and William—or Bill, as he knew him—had been trained. However, if they were used along with physical torture, Bill could have caved in. Shade wanted to put the murder out of his mind, but he knew he couldn't, for many reasons.

I'm sorry, Bill. I should be thinking of you and trying to find the son-of-a-bitch who killed you, but all I can think about is the dangerous position I'm putting Sue Ann and Betsy in if it's Tiger's Eye ONE. And there's Tuyen. There's always my precious Tuyen. What if she somehow finds out where I am—and who I am? But then, maybe this has nothing to do with ONE, and this is all just coincidence—maybe someone wanted Bill to launder drug money and he refused.

Shade took out the envelope and opened it. He knew there would be a picture. There was always a picture, something to remind him of what he could never have. He unfolded the letter beautifully written in an almost calligraphic script, and inside it was a snapshot. She was so beautiful with her short dark hair framing her petite face filled with blue eyes, his blue eyes, that showed only a trace of the slant from her mother's ancestry.

Shade placed the photograph back inside the folded letter, returned it to its envelope, and put it in the inside pocket of his leather jacket. After putting the Billings newspaper inside the saddlebags on his motorcycle, he headed back to Moose Springs instead of home. He had to make a phone call to KCBD Radio in Chevak. This would be the first message he had sent on Northern Voices to warn of danger, and he was hesitant, but he couldn't take any chances. He had to get the word out fast. He knew Wolfman would be listening, as would Hattie. They all listened every Saturday night, hoping never to hear messages like the one he was about to send. After this message, they would listen every night. The only pay phone in Moose Springs was outside the trading post, not the best location for a private call, but he had no choice. This message had to go out tonight.

"Need to put a message on Northern Voices tonight." Shade spoke into the receiver, covering the phone with his hand. "Yes, that's right."

****

Sue Ann sat drinking hot cocoa and trying to plan the unit she was teaching on the Great Depression coupled with *Of Mice and Men* by John Steinbeck. The best way to teach American history and literature was by combining the two, especially if teaching multi-levels in a one-room school. She was behind on her planning, but after the previous night with Shade, she was having a hard time concentrating.

The clock ticked on, and finally it was 9:20 p.m. and Sue Ann turned on the radio. She and Betsy tried not to miss Northern Voices on Saturday nights, and many other nights, as well. If one of them could not be there to listen, the other was expected to take notes on interesting ones, jotting down each message to be shared later. Northern Voices, a product of KCBD Radio Station out of Chevak, Alaska, intrigued Sue Ann and Betsy. The station was the essence of all things bush and had been started as a religious effort to reach souls living in isolated areas, including those out on traplines. Radios and batteries were crucial to entertainment, emergencies, and just plain existence for those so far out their only communication with family and friends was through KCBD's radio waves.

Sue Ann placed her empty cup in the sink and headed back to the radio. As she began listening to the messages, she took mental notes on each, knowing she and Betsy would be trying to decipher the stories behind the messages. Every once in a while, someone from Moose Springs sent a message to a friend or family member, mostly birthday greetings, news of a new baby's birth, and sometimes of a family member's death.

At exactly 9:20, Northern Voices erupted in a volley of messages.

"Going out to Jimbo at Jill's Slough from Tater: Birthday greetings from one old sourdough to another. Safe trapping, friend."

"To Mary and Caleb at Cole's Point from Ruth and David: Baby boy, 7 pounds. Mother and son doing well. No name yet but thinking of using Caleb. Come by as soon as you get home. Love to you, Grandma and Grandpa."

Sue Ann smiled at the message. The birth of a baby was always something to bring happiness, no matter where the recipient of the message was when the news came through. She could imagine the joy on the faces of Mary and Caleb, and probably the tears knowing it would be a while before they would get to hold their grandchild for the first time.

"Going out to Wolfman and Mama Bear from Raven. Been ill in GS. Bad. Eye on the sky and boots by the door."

As Sue Ann repeated the last word of the message, she got an uneasy feeling in the pit of her stomach. Two words stuck in her mind, "Bad" and "Raven."

"Raven—could it be from Shade?" She whispered the question but shook her head, thinking there must be hundreds of people in Alaska, female and male, called Raven. And just because Raven sometimes spoke in one-word sentences, "bad" being one of them, this did not mean it was he.

Putting the message out of her mind, she concentrated on the remaining messages and turned the radio off.

****

Three weeks passed, and Shade had not returned to see Sue Ann. Betsy noticed her mother's sadness and figured what had happened.

"He disappeared on you again, didn't he, Mom." Betsy took a bite of her grilled cheese sandwich as she sat at the table with her mom.

"Who? What are you talking about, Betsy?" Sue Ann left the stove with her sandwich and scooted onto the bench across from her daughter.

"Shade Dubois." Betsy said his name slowly with a sensual, dramatic flare and watched for her mother's reaction. "I know he came to see you when I was in Fairbanks. Lena heard it at the Roadhouse and told me." Betsy caught the dejected expression on her mother's face.

"I'm sorry, Mom. I encouraged him." Betsy put her hand on top of her mother's, wishing she had not teased about Shade. "I knew you liked him. I mean, what's not to like? He's movie star good-lookin'."

"It's okay, Betsy. Not your fault. I guess I'm just not very good with men. I never should have let Shade Dubois in the cabin, or into my head. He's not a keeper." Sue Ann took a bite, hoping the conversation was ended.

"Sure looks like a keeper. You should hear the women at the Roadhouse any time one of them mentions him." Betsy took another bite of her sandwich.

"Looks aren't everything." Sue Ann picked up her grilled cheese sandwich again but stopped just before putting it in her mouth. "But they can sure make a girl forget who she is sometimes." Sue Ann gave her daughter a mischievous grin and raised her eyebrows, and Betsy choked on a sip of tea.

"Mama, you have to take up for yourself." Betsy said a few minutes later after regaining control. "Another year and I'm off to college, and I worry about you being alone. You have spent your whole adult life being super mom, and it's gonna backfire on you when I leave."

"Betsy, you are the joy of my life, and I have no regrets." Sue Ann gave her daughter's hand a squeeze. "I don't want to think of you leaving, but at the same time, I look forward to seeing you grow up and make a life of your own. I'm thirty-seven, but I'm not dead, and according to Shade Dubois, I'm quite the looker myself." Sue Ann arched her eyebrows and winked at Betsy. "I'll have other chances, Sweetie. I just hope I'm not jinxed."

"You mean losing my father?" Betsy asked.

"Yes, that's part of it. It's a little scary when you lose someone you love so much. I guess I've been afraid of men ever since your father—you know." She did not add the word "died" because she always felt guilty about lying to her daughter. "I hope you never have to experience losing someone you love, but as beautiful and charming as you are, the chances for hurt are still good, whether by act of God or through disappearance."

****

October came in like a stealthy intruder, bringing with it the first harsh winter Sue Ann and Betsy had ever experienced. But even with the falling temperatures, the mother/daughter *cheechacos* were exuberant when they woke up to the first big snow in Moose Springs.

A thin layer of ice had already formed on the slough. The edges of the Tekooni River that ran a few miles out of Moose Springs were outlined in crusted, icy fringe. The Tekooni, with its giant fish wheels dotting the banks and spread out every few miles during the winter, supplied the mushers and sled dog kennels like Jake's with salmon, especially chum salmon, the dog food of choice. Trusting the almanac's prediction of a harsh winter, Jake and other mushers and kennel owners had stored a bigger than normal supply of chum salmon, often referred to as dog salmon, to supplement dry dog food and help get them through the winter. Salmon was also a main source of protein, along with moose, for the people of the community, many of whom were subsistence hunters and fishers.

Sue Ann had not seen Shade in a month and tried to put him out of her mind. She was principal and teacher in a school that needed her wholehearted leadership and her teaching skills, jobs she took seriously. Sixteen students depended on her ability to manage their education, and she had every intention of making herself valuable to this school and community. She already felt this was her home, and there was no time to be wasted on mourning a man who obviously wanted no ties with her.

Betsy had started helping Jake in the kennel. Her goal was to learn everything she could about sled dogs. Every day, she headed there after school to help feed and water the dogs, and in exchange Jake promised to teach her to mush.

Jake and Sue Ann had a deal Betsy knew nothing about. As soon as Betsy learned the proper care and handling of a sled dog, she would have her malamute puppy. Betsy had her eye on a runt female puppy in her charge, but she was not allowed to name it. Jake told Betsy the puppy did not need to get used to a name the new owner might not want. As soon as Betsy finished her rounds each day, she spent a few extra minutes with the puppy she secretly called Noname, very close to the word Nome, the goal for mushers in the Iditarod.

One late afternoon, Betsy was putting Noname back with her mother and siblings when she saw a musher pull up at Jake's house. She knew immediately who it was. Shade Dubois had parked his Harley in one of Jake's sheds when the first snow fell and started using his dog team or his snowmobile as main transportation. Betsy watched as Shade set the brake and headed into Jake's office. Her feeling of contempt for this man who had teased and then abandoned her mother boiled over and had to be released or risk explosion. When Shade came out of Jake's office, Betsy was waiting.

"So, Mr. Dubois, how are you? Broken any more hearts lately?" Betsy was propped on the driving bow of his sled with one snowboot crossed over the other.

"I didn't mean to hurt your mother, Betsy. You

have to believe that. Besides—Sue Ann is better off without me." Shade stood close, keeping his eyes fixed on Betsy.

"If you were the man she thought you were, you'd tell her that yourself and let her make that decision." Betsy whirled and stomped to her truck. "But then, you're not a man, are you? You're just a…a…movie star…all looks and no heart." She sped down the driveway, cutting donuts in the snow as Shade watched.

Jake came out of the office and stood on the landing, looking down at Shade.

"I'm guessing our young Miss Parish is none too pleased with your exploitation of her mother." Jake started down the steps.

"Exploitation? Pretty harsh, don't you think? It wasn't that way, Jake." Shade yelled up at him.

"Sue Ann is a fine lady." Jake continued down the steps and stopped beside Shade, who was preparing to leave. "She is accepted by the majority of this community, and I, speaking for the majority, hope she stays. The school needs her, and the community needs her, and if you weren't such a damn fool and an asshole, you'd see you need her, too."

Shade realized Jake would not listen to him, so he released the brake and headed the team to the trail leading out of town.

Chapter Eight
The Wreck

Sue Ann kept the truck in four-wheel drive all the way to and from Fairbanks. The weeklong fall administrative meeting for the school district had been held in the city, just as it was every year, the last week of October. Sue Ann had attended even though she would have preferred to stay in Moose Springs with Betsy and the staff and students at the school.

She drove slowly, both because of the dangerous mountain road and because she was enjoying the beauty that was Alaska in the winter, what little she was able to see before dark set in. Betsy had begged to come with her, afraid for her mother to drive the treacherous road alone, but Sue Ann did not want her to miss a whole week of school.

Sue Ann had meant to spend Friday night in Fairbanks but at the last minute decided she wanted to go home to have the whole weekend with Betsy. A week away from her daughter was too much, especially when it was something she had never done before. She had decided not to call and let anyone know she was on her way; she didn't want to worry Betsy. If she drove a little faster, she could make it home by ten o'clock. This would be her first time to drive the mountain pass at night in snow, but she was confident she and the truck could handle it. Besides, the pass was only twenty miles from Moose Springs.

As she turned onto the eighty-mile stretch, the snow started again, and Sue Ann wondered if she had made the right decision to head out after the meeting. The roads were packed with snow already, but the truck was doing fine in four-wheel-drive, and so was the driver, who was only a little tense now that darkness surrounded her. The temperature was holding steady at twenty degrees, according to her truck gauge, and this relatively warm temperature meant the snow would probably fall for the entire trip.

Sue Ann smiled as she popped a cassette into the new player, a surprise for Betsy, who hated the long trip to and from Fairbanks without her music.

She had talked to Betsy each night while away but did not tell her about the many surprises she was bringing her. The phone had just been installed in the cabin before Sue Ann left. The quality of the sound was not like in Mississippi and had echoes and delays between caller and "callee." Betsy laughed at the echoes and began saying "over" each time she finished her side of the conversation, as if she were on a radio instead of a phone.

As the truck began the climb toward the pass, the snow grew thicker, with visibility only a few feet in front of the truck. By now, Sue Ann's nerves were on edge, and she turned the volume up on the cassette player, hoping it would distract her from the uneasiness she felt while keeping a tight grip on the steering wheel.

Australian-born Angus and Malcolm Young, of Betsy's favorite group AC/DC, one of five cassettes Sue Ann had bought as part of the surprise package for Betsy, screamed "Snowballed!"

"How appropriate!" She laughed aloud and puckered her lips while rocking her head back and forth and lifting her shoulders, keeping time to the earsplitting music. Reminded of the sheer drop-off on one side, she slowed her speed to the "tortoise-who-lost-the-race" pace, and within a few minutes she was heading over the pass.

Feeling secure after making it over, Sue Ann sped up a notch. In another twenty miles, she would see Betsy and surprise her with all the new snow gear she had bought her for dog sledding, as well as the cassettes. But the surprise Betsy would like best was the red puppy collar personalized with "Noname" on it. Sue Ann had purchased the puppy from Jake before leaving town and planned to let Betsy bring the puppy home this weekend. Sue Ann could not wait to see her daughter's face.

As Sue Ann pictured Betsy opening the collar, she reached the big curve just beyond the pass. The curve banked the wrong way, and, too late, Sue Ann realized she was going too fast as the truck began to slide. Remembering what she had been taught by her friends at school, she took her foot off the brake, but the truck already had a mind of its own, and it was not going where she wanted it to go. Sue Ann grabbed the steering wheel as the truck turned donuts in the road before veering to the right. The truck climbed an embankment and somersaulted down the road, flipping over and over before settling on its top. When the truck stopped, Sue Ann was hanging upside down by her lap belt. Her first thought was Betsy, and she knew she had to get out.

When she released the lap belt, she fell to the top

of the truck, hitting the back of her head on the way down. As she rubbed her head, she felt a patch of warmth oozing from a cut under her braid. She lay still to let her head clear, not knowing what to do but aware the temperature was low enough she would freeze to death if she could not get out of the truck and find warmth and safety. All she had in the cab was her lightweight coat and gloves, and she was wearing boots more suitable for an administrative meeting than for plodding through snow. If she could get to it, she could put on the snow gear she'd bought for Betsy and maybe survive the night.

It was late, with no chance of anyone finding her tonight on this high mountain road. The snow pummeled down, its icy flakes making tapping sounds as they hit the cracked windows surrounding her. The snow was building up rather than "tapering off," declaring the weatherman to be a liar. She turned the hand cranks on both windows, but neither of them would roll down—or rather up, since the truck was upside down. She tried sliding the back window, to see if she could break through to the camper shell window, and mouthed, "Thank you, Jesus!" as both of those windows slid open.

Sue Ann crawled low through what was left of the camper shell. Her face was hit by the cold snow blowing through the side that was barely hanging on but not crushed flat like the other. She was about to grab the bags of snow gear when she smelled it—smoke!

Within seconds, flames shot from the truck hood, and Sue Ann knew she had to get out fast or be burned to death in the explosion likely to follow. Forgetting about the bags, she dove at the torn camper side, squeezing through twisted, jagged aluminum. Sharp pain shot through her hands and the arm she had used to twist the aluminum up and out of way. As she belly-crawled through the tight, twisted side of the camper, sharp edges of aluminum tore at her sweater and thin khakis. In seconds, she felt the frigid snow beneath her, but she knew she was still not safe. Smoke and flames leapt into the darkness, pushing her to escape even as her breath froze in front of her like hoarfrost. The frigid night air stung her throat and lungs as she gulped it in with a rush of adrenaline.

The first pangs of soreness hit her as she steadied herself on her knees. As she stood, she noticed a stream of blood trickling down her hand, leaving a ghostly red handprint in the white ground. The hissing flames took away any comfort she felt at being free from the deathtrap as she shook from the intense cold, her teeth chattering out of control.

She hurried, limping blindly away from the burning truck, unable to see exactly where she was going through the icy snowfall.

"Betsy!" She whispered her daughter's name over and over, reminding herself of the reason she must live and not give in to the pain that swept through her body like a thousand needles all trying to escape through her skin. She tried to run, but her slick boots got no traction. Without being able to stop herself, she slipped, careening out of control on her back like a human bobsled. Turning on to her side, she grabbed at the icy road, tearing her fingernails and skin but finding nothing to grip. Just before she catapulted over one of the lesser drop-offs, a spindly spruce tree stopped her.

The impact took away all consciousness; her world went black.

****

Shade stood at the easel in his cabin and tried to paint but could not wrap his mind around the piece. He had a deadline to meet, but he was struggling to finalize the project. Besides, Bill was dead, and he was the main person responsible for selling Shade's paintings in the lower forty-eight.

Shade's forte was painting the Northern Lights using oils on oversized canvases, although he had painted other genres in the past. With the addition of slow-moving strobe lights without color, he was able to enhance the colors of aurora and give the lights the illusion of actually moving on canvas. Shade's painting was unique and vibrant, and in serious demand. In his profession as an artist, he had painted a path to success and wealth. But in his old profession, he had painted a path of destruction for himself and anyone too close to him. His Northern Lights paintings earned him a nice amount, but he kept none of this money for himself. He had another responsibility, and the paintings were sold especially for her livelihood and care. His parents had money, but he was no longer alive to them, nor they to him. His real family, a family of one, only knew him through letters, never photographs, but he had photos of her, and each picture received was enough to keep him hiding and painting for a long time.

Once he had taken a big chance and followed her as she enjoyed a school outing when she lived in Seattle. Her reaction from the lookout deck on the Space Needle was pure exuberance as she ran from side to side, breathing in the panorama of mountains, water, and cityscape. She was a beautiful little fairy, her thick dark hair always cut short and outlining the face of a real live doll with only hints of her Southeast Asian ancestry. Her pictures did not do her justice, and he wanted to approach her and take her in his arms, but that could never happen.

Keeping his distance and hiding his identity were hard, but he had to remain incognito for the girl's welfare and safety. He kept his overcoat collar pulled high around his face that day but did not have on sunglasses. He knew he needed to leave, yet it was impossible to pull himself away from the young teenage girl dressed in the school uniform of the prestigious girls' boarding school he paid for along with everything else.

The highlight of the observation came when she isolated herself from the rest of the students and their chaperone and pulled out a sketchpad. Shade moved close behind her and cast glances over her shoulder at the drawing that magically took shape as she looked from scene to pad. He smiled, forgetting himself momentarily, and watched. Tuyen, Vietnamese for "angel," had inherited his artistic talent. He stared too long, and the girl, sensing his presence behind her, jerked her head around. The girl's light blue eyes, his eyes, met the stranger's, and they stared briefly until each smiled at the same time, their eyes looking like pieces of the same sky had fallen from above and found refuge on each of their faces.

"Hello," she said as she looked at him, and he was sorry he had taken his sunglasses off.

"Hi." He answered and turned away, moving to the other side of the deck. Each time he turned back, he found her eyes following him and knew he had to leave. He had stayed too long, taken too big a chance, and it was dangerous for Tuyen. Hattie, the girl's adopted mother, would have to be told about the encounter the next time he met her in Fairbanks.

****

As Shade tried to capture the magic of the Aurora Borealis, his mind wandered to the articles he had read in the Billings newspapers. The news of the murder of William Donovan was hurtful and alarming. He and Bill had gone through so much together in Vietnam, Cambodia, and Laos, and on other jobs, places much more dangerous than Billings, Montana. But Bill was dead, tortured and executed in his own home. Shade had sent out the warning to the others, but none of them had any way of knowing if Bill had caved with the torture and the barbiturates. Now that Bill was dead, Shade knew he would have to depend on Hattie alone for selling his paintings. Somehow he had to find a way to talk to her, but with Bill's murder, he had to be even more discreet. Hattie was a good friend and confidante, one of only two persons in Alaska who had known him in his other life, but then she had another life, as well. He and Hattie had many things in common, not the least of which was Tuyen.

Shade turned his thoughts away from Bill's murder and Hattie, replaying his encounter with Betsy a week ago. Betsy was angry and had looked so much like her mother as she yelled at him, accusing him of hurting Sue Ann intentionally. But it was Jake's use of the word "exploitation" that hit hardest. Yes, he had been guilty of exploiting a woman once, a long time ago, and his conscience made him pay for that mistake every day of his life. Now Sue Ann was being hurt indirectly, and the jugular hold of his hidden past tightened another notch.

"Damn!" he yelled and threw the brush at the canvas. "I can't get it right! I've got to get out of here before I go crazy."

He was talking to himself like he did when in his cabin alone for too many weeks. The perfect cure was to go see Sue Ann, to kiss her, to make love to her over and over like he had done that night—but he couldn't. It was too risky, and he might put her and Betsy in harm's way.

After pulling on his snow gear, he grabbed the keys to the snowmobile and his high-powered camera in its insulated case that kept it and the batteries warm. He climbed aboard the powerful snowmobile and was soon heading down the trail. Next to his Harley, the dog team provided his favorite mode of transportation, but what he needed right now was a quick trip into the Alaskan wilderness with the Sky Dwellers dancing their way into his "artistic inner voice," as Hattie called it, where mental images could be teleported onto canvas. He knew where he'd go for inspiration, the same place he always went, the hill overlooking Old Sawyer's mine.

Chapter Nine
Snowballed!

The snow was coming down lightly, but Shade knew it would soon stop. He turned his running lights on, although he didn't really need them. He knew the trail well; it was his pathway to the "spirit voices" who whispered images into that secret place in his mind he shared only with them. When he reached the top of the hill, he cut the motor and cast his eyes above. The snow had stopped, and the heavens were alive with yellow and green strobes of magic, God's masterpiece, the Aurora Borealis.

As he stared into the green, all he could see was Sue Ann's eyes, eyes he thought could love him, but he was a monster with a past that kept him from her. Betsy and Sue Ann were like identical twins with those tantalizing eyes, and from the first minute he'd looked into Sue Ann's eyes, he wanted to dive in, search for the source of the enchantment, and perpetuate it on canvas. But it could never be.

"Exploitation!" He said the word aloud. It was the most negative and descriptive term for his many transgressions he had ever heard but was so fitting.

The banging of loud guitars and the high-pitched repetition of one word, "snowballed," screamed over and over, breaking the silence of Shade's world until he thought his ears would explode.

"For God's sake! What parasite dares disturb the reverence of the lights by playing their radio loud enough to break the sound barrier?" Ordinarily, he liked AC/DC, but this time he got off the snowmobile and pulled the fur earmuffs away from his ears, turning his head like radar to seek the source of the loud music, wanting to stop it. Shade figured it was coming from the pass, where more than likely the snow was pounding down. The pass was not that far away from his property as the eagle flew, and he wondered what juvenile delinquent had intruded on his and Old Sawyer's haven.

Ten years ago, Shade had purchased the hundred acres from the estate of Old Sawyer, a gold miner who left his entire fortune and assets to the town of Moose Springs, not that the town was endeared to him but because he had no heirs. Old Sawyer hated bureaucracy and was afraid the state would take over his paradise if he didn't leave a will. Shade paid dearly for the property because of the gold still in the ground and in the streams, where finding nuggets was still possible. He had no interest in nor need of gold. His gold was the lights, the Northern Lights. Aurora was his lover, the only woman allowed into his heart and soul and the only woman who had ever consumed his thoughts…until now.

Shade pulled his earflaps down, attempting to drown out the band as he gazed upward trying to memorize the most beautiful ballet ever witnessed. But AC/DC "snowballed" his efforts to gain inspiration.

"Damn!" He yelled and kicked at the snow. "I should go down there and break that son-of-a-bitch's neck and teach him to respect the wilderness and the silence."

Shade got back on his snowmobile and revved up the motor, ready to leave since his space and his nighttime concentration had been disturbed beyond repair, but as he turned to leave, a blast shook the ground beneath him. Fire shot upward from the pass, and Shade knew the "parasite" was in serious trouble.

Gunning the snowmobile, he headed straight down the long, steep hill, the quickest way to the road that led to the pass. He felt guilty at the prospect of someone being hurt, or more likely killed, and put the Sky Dwellers out of his mind, turning his attention to reaching any potential victims.

****

Sue Ann came to but couldn't move. Her body felt as if she had been run over by the City of New Orleans and then backed over again just for good measure. Her out-of-control shaking intensified her agony. She was on the verge of freezing to death, and she had to do something about it, fast. Fires, burning debris from the truck, dotted the road like campfires from a national Boy Scout Campout and lay between her and the burned-out truck frame. Her only hope was to drag herself to the closest fire.

As her body quaked, she thanked God for saving her, even though the pain was almost unbearable. Death and leaving Betsy would be more intolerable. Her sweater was in shreds where the icy road had eaten it and burned her skin beneath as she'd done her bobsled imitation. Sue Ann forced herself to move through the pain, moaning and shaking. Her teeth clicked together so loudly and so fast they sounded like a Maraca band being played by drug addicts on speed.

"The truck...Noname's collar...Betsy!" she whispered in repetition as her tears gushed—only to freeze on her eyelids and lashes before given a chance to flow. She pulled with both arms, even the one caked with frozen blood, inching her body toward the fire. She needed to stand but feared a repeat of her bobsled experience, so she crawled or dragged herself. As she got within a few yards of the blaze, she realized it was the seat from her truck.

Closer! I have to get closer.

She talked to herself, and with every few inches gained, she could feel the warmth from the fire.

"Don't go out! Don't go out!" Sue Ann begged the flames as she curled into a ball only a couple of feet away from them. The fire helped, and her shaking diminished. As the warmth overpowered her, she could no longer keep her eyes open. She hoped her sleepiness was from the warmth from the fire and not from hypothermia.

****

Shade hit the road just below the pass and stopped to cover his mouth to prevent inhaling smoke from the explosion. He followed the smoke and the small fires that had erupted, and within a couple of minutes he saw what remained of the truck, still smoldering, with small flames coming from what was once a hood. The smoke made his eyes burn, but he strained to see if he could find driver or passenger, hoping they had gotten out before the truck became a bomb. He left his snowmobile and walked to the back of the truck bed, and it was then he recognized the vehicle by its Mississippi personalized tag with "BETSY 2" in bold letters.

"Sue Ann! Sue Ann!" Shade yelled and ran in circles around what was left of the truck. He bent over and coughed after getting too close and inhaling smoke. She was not in the area of the burned wreckage, and neither was Betsy or anyone else that he could see. As he ran away from the truck in the direction of Moose Springs, he hoped and prayed Sue Ann was out and attempting to walk to town, just the type of thing she would do. He hoped Betsy had not been with her but figured the teenager was the culprit behind "Snowballed."

"Sue Ann!" Shade was frantic as he yelled her name every few feet of road and embankment but got no reply. He was about to turn around and go back for his snowmobile, to make the search go more quickly, when he saw something in the road ahead, close to the truck seat that had only a little flame and smoke curling from its remains now.

"Sue Ann!" He continued yelling as he ran toward the charred seat.

****

Sue Ann opened her eyes and thought she was in heaven. Bright, colored clouds hovered over her, moving like rainbows caught in massive tornadoes, furling and then transforming into waving, undulating sky magic backed by millions of stars twinkling in sync. Heaven beckoned to her through choral whispers.

"Come back to the light! Come back to the light!"

She moved her good arm and held it up, thinking herself close enough to touch the lights, but she did not have the strength. The sound of someone calling her name made her realize she was not dead after all. She lifted her head and looked in the direction of the voice, and there he was, running toward her.

"Sue Ann!" Shade's voice cracked with emotion as he grabbed her up and held her to him, but her cries of pain forced him to gently lay her back down.

"Can you hear me, sweetheart? Was Betsy with you?" His voice was frantic as he removed his heavy coat and secured it around her. Then he took off his hat and pulled it tight over her head despite the matted, frozen blood.

"No. I'm alone," she whispered and tried to smile as Shade gently lifted her, holding his coat firmly around her.

"Thank God you're alive." His voice shook from cold, fear, and what sounded like joy. He had reached her in time. "Let's get you to a warm place."

Chapter Ten
"Come Back To the Light!"

Sue Ann awoke under a pile of down comforters and blankets. Her body ached, but she had to move even though she did not want to leave the warmth. Then she realized she was not alone. Someone was next to her, right next to her, adding his body heat to hers. "Someone" raised his head and smiled at her.

"Shade?" Again she tried to lift her head and this time succeeded enough to roll from her stomach onto her side, where she could face him. "Oh!" Sue Ann cried as the first wave of pain hit her. Shade put his arm around her and rubbed her face.

"Where does it hurt?" Shade's face looked serious. His hands began gently touching her arms before reaching over her to her back.

"Everywhere—and then some. There doesn't seem to be one certain spot." Sue Ann's eyes were wide open now, and her facial expression matched his. "I thought I was dead. The lights wanted me."

"The lights?" he asked.

"Vibrant green and yellow lights surrounded by millions of the brightest stars I've ever seen. They were so close I thought I could reach up and touch them, but I couldn't. They whispered to me with hundreds of voices, all blended together as one. 'Come back to the light! Come back to the light,' they pleaded with me, and their dancing kept time with their whispers. It was the most—the most spiritual thing I've ever experienced."

Sue Ann cried, and Shade put his arm around her and rubbed his cheek to hers.

"You're not dead, Sweetheart. Those were the Northern Lights, the Aurora Borealis, reminding you that you are very much alive, and I am more alive than I was because I found you before you went to 'the light.' " When he kissed her lips gently and felt her tears running down her cheeks, he had to turn his head and wipe his own moist eyes, hoping she didn't see him and think he was weak and way too sentimental.

"You disappeared again." Sue Ann made it a statement.

"Yes, but my disappearing is over—unless you want me to leave."

Shade moved closer. He wanted to cuddle her but was afraid he'd hit a sore spot. As he placed his knee between her legs and his lower body joined hers, she realized they were both naked. Sue Ann lifted her head, groaning, and held up the cover to peek under but put it down in a hurry.

"You took my clothes off?" Her question came with not only surprise but also anger. "And yours?"

"It's the quickest way to warm someone when the person is on the verge of hypothermia. Besides, your clothes were ripped to hell and back." Shade cut his eyes down at her, frowning. "And I can assure you, lying next to you like this, my body temperature was at an all-time high. It was necessary—you know, to save you."

"Yeah, right!" Sue Ann rolled over and cried out as

her scratched back met the sheet too quickly. Fighting more tears, she changed the subject.

"I need to get to Betsy before someone finds the truck and tells her. She'll be terrified, thinking I'm dead."

"I've already taken care of that. I have a shortwave radio. Jake also has one, so I radioed him and told him about the wreck and that you are okay. He's going to tell Betsy later this morning. I also told him you are too scratched up and bruised for me to bring you home today."

"What?" Sue Ann jerked up too fast, grabbed her head, and lay back down, shivering from the jolt of pain.

"Yep." Shade pulled the cover tighter around her. "You're alive and back with the 'What' game."

Shade left the bed and turned on another light. Sue Ann's eyes followed him as he walked across the room and put more logs in the woodstove. For the first time, she noticed a long, raised scar starting just below his waist on his back and extending down on to his hip. Another scar covered the back of his left shoulder but was less noticeable. He walked to a cupboard and reached to the top shelf for a bottle of pills. Sue Ann's eyes continued trailing him as he left the bedroom. In a few minutes, he reentered the bedroom holding a glass of water. It was hard to keep her eyes on what was in his hands when she had such a great front view of him walking back to the bed with his thick black hair surrounding his crown jewel like a black lion's mane. "King of the Jungle," a phrase from one of her daughter's favorite bedtime stories as a child, came to Sue Ann's mind, and she smiled in spite of herself.

Even through the pain she grew warm and could feel her face flush.

"Here. Take these. It will help with the pain." He held the pills out to her, but she just stared at them.

"They won't knock me out, will they?" She watched his face, waiting for an answer before putting the pills into her mouth.

"Afraid I might take advantage of you?" Shade smiled and sat down on the edge of the bed, still holding the glass of water.

"No. I just know Betsy will show up when she finds out I had a wreck."

"It's just a mild painkiller. I take them all the time. They won't knock you out, Sue Ann."

She took the pills and the glass of water. With the first sip, she discovered her throat was parched, and she downed the entire glassful.

"You must have back pain from your old injuries." Sue Ann held the glass out to Shade. "I saw the scars on your back. Whatever caused those must have been painful."

Shade did not make eye contact or answer her probe as he took the glass and headed back through the door without answering her question. When he returned, he was carrying a stack of towels, two plastic bottles, and a glass pitcher. After placing them on the dresser, he opened double doors to uncover an enchanted glassed-in garden.

"The Garden of Eden," she whispered, pulling herself to a sitting position to get a better look.

He smiled when he heard what Sue Ann called his own little piece of paradise.

"You have…a…a…" She was speechless and just

sat staring with her mouth wide open. "A solarium! How beautiful!"

He sat beside her on the bed and continued to smile.

"How about you and me play Adam and Eve?" Shade started to pick her up, but she balked, holding her hands up and keeping her eyes on the solarium.

"How did you...?" She just could not find the words to express what she was seeing. "It's a garden with flowers, and—is that grapevines? How did you do all of this, Shade?"

"It is, and they're ripe for the plucking. It's all fed by the same hot springs that run through Moose Springs, so I trapped it and made myself the perfect bathhouse/garden/solarium. Actually, if you look over to the right, you'll see a gym area with all kinds of work-out equipment, both weightlifting and aerobics, but it is well hidden since I didn't want to detract from the natural beauty and ambience of the garden. It took a little ingenuity, but I managed. I enjoy cleanliness, and I like surrounding myself with beauty—like you." He sat beside her, and before she could stop him, he kissed her, not as long or as deep as that night so long ago, but his kiss said a lot.

"When I'm in town, I get a room at the Roadhouse, mostly to enjoy the luxury of a manly shower."

"And to take advantage of the ladies who throw themselves at you." She gave him a catty grin as he opened his mouth to speak. Before he could ask where she'd heard this, she answered, "As someone once told me, 'Small town; get used to it.' "

"I don't take advantage of anyone, Sue Ann. You should know that. Do I always succumb to beautiful women 'throwing themselves at me?' Not always, but I am a man, or haven't you noticed?" Shade turned his head away briefly. "Actually, I haven't had a woman in months, before my night with you, and that's a good thing, since you recently lost your virginity—again. Neither of us is harboring any nasty diseases, so we can be as wild as we want without anything unnatural between us."

"I noticed—you're a man, that is. As for your escapades in the last few months, I only know of one, and that is quite enough." She lay back, groaning, but kept her eyes on him.

"The only problem with my solarium, as you call it, is I've had no one to share it with until now." Shade turned to Sue Ann and smiled. "But a bigger problem is that I can't make love to you with you in so much pain." He stared at her, smiling as he gently pulled the covers off her. "Ready for a nice, warm soak in a natural hot tub, Sweetheart? Maybe I can at least get your mind off your pain with a little caressing and massaging in the right spot." He ran his hand between her breasts and continued down her stomach, letting his fingers stop when he reached her sensitive area. She closed her eyes and held her breath but did not protest.

"Relax, baby. Breathe. Let some of that tension flow from your body." His fingers were gentle.

"Shade, I..." She shivered, and he realized what she needed.

"You're freezing, Sweetheart." Shade stood, looking down at her. "There's a better way of helping you relax and see what hurts the most."

He leaned over the bed and lifted her up into a sitting position. She tucked the covers around her, feeling uneasy with her nudity. Easing himself to a position behind her, he straddled her hips, with his legs stretched out on either side, and began taking down her braid, which hung loose and disheveled down her back.

Sue Ann carefully leaned back against him, cringing a little as her raw back met his bare skin. She liked the feel of his muscular chest—and other parts of his body—and swallowed the desire to cry out when he hit the sore spot on her head. Soon she felt her loose hair moved to the front, over her shoulder and away from her injuries.

"Your left arm and your back seem to be the biggest problems, but we need to wash off the dried blood so we can see the damage. Besides, the mineral springs will do wonders for your soreness." He moved to stand beside the bed, looking down at her.

"Are you ready?" He put a hand under her hips and one on her lower back to lift her from the bed.

"No! Stop, Shade!" Sue Ann held up her hands. "I've got to do this on my own. The sooner I'm up, the sooner I'm home with my daughter." She held out her good arm and tried to pull her legs around to the edge of the bed.

"Here, I'll help you, Sweetheart." He moved closer.

"No, I'll do it. Just give me a minute. I can't look or act like I belong in a hospital, or somebody might take me back to Fairbanks."

He smiled an approving smile at her will but stood close, ready to help her if she needed it.

Slowly, she inched her way to the side and let her legs fall to the floor. She tried to wrap a sheet around her, but when she almost tripped over it, she decided it was not such a good idea. Besides, Shade did not seem to be bothered with his own nudity.

"Okay...if you'll just let me lean on you a little bit so I won't fall..." Sue Ann stood but had to sit back down when dizziness overcame her.

"Are you okay, Sweetheart?"

"Why are you calling me sweetheart? You barely know me, and you obviously don't like me much, since you keep leaving."

"I'm sorry. I won't call you that anymore. I guess it sounds demeaning to a hardheaded woman who's hell bent on being independent even when she's covered in cuts and bruises, but I can assure you I didn't mean it that way." He let her hold on to him as much as she needed as she took a step.

"Sue Ann, you do realize we made love—a lot of love, even if it was all in one night. That should count for something."

"It might have, if you had ever come back." She stopped before getting to the bathhouse. "Please tell me you don't have an outhouse, Shade. I've really gotta go, even if it's just a honey bucket, but I hope to goodness I don't fall off of it."

Shade laughed and led her to a door on the other side of the bathhouse.

"Hate to bust your bubble, but you're not the first one to come up with the idea of an inside outhouse." Shade opened the door, and Sue Ann held to the wall and stepped inside to find a shiny stainless steel toilet.

"Can you make it, or do I need to help you?" He cut his eyes at her.

"I prefer to pee alone, but thanks for the offer. It's very romantic." She was back to sarcasm. "Even though we're walking around in the buff like two old lovers, I still have modesty where some things are concerned." She shut the door in his face.

"I don't even want to know what your space-age honey bucket cost, but just know I've found another reason to hate you." Her voice echoed from the room.

****

Sue Ann lay still, soaking in the warm water, and let Shade sponge her wounds. For some reason, she felt no shame, as if it were natural and reasonable.

"Now for those long curls I love. Are you ready?"

When all the dried blood was gone from her hair, he shocked her by sliding into the water with her.

"I'm really not up to it, Shade. Give me a week or so."

He laughed and began bathing himself.

"Conservation of water, Sweet...Sorry, I mean Sue Ann. Of course, there is an endless supply of the mineral springs here. Look around. This was Old Sawyer's at one time, but he did not have it quite as magical as I do. He used the heat from the mineral springs to grow vegetables year round." Shade slid over by Sue Ann and put his arm around her, pulling her to his chest.

"I missed you so much, Sweet...Sue Ann. I promise I wanted to come back and make love to you and almost did, several times."

"And you expect me to believe that because...?" She wanted to argue with him, but it felt too good to have her head on his awesome chest, there in the paradisiacal world of Shade Dubois.

"Because I'm telling you, and if you'll trust me, I'll show you." He kissed the top of her head and held her close. "Just relax, now. You are safe. I'm just so thankful you're alive and here with me."

After a few minutes, Shade left the bath, wrapped a towel around his waist, and sat on the edge looking down at Sue Ann. She had her eyes closed, ignoring him.

"I just want to stay in here until I heal." Her voice was hardly audible, only a weak whisper.

"What happened to that strong, independent woman I just shared a bath with?"

"She shriveled away to nothing, just melted away in the warm mineral water." Sue Ann pulled herself into a sitting position with her good arm and then held up her hand to Shade, who was already reaching for her. This time, he lifted her from the tub and carried her to the bed, where he dried her with the soft towel.

"I don't know about not going to the hospital. These cuts on your back are pretty deep in spots. You really need stitches." Shade patted the cuts with the towel, being as gentle as possible, while Sue Ann grimaced.

"A little Neosporin and a couple of Band-Aids, and I'll be good as new," she assured him. "Ow!" she yelled when he hit a tender spot.

"A couple of Band-Aids? Hmm. I'm thinking I'll need to cut up one of my sheets to cover all of these scrapes and cuts. Could just rub Neosporin all over you, cover you with sheet bandages, and wrap duct tape around you like a mummy. Duct tape can fix anything, you know. Alaskans don't call it 'ninety-mile-an-hour tape' for nothing." He put ointment on each spot on her back, being as gentle as he could. "This is not how I envision caressing you when I think about our night together."

"Which night was that? We've had two now." Sue Ann laughed and leaned back on her side, holding her ribs.

"You think you might have some broken ribs, Sweet...? Damn it, Sue Ann, you're making it hard for me to pamper you when you won't let me call you Sweetheart." Shade was quiet for a few seconds as he finished dabbing ointment on her back.

"Okay, I've got this." He lay close to her back and reached over with one hand, gently placing it on her breasts, caressing each tenderly while feeling for sore spots under and around each one.

"Just checking for broken ribs"—he paused—"Darling?"

Sue Ann held her breath and then exhaled in one big gush, both from twinges of pain and from the sensations Shade was stirring in her. As he leaned over her to look in her eyes and check if she was all right, she put her good hand on his face and traced her finger from his upper cheek to his mouth, where she parted his lips. He sucked on her finger and pulled her hips to him as gently as possible. She turned sideways to face him, and he covered her lips with his, and it was clear the passion he felt for her was real. She had the same wanting he did, but it was too risky not knowing the full extent of her injuries. When their lips parted, his blue eyes sparkled.

"We better get some clothes on, Darling. Don't think your daughter will appreciate seeing us like this, especially not me with a hard-on the size of Alaska, and if that daughter of yours is like her mom, she could show up any time."

****

Shade was careful as he towel dried Sue Ann's hair; he'd seen the cut underneath. She sat swaddled in a pair of his long johns rolled over and over at the waistband, one of his thick ribbed Henley shirts with the sleeves rolled up, and wool socks pulled to her knees over the long johns. While he sat straddled behind her, detangling her hair with his hairbrush, she got her first good look at her hospice.

"Nice." she said.

"What's nice? My fooling with your hair, or the feel of my most prominent male feature growing against your delicate little hips?"

"No. Your cabin. It's amazing! Functional and excessively large."

"I would that you should be talking about my man parts, but thank you anyway. It took me six months to finish it after the crew from Fairbanks put the logs and roof up and installed the complex generator system. I'm a bit of a perfectionist in things I design and create." Shade put the brush away and sat by Sue Ann on the sofa, a new one upholstered with a fabric imprinted with vintage fly rods, flies, and creels to coordinate with easy chairs upholstered in solid, bright colors, a recliner, and a loveseat, all oversized to fill the space in the main room.

"So, Shade, if you can afford all of this, you obviously did not need the money for repairing my roof, not that I ever paid you anyway since you never gave me a price, but why did you take the job when Jake asked you?"

"Because Jake is a friend and asked me to do the job, and because I'm good with my hands and enjoy restoration projects. I love all things vintage, whether a historical cabin like Old Sawyer's town house—now yours, of course—or a 1950 Harley Davidson Panhead like mine."

She rubbed her hand over the fabric.

"So are you a fly fisher?" she asked.

"Yes. I love the sport but don't take time for it much anymore. Jake told me you and Betsy fly fish."

"We do. Caught some northern pike when we first got to town. Betsy's father taught me a long time ago, and I passed it on to Betsy." She was hoping he wouldn't ask her any questions about her phantom husband and was relieved when he didn't. As she continued to look around, she noticed another door.

"So what's behind door number"—she put her finger to her head, counting—"four, I think?"

Shade hesitated, not sure if he was ready to share this complicated part of himself with Sue Ann, and then decided he would.

"I tell you what. I'm going to make coffee and pancakes, and then I'll show you. Deal?"

Sue Ann nodded her head, letting him know she liked the sound of breakfast, and leaned back on the sofa. He got a fresh pillow and a blanket out of the closet and returned to her. After placing the pillow on one end of the sofa, he made her stretch out, then covered her with a blanket. Before heading to the kitchen section, he bent down and pulled her hair over her chest, where her hands were crossed, like he was posing her.

"Do you want to put a bouquet of flowers in my hands, and maybe quarters over my eyelids?"

He ignored her comment and used his fingers to

crimp her curls with his fingers like he'd watched her do, and then gave her a quick kiss. He started to move away but turned back.

"Oh, what the hell!" He sat on the edge of the sofa, bent over, and kissed her again, another of his long steamy kisses with his tongue expressing what he felt for her. She put her good arm around him and began massaging his neck, and he prolonged the kiss. When he pulled his lips away, he kept his face close, staring into her eyes.

"Did I tell you how hypnotizing your eyes are? They make me crazy, wanting you. If I could just dive into those emerald green pools..." He rubbed his fingers over her face, kissed each eye, and had started to leave the sofa when she grabbed his arm.

"Why'd you leave and not come back, Shade? You broke my heart and made me feel like...like some old whore."

He took her hand, kissed it, and placed it on her stomach. He walked away a few feet and began pacing, running his hands through his hair.

"Not now, Sue Ann. I just can't talk about it right now. Something happened—something bad—and I've got to figure everything out, but I promise I won't disappear on you again."

"Not good enough. If you ever want to make love to me again, you'll have to tell me why you left me." She stared at him without smiling. "And that, Sweetheart, Darling, is an ultimatum." She closed her eyes and turned her face toward the back of the couch.

"Then I better figure out what the hell I'm going to do to meet that ultimatum before I explode like that truck of yours." Shade walked to the kitchen cabinet and pulled out pancake mix.

****

Shade took Sue Ann's plate, after she'd eaten her last bite of pancakes, and gently lifted her from the sofa. "So, door number four it is."

Once through the door, he placed her in an oversized leather chair, the only piece of furniture in the large open room, and placed her feet on the ottoman. She leaned up and looked around, absorbing the details of wood and glass; this room, like the rest, was a modern version of the log cabin. Sunshine filled the room with warmth and natural light from oversized windows, and shooting beams of light landed on large canvases that stood propped on easels. All were covered, playing "I've got a secret" like the master artist, or so she suspected, who painted them before covering. Another wood-burning stove stood in the middle of the room, but this one was magnificent, like the room. It looked like green marble, and even from a distance she could feel the heat radiating from it.

"That stove is beautiful. What's it made of?"

"It's soapstone, a natural heat retainer made by Mother Earth herself." Shade smiled, enjoying sharing his side of heaven with Sue Ann, even though circumstances were less than perfect.

Only one partial wall was solid in the room and stood tall and empty, sitting several feet out from the rest of the wall.

"You need to finish some of these paintings and fill that wall, Shade, assuming you are the artist."

He reached into the drawer in the small table beside the chair and pulled out a remote. With one push, previously invisible drapes blackened the windows, giving the illusion of nighttime; the empty log wall separated down the middle, with each half disappearing into nothingness. Native American flute music, somber yet beguiling, surrounded the room; spirit voices emerged from every corner as an oversized painting faded in with light as brilliant as the second coming.

Shade watched for Sue Ann's reaction.

She forgot her pain and moved to the edge of her chair as the mixture of hues and movement came alive on the stage, Shade's stage, its giant curtain swaying in radiant colors, irrepressible majesty in a room filled with magic. Aurora, the Roman goddess of dawn, danced, perfectly choreographed in the most beautiful ballet ever performed. Sue Ann's eyes traveled the full height of the canvas, almost as tall as the vaulted ceiling. She stared, mesmerized by green and yellow hues with a hint of red, as silvery streaks cast mini shadows over twinkle-toed, illusionary ballerinas. Huge and impressive, the painting captivated her, filling her with a sense of jubilation at the sheer splendor of it.

She sat gasping for breath, her gaping mouth and quivering chin covered by a hand shaking with emotion. She was filled with the beauty and wonder of the three-dimensional illusion appearing to move yet captured in oil on a two-dimensional static canvas.

"Come back to the light!" she whispered, not wanting to break the spell, unable to remove her gaze from the giant likeness of the same heaven she had witnessed. "Come back to the light!"

She sat still and quiet, her tears pouring, with no thought of wiping them away for fear the night dancers would disappear if she moved. Reality hit hard as the lights brought the wreck back to her in a storm of emotions: terror, relief, and the secret desire to go to them. All that had stopped her the night before was the thought of dying without getting to see and hold her precious daughter again.

Shade picked Sue Ann up out of the chair and took her place, cuddling her in his lap with his cheek rubbing the top of her head and his arms wrapped around her, soothing her and letting her cry it all out. Her eyes remained fixed on the painting, as did his as he tried to see and feel what she was experiencing. With her last sniff, she closed her eyes and fell asleep in his arms.

****

He didn't know how long she'd been asleep. All he knew was he was holding the only woman he could ever love. He would not leave Sue Ann Parish again, not for any reason other than to give his life for her if required. As he stared at his most perfect work, the Sky Dwellers drew him in and would not release him until he said aloud the words he'd sworn he would never say to any woman.

"I love you, Sue Ann Parish."

****

Shade heard the snowmobile motors grinding as they climbed the steep hill to the cabin and knew immediately Jake had gotten word to Betsy. Picking up the remote, he closed the wall, concealing the treasure he had shared for the first time, and uncovered the windows, letting sunshine fill the room again. He never left the chair, not wanting to disturb Sue Ann's deep sleep, knowing it was exactly what she needed right now.

Within minutes and without knocking, the back

door flew open, and Betsy hurried in with Jake on her heels.

"Mama?" Betsy called through her sobs.

"In here, Betsy," Shade called back.

Betsy dove onto the ottoman, fully clad in winter gear, including boots covered in snow, and wrapped her arms around her mother, putting her head in her lap, and crying. Shade reached his hand around the girl who was so much like her mother and caressed her hair.

"Mama," she said again but this time as a statement, in a soft whisper as if realizing her mother was truly okay.

****

Sue Ann was awake and holding to her daughter, who refused to leave her side until Bonnie, the physician's assistant for Moose Springs and other villages, told Betsy her mom needed a thorough exam. Jake had gotten Bonnie from her cabin that morning before going to Rose's to tell Betsy about her mother's wreck. He knew Betsy would demand to go to her mother immediately.

Jake, Betsy, and Shade left the studio so Bonnie could examine Sue Ann. In a few minutes, the P.A. came out and told everyone they could come back in now.

Betsy had a million questions, and Bonnie answered each one but qualified them by saying she could not be sure about internal injuries without the proper equipment only a hospital could provide.

"Then we need to get a Medevac and take her to the hospital." Betsy was pacing now and casting worried glances at her mother.

"Betsy, I told you I'm fine. I feel so much better

already, mostly because of seeing you. It was you, my daughter, who kept me determined to survive; well, and the lights watching over me."

"Lights? What lights, Mom? Did you have an out-of-body experience like that guy was talking about on RAT Net the other night?"

"We'll show you tonight, Betsy. Your mom doesn't need to be moved right now, and I know there's no way you two can be separated. You are both staying here." Shade looked from Betsy to Sue Ann, waiting for them to turn him down flatly.

"Mom, are you okay with that?" Betsy smiled and took her mom's hand. "At least if we're here, he won't disappear again." She frowned at him. "Isn't that right, Shade?"

"I won't disappear, Betsy." He looked at Jake. "That's a promise."

"Cross your heart and hope to die?" Betsy folded her arms and glared at Shade.

"No, Betsy! Never, ever say that again! Death is not something to joke about."

"Okay, Mom. No jinxes." Betsy hugged her mom and headed to the door.

"Where are you going, Bets?" Sue Ann called.

"To get my pack off the Snow Go." She glanced back at her mom. "No offense, Mom, but Shade's long johns are not making a fashion statement even for the bush." Betsy headed out the door.

"You made another call, didn't you?" Sue Ann grinned at Shade and took his hand.

"Yep." He bent over and kissed her while Betsy was outside. "But I kind of liked what you were wearing when we woke up together this morning."

Chapter Eleven
Sky Dwellers

Shade left mother and daughter talking about the wreck and went outside to cache number two. He had three caches, at least that were visible, but only one contained game he had killed. As soon as he saw Sue Ann and Betsy sitting side by side, he knew what he wanted to do, had to do. It was in the stars. After climbing the tall ladder steps to the platform where he had built the cache, he brought down a plastic bag and laid it in the arctic entry so he would not forget it when he headed into Moose Springs with Sue Ann and Betsy. He rubbed his hands in eager anticipation of starting what he knew would be his second great masterpiece.

That night, the three sat eating moose stew, Shade's specialty, with drop biscuits Betsy made from a mix. Dessert was buttered biscuits with wild raspberry jam, a gift from Jake's wife.

Sue Ann hid the pain she felt and even hastened her step a little with Betsy beside her, making sure she didn't fall. As darkness descended on the cabin, Betsy became antsy.

"Shade, could I speak to Mom in private for a minute?"

"Of course. I need to bring in a load of wood anyway."

After he closed the door, Betsy sat by her mom and

took her hand.

"You love him, don't you, Mom? I can tell by the way you stare at him when you think I'm not paying attention."

"I hardly know him, Betsy. Don't jump to conclusions just because he saved my life." Sue Ann put a finger to her chin. "Hmm! Well, that does count for something, I guess."

"Shade loves you, Mom. He can't take his eyes off you, and every time you groan, he puts his hands out like he's trying to save you all over again."

"Betsy, this is not the time or the place. It's too soon. Can we change the subject, please?" Sue Ann leaned her head back on the sofa and took her daughter's hand. "Besides, you and I have done just fine without a man in our lives for almost seventeen years, don't you think?"

"Well, you don't have to marry him tomorrow, you know." Betsy sat in silence. "But..." She didn't finish her thought.

"Do I even want to know what you're about to say?" Sue Ann scowled at her.

"I think you already know." Betsy left the sofa and opened the bedroom door. In a minute, she was back, carrying a blanket for herself. "I knew it."

"Knew what, Betsy?" Sue Ann kept the frown on her face.

"You slept with him—again." Betsy sat back and crossed her arms over her chest.

"Betsy, I was injured, only half conscious, and I didn't know where I was until I woke up with him trying to thaw me out with his body heat and a mile-high stack of down comforters and blankets. We certainly didn't do anything, if that is what you're suggesting."

"And why not?" Betsy cocked her head at her mother and folded her arms. "Oh, yeah. The wreck."

"Why not? You, my sixteen-year-old daughter, are asking me why I didn't have sex with a man I hardly know?" Sue Ann tried to get up, but a pain hit her. "Oh! That hurt." She sat back, leaning her head against the back of the sofa.

Betsy picked up her mom's hand. "Well, one of us has to be mature about this situation. You're thirty-seven and not getting any younger, as the cliché goes. And Shade is forty-two. That's perfect, Mom, and it's settled."

Betsy got up and headed for the coffeepot.

"What's perfect and settled?" Sue Ann cut her eyes at her daughter.

"I'm sleeping on the couch tonight, and you are sleeping with Shade. Just pretend I'm not here. You know I'm not a light sleeper, so this time, do something!"

Shade opened the door with a load of wood in his arms. His face was covered in a grin, and Sue Ann knew he had caught Betsy's last remarks.

"Don't you agree, Shade?" Betsy asked as she poured three mugs of coffee. "Black, right?"

"You are a very perceptive young lady, Miss Parish." Shade took his cup of coffee from Betsy. "In every way." Shade looked at Sue Ann and raised his eyebrows while he took his first sip of coffee. He sat in the chair by Sue Ann and reached for her hand. She did not object.

"Ready to join the Sky Dwellers in a little magic

show, ladies?" Shade asked a few minutes later.

Sue Ann looked at him and shook her head. "I don't think I'm ready to get back on that snowmobile, but you and Betsy can go."

"We don't have to leave the warm, cozy cabin." Shade stood and took a big gulp of coffee, almost burning his mouth. "Damn, that's hot! Sorry. I shouldn't be using profanity around a child." He smiled, knowing this would get a rise out of Betsy.

"Child indeed! I believe I'm more mature, in some matters, anyway, than my mother and her—whatever you are." She had her hands on her hips, casting frowns back and forth between Shade and her mother.

He couldn't help but laugh but stopped himself when he saw Sue Ann's serious expression. "Help me get everything ready, Betsy Boop. It's going to be a great show tonight."

Shade and Betsy grabbed the stack of down comforters from the bedroom. When Betsy saw the blood on the sheets beneath, she sat on the bed and started crying softly. Shade sat down by her and put his arm around her.

"She's okay, Betsy. I'm going to watch after her. I promise." He crossed his heart.

"No, Shade!" Betsy took his hand away from his heart. "Don't jinx it." She got up to leave. "We'll have to change those sheets before you and Mom go to bed," she announced matter-of-factly, her arms laden with comforters and pillows as she headed out the door.

Betsy and Shade spread the blanket on the floor in the room behind door number four, and made sure the thick comforters were on top. Pillows were added, and Betsy wondered if Shade had plans of the three of them sleeping here so no decision concerning sleeping arrangements would have to be made.

Betsy announced it was time, and Sue Ann started to get up off the sofa, but had grown stiff from sitting too long.

"Give me your hand." She held out her hand, but before Betsy could reach the sofa Shade scooped her mother up in his arms.

"Okay, Darling?" he asked without a hint of a smile.

"I can walk, Shade. Just let me lean on you," she scolded.

"Nope. I told Betsy I'd take care of you, and I'm not breaking my promise." He dropped to his knees by the pallet and eased Sue Ann down in the middle, making sure her head was on the pillow. "Are you comfortable enough, Sweetheart?" He asked as he spread the down comforter over her.

"Yes. I'm fine, thank you." Sue Ann glanced up at Betsy and noticed a quirky grin forming at the corners of her mouth. She was enjoying this far too much.

Betsy, who had changed into her flannel pajamas and a pair of Shade's wool socks, joined her mother on the other side of the pallet.

"This should be fun...whatever it is...probably a cop-out to keep from doing the sleep-together thing, but it's a good one, Shade." Betsy snuggled next to her mother.

"Time to get settled." Shade pulled his jeans off, leaving his long johns, and removed his shirt. Sue Ann stared at his muscular chest and could feel Betsy's eyes on him, as well. Sue Ann looked at Betsy and frowned. Putting her hand on her cheek, she turned Betsy's gaze away from Shade, but not before Betsy whispered, "Movie Star."

Shade heard the whisper and grinned as he nestled in on the other side of Sue Ann and held up the remote.

"Oh, wait! Need to turn the light out in the other room. It has to be totally dark. And you might better pull that down comforter up around your chins. It's about to get a little chilly." Shade added a stick of wood to the soapstone stove, with two sets of eyes on him as he moved from the stove back to the pallet.

He held the remote up and clicked. The blackout curtains covering the windows disappeared, exposing the bright winter wonderland outside through the massive walls of windows. With the next push of a button, another sound was heard above them. Betsy and Sue Ann cast their eyes up as a huge skylight opened, revealing luminous spheres of brilliance sparkling on a blue/black background. Betsy sat up to stare at the skylight.

"It's not glass! It's an actual hole in the ceiling! Far out!" Betsy let her head fall back on the pillow.

"A little night air will get to us, but the fans up near the ceiling will blow most of it back up."

"The man's a genius, or he's got more money than he can spend. Either way, can we keep him, Mom?"

Shade laughed, a good, hearty belly roll, and Sue Ann followed, holding to her ribs.

Shade hit the remote again, and the faint sound of Native American flute music filled the room, the same kind of music Sue Ann had heard that morning when Shade wowed her with his masterpiece. The music was soothing, like eagle wings on mountain breezes, and set the stage for what came next.

"I see it!" Betsy screamed and pointed. "It's Sirius, the brightest star!"

"Nope, you're wrong." Shade grinned. Betsy couldn't see him, but he took Sue Ann's hand and squeezed it.

"Am not! I learned it in physics. Besides, I have very intelligent genes. My mother has her doctorate, you know." Betsy crossed her arms but continued staring up. Her mother smiled beside her.

"I don't care what your genes are; Levis, Calvin Kleins, or Guess, that is not Sirius." Shade argued with vehemence and a good sense of humor. He left the floor bed and walked to a switch on the wall, lowering the fans' velocity so their sound would not overwhelm the ambiance he was trying to create.

"Mom, tell him. He is such a hardhead. Maybe you'd better keep looking after all. You were right. Shade is not a keeper." Betsy grinned. That would get a reaction from him.

"What? Did you say that, Sue Ann?" Shade's silhouette appeared against the bright windows of snow light. He was staring down at Sue Ann, and Betsy was laughing.

"Guilty!" Sue Ann announced. "But you're not too bad in an emergency."

"Well, I'm glad to know I redeemed myself." Shade crawled back under the covers and looked over at Betsy, who could see him now that her eyes had adjusted to the snow light.

"Okay, it's Sirius." Shade propped on one elbow. "But I have a better name for it—the brightest name I can think of." He went silent.

"We're waiting…" Betsy sang. "And it better be

good, after this drama."

"Betsy Boop." He put his arm around Sue Ann and drew her to him as he snuggled under the comforter. Betsy sat up and looked across her mother at Shade.

"He's just trying to impress me, Sue Ann, so he can get at my mother." Betsy lay back down and crossed her arms over her chest. "Well, it's working."

Sue Ann laughed so hard she snorted and then drew her knees to her chest as she groaned. Shade and Betsy butted heads as each reached across to console the patient.

"Okay." The dial on Shade's watch glowed as he punched it. "According to the last report I received from the Alaska Geophysical Institute, the show should begin any minute now."

"You are such a name dropper, Shade. You don't have a clue about the Geophysical Institute, but Mom does. She gets newsletters from them."

"I am a paid supporter, thank you very much, and well thought of in the geophysical community." Shade turned his gaze upward.

The room grew silent. First, a light mist wafted over the stars like it was being blown by an arctic breeze. The mist gave way to a blanket of light standing stationary, a galaxy.

"It's the Milky Way!" Betsy yelled.

"It is a galaxy," Shade interjected. "One of one hundred seventy billion known so far."

"Beautiful!" Sue Ann chimed in.

"Okay, are you naming this one after me, Shade?" Betsy propped on her elbow and looked across her mother, waiting for his reply.

"No. I'd never name a galaxy after you, princess.

You could never be a rejected child. Your mom loves you too much, and so does everyone who comes in contact with you—and can overlook your sarcasm."

"Gee! Thanks, but I'm not following your drift on this one." Betsy crossed her arms over her chest and gazed at the sky.

"I know," Sue Ann added and then waited until Shade and Betsy were settled and ready.

"Zeus, that Greek god who was so very stuck on himself, liked the women, not just the heavenly goddesses but us good old, down-to-earth mortal women, as well. Just as often happens, he had a baby boy, Heracles, by a mortal woman. Zeus loved his baby boy, but he was worried about him." Sue Ann paused, thinking about Betsy as the product of her and the man she had loved beyond the bounds of reason, the man who had made her not care to ever love again—until now. Her thoughts drifted to her own baby boy, Tobi, Betsy's twin brother who had died at birth. Sue Ann could feel the lump forming in her throat.

"Worried about what, Mom? What could a god like Zeus be worried about, especially with a brand-new baby boy? Isn't that what every man wants? A son?"

"Zeus knew his son was half mortal, and that meant..." Sue Ann's voice began to quiver. She knew she would not be able to finish the story and hoped this extreme emotionalism was due to her injuries. It was totally out of character for her. Shade squeezed her hand and, as if reading her mind, took up the story.

"Zeus knew his son, being half mortal, would die some day." Shade's deep, melodic voice was perfect to tell Zeus's story.

"While Hera, a heavenly goddess, was sleeping,

Zeus placed his baby boy at her breasts so he could drink her milk and become immortal. Zeus knew he was taking a chance but was determined his son should live forever as a god like himself.

"But Hera was a ruthless woman who hated Zeus's lovers and his offspring with them. As the baby suckled, Hera awoke and discovered the baby, a stranger, feeding at her breast. Heartlessly she shoved the baby away, and a jet stream of her milk splattered across the sky, forming a faint band of light perpetuated in Greek mythology as a galaxy, better known as…"

"The Milky Way!" Betsy and Shade finished in synchrony.

Soon the galaxy grew fainter, giving the night sky back to the stars, which seemed to sparkle more than usual, perhaps out of excitement at what would happen next. Then, as if by a giant bolt of electricity—or perhaps God spread his hands in one giant sweep—the sky undulated in green and yellow waves cascading across the sky. Across the flickering array of starlight, Aurora, madam of the night, drew her celestial wand and cast more brilliant flashes of awe for her earthly audience. As she danced, her colorful gown infused more hues and more movement, until the whole sky rolled in and out like a tumultuous sea, a kaleidoscope of colors that hit the shore and then bounced back to replay itself over and over.

Oohs and aahs dominated the scene, and Shade smiled in the dark. No one spoke as the Northern Lights moved rhythmically, keeping perfect time to the low melodic Indian flute in the background, until Betsy spoke.

"Tell the story, Shade."

"The story of the Northern Lights?" he asked.

"Yes. There has to be a story as magical as they are."

"There are so many, but I'll tell you my favorite."

Betsy turned her eyes upward, waiting for the dramatic voice she knew was coming, and hooked her arm through her mother's, putting her head next to hers.

"My favorite is told by the explorer Ernest Hawkes in his book *The Labrador Eskimo*, published in 1916. Hawkes was an explorer and an anthropologist who studied the indigenous peoples of Canada and Alaska. Anyway, here's how the Eskimos of Labrador explained the Northern Lights. I believe it to be true, and someday I will experience it firsthand.

"The magnificent canopy you see up there is not heaven, regardless of how celestial it appears. It is actually a hard dome arched over the earth. What is beyond, outside our reach, is the true heaven. If we could somehow be given the eye to perceive paradise, it would be through a tiny hole that allows the spirits passage to this mystical place, but only the spirits of those who have died a voluntary or violent death, and the raven, have been over this secret pathway. The spirits carry torches, lighting the path for those fortunate enough to enter. When the new spirits arrive, a big feast is thrown, and you can see them moving about, playing football with a walrus skull."

"Sh! Listen!" Shade put his finger to his lips and whispered. His voice was full of melodrama as he waited a few seconds before speaking barely above a whisper.

"Do you hear it? The crackling noise?" He paused again. "It's the voice of the spirit beings, *Selamiut*, the

Sky Dwellers, trying to communicate with you, Betsy, and you, Sue Ann, and even me, although I don't deserve them. The Sky Dwellers, or spirit people, only speak to those of us who believe. Always show respect, Betsy. Never shout or shake your fists at them. Speak in a whisper, and sometimes you will hear what the Sky Dwellers are telling you."

Silence followed, and Betsy, still nodding her head in agreement with the storyteller, held her gaze on the lights, listening.

"I'm never leaving Alaska." Betsy sniffled. "That was…was…amazing, Shade. Thank you."

Silence dominated the scene: Sue Ann nestled against Shade, who kept his arm around her, and Betsy snuggled tight, as close to her mom as she could get while lying on her back looking up. As she stared through the exposed ceiling at the sky that brightened and swirled with each color change, she wondered if Tobi was up there, kicking a walrus skull around. Betsy smiled and listened closely, hoping the spirits heard her thoughts, but she received no answer, not even a whisper. Betsy heard her mother's soft breathing and knew she had dropped off to sleep.

Shade held Sue Ann tight. He thought Betsy was asleep, too, as he moved his arm from under Sue Ann's head and propped on his elbow where he could look down at her. He leaned over and kissed Sue Ann, a soft gentle kiss on her lips as if trying not to wake her. With his eyes still looking down, he rubbed his fingers gently across her cheek before cuddling her back against his chest.

Betsy smiled.

Chapter Twelve
The Homecoming

The next day, Betsy helped Shade get the sled and dog team ready to take her mom back to Moose Springs. Shade packed the sled with down comforters and everything else he could find to pad the basket and prevent Sue Ann from being jostled and bumped on the long ride.

"Are you sure Mom will be all right, Shade? What if she has broken ribs, or some internal injuries we don't know about?" Betsy's face was outlined in worry.

"You tell me, Betsy. You know how stubborn your mom is. She's determined to get home today, although I don't know what's wrong with my cabin." Shade laid out the harnesses in preparation for bringing the dogs over.

"Yes, she is stubborn, but she loves our little cabin. I know you don't understand that, with this fine place of yours, but it is the first piece of property Mom and I have owned that is really ours, and we're quite proud of it. It's home, Shade."

"I do understand, Betsy, but I'm going to warn you, I'm not leaving your mom tonight—maybe not for a few nights, and maybe not forever." Shade looked away as if trying to gather his thoughts. "And I'm not sleeping on the sofa. If you're not prepared for that, you need to let me know now. I'm in love with your mama,

Betsy. It's not the wisest decision I ever made, not for you and her, anyway, but I love her, and for right now, I've got to know she's all right."

Betsy stared at Shade, and then out of the blue she walked to him and gave him a giant hug. Shade put his arms around Betsy.

"Thank you, Shade, for loving my mama."

Shade was speechless but loved the hug. He took it to mean he met with Betsy's approval.

"What's not to love, Betsy Boop?" Shade smiled at the girl who was a younger version of her mother. "Now. Let's get those malamutes hooked up and get your mother back to her little piece of Alaska. Are you ready?"

"Yes, sir!" Betsy answered with a smile at Shade as she headed with him to get the dogs.

Shade took a longer route than usual to Moose Springs, but it was a much smoother trail. Betsy drove the snowmobile and followed the dog team, letting them break trail for her. Shade stopped every few minutes and asked Sue Ann if she was okay. She finally told him to just get her home and she would truly be fine.

When Shade pulled the dog team into the cabin's parking area, a crowd of townspeople waited to greet their school principal. Every student and staff member plus most of the fifty-six locals were there. Even Don stood in the yard and offered his hand to help get Sue Ann into the cabin.

"Thanks, Don, but I've got her." Shade did not give Sue Ann time to argue as he swooped her up and carried her inside, putting her gently down in Old Green, where she was inundated with hugs, handshakes, and well wishes. Jake took charge of the team as soon as they pulled up and he had given him a firm handshake and a pat on the back. Shade had indeed redeemed himself.

The table and kitchen counters were covered with food, everything from baked salmon to Bernice's moose stew to a plateful of fry bread made by Rose and Lena.

"I put you a half gallon of ice cream in your freezer, Sue Ann. I wanted to bring you French vanilla 'cause I know it's your favorite, but I was sold out. Afraid you got Betsy's strawberry instead." Don smiled, something Sue Ann had never seen him do.

"I appreciate that, Don. I just hope Betsy will share with me. Thank you." Sue Ann held out her hand to him, and Don grasped it with both hands for a quick second before heading out of the cabin. Sue Ann knew she had another friend to add to the list.

The crowd left soon after, knowing Sue Ann needed to rest, but she refused to go to bed, preferring to recline in Old Green and just look around and admire her little piece of heaven. Bonnie came by later to check Sue Ann's injuries and take her vitals, and she announced to Sue Ann, Betsy, and Shade, "the patient seems to be recovering nicely." With orders for Sue Ann to take it easy for a few days and not to go back to work, Bonnie got ready to leave. Betsy insisted that Bonnie make herself a big plate of food to take with her. After Bonnie left, Sue Ann's quiet healing began.

She moved to the couch, at Shade's insistence, so he could hold her head in his lap and kiss her any time he wanted. Betsy tried to give her mother and Shade a little space and even decided to go over to Lena's for a while.

Jake had taken the dog team home with him to take care of them until Shade went back to his cabin, something unlikely to happen before Sue Ann was pretty much back to normal. But the last visitor for the day was a repeat: Jake returned with some surprises. He and Don had gone to the wreck site and salvaged what had not burned in the truck.

"I'm afraid we didn't find anything worth keeping, Sue Ann, but there was one little something I found that must have gotten slung out of the truck, or maybe was blown out in the explosion, but it seems to be in perfect condition." Jake held it out to her, and she took it, turning it over and over in her hands.

Her eyes filled, and Shade put his arm around her.

"Out of everything I lost, this simple little item was the most important for me to bring back to Betsy. Could you bring Noname to us, Jake? I'd like for Betsy to have her tonight. I never break a promise to my daughter."

"It just so happens Miss Noname is curled up on the seat of my truck as we speak."

Betsy cried when she saw Noname with her red collar.

"How did...?" For once the sixteen-year-old was speechless.

Sue Ann explained how Noname was already purchased before she left for Fairbanks and how Jake had salvaged the collar from the wreck, the only thing saved.

"It's a sign, Mama!" Betsy attached the leash Jake had left on Noname's collar and was ready to take off to Lena's house.

"Don't stay long, Betsy. It's almost dark," Sue Ann called but was glad to have a little time alone with Shade.

Shade held her and kissed her, being careful of her injuries, as they sat together on the couch. He leaned back and pulled her head to his chest, where he played with her hair and rubbed her hurt arm gently.

"Shade, I don't know how to thank you for…"

He put his finger over her mouth and stopped her.

"I love you, Sue Ann. I know we haven't known each other long, and I know I almost screwed everything up, but you need to know. I love you and have since that day you claim I tried to kill you." He watched for her reaction.

"How can you be sure, Shade? You've had plenty of women. Look at you. You're…you're…"

"Please don't tell me I'm 'movie star good-looking' as Betsy puts it. I'm not a movie star, Sue Ann. I'm just a man, a man in love for the first time in his life. I've never allowed myself the pleasure of loving a woman until now, and God help me, I shouldn't, but I do love you." He pulled them both upright and turned her face to look into his.

"I'm a man with a past, a very bad past. I'm not proud of it, but it happened, and I'll be paying for it for the rest of my life."

"Is that why you disappeared on me?" She kept her eyes glued to his.

"Yes. And if I were not such a weakling where you are concerned, I'd disappear for good right now, to protect you and Betsy. You have no idea who you're dealing with, or what the consequences could be." He sat up on the edge of the couch, running his fingers through his hair like a man distraught, a habit she would become accustomed to in him. He propped his elbows on his knees and clasped his hands, his eyes on the floor. Sue Ann put her arm on his back and rubbed his neck.

"Tell me, Shade. What has you so upset and so fearful you would disappear on me? Especially if you love me like you say you do."

"I can't tell you. Not now. You have to understand and trust me." He left the couch and stood facing her. "If I disappear again, and I could, it won't be because I don't love you. It will be to protect you and Betsy. If that happens, promise me you will move away from here fast. I'll leave money with Jake. It will be enough that you and Betsy can disappear if need be, and start over somewhere else. You have to swear you'll do this, Sue Ann. This is not a joke." He turned away and paced back and forth several times before stopping to face her again.

"What the hell am I doing? I should leave right now because I love you."

Before Sue Ann could argue with him, the back door opened and Betsy and Noname flew in. Betsy unfastened the leash, and Noname bounded into the living room, stopping at Shade. He reached down and ruffled the dog's thick fur around her neck.

Betsy took her snow gear off in the arctic entry and walked in, grinning from ear to ear but stopped when she saw her mom's and Shade's faces.

"You two have a fight or something?" Betsy sat down by her mom. "You're not leaving, are you, Shade?" Betsy took on a serious look. "You said you loved my mama." Betsy turned to her mom. "What's going on?"

"Betsy, it's just a little disagreement. Everything will be fine. Don't worry." Sue Ann looked at Shade. "You're not going anywhere, are you, Shade?"

Shade hesitated and moved his gaze to the darkness outside the window. The Northern Lights spoke to him, saying, "Follow your heart." He was not sure if they meant "Follow your heart and stay," or "Follow your heart and leave," but he knew what he would always do would be to protect Sue Ann and Betsy.

"No. I'm staying right here—unless you and Betsy come back to my cabin." Shade moved from the window and sat on the other side of Sue Ann, putting his arm around her.

"Shade, I think that is a bit much for a commute to school, even by snowmobile, but let's not talk about it now. I'm hungry. Moose stew and fry bread are calling my name, and maybe some of Don's strawberry ice cream, too, if my daughter will let me have some."

"I'd say, from the look of the spread folks left and the greeting you had today, you are no longer *cheechakos*." Shade sat on the bench by Sue Ann with a heaped plate in front of him. Holding up his glass of sweet tea, he proposed a toast.

"To Sue Ann and Betsy, newest inductees to the SFABD, Sourdough Fellowship of Alaskan Bush Dwellers." They clicked their glasses together with all three smiling, but Shade knew Sue Ann could see the worry hiding behind his façade.

****

Betsy took Noname to her room, and soon no sound could be heard coming from the upstairs. Betsy, with Noname snuggled beside her, was sound asleep with the door closed. Sue Ann knew what this implied.

Shade looked at his watch.

"You do have a radio, don't you?"

"Of course. Have to listen to Northern Voices when I'm still awake at 9:20 each night. Is that what you want to hear?" Sue Ann asked. "The radio is in the old pie safe. Just open the doors and turn it on."

"We have a few minutes, but I'll go ahead and get it going. It wouldn't hurt for us to listen to a little gospel music before we go to bed." He raised his eyebrows and winked at her, asking, "How's the soreness?" before he opened the doors to the pie safe, a primitive antique cupboard, and bent over to examine it closer.

"Still there, but getting better every time I look at you." She waited a few seconds for her words to sink in. "Nice butt!"

Shade looked around at Sue Ann, saw her smile, and then turned his head around as far as possible trying to see his butt.

"Thanks. I'll leave that verdict up to you, my pretty." He grinned. "But I'll be the judge of yours."

"Betsy said you talked to her about our sleeping arrangement. I'm just not sure about this, Shade. I know she's almost seventeen, and she is so worried about me being alone when she goes off to college, but…"

"I won't force you, Sue Ann, but I plan on this being a long-term commitment, something I've never had, never wanted until now. I'm forty-two and, as Betsy says, "not getting any younger." Shade turned his attention back to the pie safe but not to the radio.

"You didn't get this at Moose Springs Mall. It's walnut, and really old, way over a hundred, for sure."

Shade ran his hand along the walnut surface and then examined the six tin inserts in the two doors. Each insert had holes punched to provide air for the home-baked delicacies once tucked away inside.

"The children of this pie safe's day didn't unwrap a cupcake from a cellophane wrapper; nor did they take candy or cookies out of a box. They just opened the pie safe doors and checked out what Mama had baked in the oven of her woodstove that day." Shade was captivated by the old antique piece and the human history embedded in it. "Amazing! The pie safe is definitely my favorite piece of furniture in your cabin, although Old Green is still pretty comfortable."

Shade had turned to leave the pie safe when he noticed the design made by the holes punched in the tins on the doors. All six were the same design.

"As if it needed anything to make it more perfect, check out the design on the doors, Sue Ann. Six stars and a moon surrounded by holes I think represent more stars, or lights in the sky. I'm thinking it's the Aurora. How perfect is that?"

He left the pie safe and returned to Sue Ann.

"See, I can kiss you under the Northern Lights whether we're in my cabin or yours. Yep, it's a sign, all right." Shade mocked Betsy, who was always looking for a sign, a good omen for her mom and her, and now for Shade, too. He kissed Sue Ann as Northern Voices began pouring messages over the waves to and from people living in the bush: people keen on living a subsistence lifestyle, providing for self and/or family through living off the natural resources of the wild; people isolated from society by choice just to live on their own terms; and people isolated out of fear of their past creeping up on them. Most were normal honest folks experiencing the best part of Alaska, freedom to be one's self and enjoy the surreal beauty and natural resources of the Last Frontier. Some were loners escaping from hell. And a few were the hell from which others escaped.

"This one is sent out to Sadie and the kids at Sleetmute from Papa Norm. Done good trapping; home on the weekend."

Ten minutes of chatter later, Shade had not received a message, always a good sign, but he knew he'd better listen until the end. He was getting coffee for Sue Ann and himself when he heard it. He put the cups down too fast and spilled a little from one cup. Not taking the time to wipe it up, he turned his attention to the radio, listening from the kitchen.

"Going out to Raven from Mama Bear. Baby Bird is good, but Fox is not good. Sorry to hear about your old home place. Good All Hallow's Eve."

Shade headed for the cabin door, leaving the coffee cups and the spilled coffee on the cabinet. He stood looking up, hoping the lights would come and wake him from his nightmare. He had not even taken the time to put his boots on, and he stood in the snow in his sock feet. His mind was rushing like the Tekooni after breakup, but he didn't know which way to turn. The stars covered the sky, looking like the tin punches in Sue Ann's cupboard doors, but no heavenly lights spoke to him this night. Grabbing three sticks of wood, he headed back in to pretend replenishing the stove was his reason for going outside. He needed to get back to Sue Ann and hoped she had not noticed his quick exit. First stop tomorrow on his way to the cabin would be the Trading Post for a copy of the *Fairbanks Daily News Miner* to see what had happened at his old cabin in Fox.

When Shade reached his cabin the next morning, he rushed in and spread the newspaper on his table and began scanning it. He didn't have to go past the front page.

State troopers report two residents have gone missing in the Fox area in the last five days. David Fielder of 209 Beaver Road and Monica Shelby from 148 Aspen Circle were last seen at Fielder's cabin five days ago. Vehicles of both were left parked in front, and the lights and radio were left on in their cabins, arousing the curiosity of neighbors. A neighbor who doesn't want to be identified reported the disappearances to police after noticing Fielder's dogs had not been fed or watered in days. Fielder has lived in the cabin at 209 Beaver Road for the last ten years, but Shelby is a newcomer to the area. Law enforcement has named one person wanted for questioning. Fielder had expressed distrust of a drifter who called himself "Shockey" who rented a small shack in the back yard of Fielder's property. As a neighbor related, Fielder said he was planning to "run Shockey's ass off." The police are requesting any information available to help find the two missing residents and "Shockey."

Chapter Thirteen
Tulen

Sue Ann watched as Shade paced from window to window, looking out as the snow piled up, banking against the cabin. He had been with Sue Ann ever since the wreck, and even though she'd told him he was free to return to his cabin whenever he wanted, Shade refused to leave her. Sue Ann was not sure she was doing the right thing by having Shade live with her and sleep in her bed at night, with Betsy just across from them, but Betsy assured her mom she was comfortable with the arrangement. Sue Ann loved falling to sleep in Shade's arms—and the lovemaking, though toned down tremendously in the close confines of the little cabin, was the snowcap on the mountaintop. But as the days grew shorter, Shade became restless.

During the day he would go to his cabin, but before nightfall he was back with Sue Ann and Betsy. With Jake's help, he had built a dog yard for his team out by the old cache so he could tend to his animals himself, but Betsy loved taking care of the dogs and always helped. She had learned how to handle the team and the sled, and Shade had said she would soon be ready to take a few dogs out on her own, but only around town.

****

"Shade, we need to talk." Sue Ann brought two cups of coffee to the living room and handed one to

Shade, who stood looking out into darkness as he had done several times this week.

"What about?" Shade asked as he took the cup from Sue Ann's hand.

"I think you need to spend more time at your cabin. You need to finish the paintings you've started. I'd be willing to bet you haven't picked up a brush since you saved my life."

Shade put his cup down and moved to Sue Ann.

"Are you tired of me, Darling? Am I not man enough for you anymore?" Shade put his hands under Sue Ann's sweater and caressed her breasts. Reaching down, he unfastened her jeans, moving his hands inside to grope her hips and pull her close to him. Weak at the knees, Sue Ann put her arms around his neck and her head on his chest to balance. Before she knew what was happening, Shade had whisked her up and headed upstairs.

"Are you sure Betsy is spending the night with Lena?" he asked as he removed her clothes and then his.

"I'm sure. I talked to her just before you came in."

"Then get ready, Sweetheart. Your man is back!"

****

Thanksgiving was spent in Shade's cabin, but Betsy would only spend one night. Her plans were to go to Fairbanks with Rose and Lena to do some early Christmas shopping.

On Thanksgiving eve, Shade presented Sue Ann and Betsy with large, wrapped gifts.

"It is Thanksgiving, not Christmas, Shade. What is this?" Betsy tore into her package but decided to wait for her mom before opening the box.

"Oh, before you two open those, I need to tell you I have an ulterior motive for giving you these, but I'll explain when you've opened them."

Sue Ann and Betsy each lifted her box top and reached in at the same time, pulling out emerald green velvet down parkas adorned with white fox ruffs.

"These are beautiful, and green is our signature color." Sue Ann pulled the parka over her head and posed. "It's so beautiful! Put yours on, Betsy."

Betsy quickly pulled her parka over her head and posed beside her mom.

"Wait!" Shade moved in front of Betsy first, reached inside the white fox ruff that edged the hood, and pulled out handfuls of golden ringlets. Her long strands cascaded over a background of emerald green velvet.

Shade moved to Sue Ann and repeated the ritual, but added a kiss as magical as the scene he created.

"Bernice made these for me. Jake traded for the white fox, and I bought the pelts from him. I had the velvet left over from another project and knew what I wanted to use it for the first night you two slept here."

Shade checked his watch, grabbed his own parka and his camera, led his models to the arctic entry to put on snow boots, and took Sue Ann by the hand with Betsy following to the outside to present the green-eyed lookalikes to the Sky Dwellers.

Shade captured shot after shot of the two females he adored, stopping every once in a while to warm the camera batteries inside his parka and to re-pose his models against the green-and-yellow spectrum of the Alaskan sky.

As they started back to the cabin, Betsy stopped

them.

"My turn to play photographer. I need to take your picture together. You've brought magic into my mom's life, Shade, and it needs to be perpetuated here and now—under Northern Lights."

Shade smiled and took Sue Ann's hand, leading her to a spot away from the cabin, where the snow gleamed pure and white against a forest backdrop of evergreens tipped in the same purity. With his arms around her, he pulled her hood off her face and released her mass of golden curls that sparkled under the heavenly lights. Then he lifted her face, not posing—only doing what came naturally to someone in love. Sue Ann placed her gloved hand on Shade's cheek and caressed it before putting her arms around his neck. She stood on her tiptoes as he leaned down and kissed her. Aurora danced above, showing her approval of the scene below.

Later, as the three stretched out on the pallet under the heavens of Shade's art studio, silence dominated. No mythology; no Eskimo legends; no Betsy Boop jokes; no reminders of babies lost at birth. Just three people huddled closely together staring, enamored, at the ethereal dramatization they loved.

****

After Betsy left with Rose and Lena, Shade filled every waking moment with lovemaking and showering Sue Ann with tender affection.

"So when will you finish the painting of Betsy and me?" She smiled and placed her hand on Shade's. "It's obvious photography is not your main medium of art, not with the display you showed me that day after my wreck."

"If you think what you witnessed on that big wall was something, wait until you see what I have planned for you two. But, I need to warn you, it will not be a quick process. As I told you, I am a perfectionist when it comes to my creations."

"Is that what Betsy and I are to you? Creations?"

"Let me rephrase that. I am a perfectionist when it comes to my creations and re-creations. With or without my paintbrush, you and Betsy are the embodiment of all that is celestial, all that can be recreated on canvas. You are perfection, Dr. Sue Ann Parish, and I promise to do you and Betsy justice in my studio. But there will be no sneak peeks and no chances to play art critic. My subjects—my painting."

****

The days were getting shorter and shorter, and the temperature plummeted each night. Shade spent less and less time at Sue Ann's, but she knew he was working on his second great masterpiece, as he called it. Still, sometime in the wee hours of each night, he eased into bed beside her.

Christmas holidays were about to begin, and all Betsy wanted for Christmas was to spend her break in Mississippi with Annie. It would be Sue Ann and Betsy's first Christmas apart, but Sue Ann agreed to let her daughter go, having witnessed how much she missed Annie.

Shade picked up Sue Ann and Betsy in the huge four-wheel-drive truck he kept parked in a shed down from his cabin. Sue Ann had bought a new truck after the wreck, but Shade did not want her alone on the treacherous road again.

After putting Betsy on the plane, Shade took Sue

Ann to eat at the Turtle Club outside Fairbanks, his favorite place to eat dinner and the place having the best halibut in the Interior.

"Do you mind if I order wine to go with the halibut?" Shade asked, knowing already what Sue Ann's answer would be.

"Please do." Sue Ann figured fish, white wine, but was no connoisseur of fine wine.

Shade ordered a Pinot Noir and specified, "with no heavy oak taste."

"Isn't that a red wine? I was taught red with meat, white with fish, but I've never been privileged with a lot of fine dining or fine wines." Sue Ann smiled at Shade. "So are you a master sommelier as well as master artist, master designer of luxurious log cabins, master roofer—"

"Yes, it is a red wine, and no, I'm not a master sommelier. I just know what I like and learned from the best, and that would be Pinot Noir with halibut." He stared across the table at Sue Ann with her green cowl-necked sweater pulled just below her chin accentuating her haunting eyes. Neither food nor wine was the main thing on his mind.

"What I really want to be is master lover to the woman I love, who is sitting across from me, the same woman who is making me wish we could cut out of here and head for my cabin." Shade reached across and took Sue Ann's hand in his. "I'd like to make insane, passionate love to you the rest of the night while Aurora, the other woman in my life, looks down turning green and yellow with envy."

Shade rubbed the empty fingers of Sue Ann's left hand.

"Why don't you wear rings, Sue Ann? You're the only woman I have ever known who isn't strung up with every stone, real or otherwise, known to mankind."

"Empty hand—empty heart!" Sue Ann quipped. Looking down at her ring finger, she wished she could take back her words, fearing it would bring up a barrage of questions she did not want to answer.

"Your husband, Betsy's father." Shade made it more as a statement than a question.

Sue Ann became quiet as if in deep thought.

"When you decide to go to confession, I'll go to confession, but not a moment sooner." Sue Ann removed her hand from Shade's and took a sip of wine, her eyes sparkling more than the expensive Pinot Noir so well balanced with the flaky halibut steaks just as Shade had said it would be.

"Well, I'll just have to wait, I guess." Shade picked up Sue Ann's hand again. "Tomorrow is our last day in the city. You've seen very little of it, so what's your pleasure, Darling—other than me."

Sue Ann put her finger to her puckered mouth as if thinking.

"Art gallery." She answered after only mild reflection. "I want to go to the best art gallery in Fairbanks. I know your work has to be there some place, even though you refuse to talk about it."

Shade looked away, and Sue Ann sensed his uneasiness with her request.

Okay," Shade answered and attempted a smile.

****

After a healthy session of lovemaking in the hotel, Sue Ann fell asleep, a deep sleep filled with worry for her sixteen-year-old daughter, who was flying thousands of miles by herself with only the promised assistance of the flight attendant.

In the night, Sue Ann awoke to find Shade's side of the bed empty. She noticed the phone cord stretching to the closed bathroom door and left the bed. As she stood at the door, she could hear a phone ringing on the other end, but no one answered.

"Damn it! Pick up!" she heard Shade say under his breath. As he slammed the receiver down, Sue Ann hurried back to bed. In a few minutes, she turned toward Shade, who lay on his back, the back of one hand resting on his forehead as he stared at the ceiling.

"Can't sleep, honey?" Sue Ann combed her fingers through his chest hair, letting her fingers stop to play with his nipples.

"I'll be fine." Shade put both arms over his head as she moved her lips to his nipples, pulling them with her lips.

"Oh, god, woman! What you do to me!" Shade moaned and reached to free his erection from the covers, letting it grow unfettered. "Most men think, just as I did, that only women get aroused by their nipples getting teased, but you taught me different."

Sue Ann moved down on him, enjoying the sounds of pleasure emanating from him, making him forget whoever did not answer the phone. When she felt he was ready, she straddled him, preparing to ride to the finish line.

"Maybe this will help you sleep, baby." She gently swayed, keeping rhythm to his heightening thrusts, until Shade reversed their positions and broke for the home stretch, taking her with him.

****

The Alaska Museum of Art, located in the heart of downtown Fairbanks, was a huge but unassuming structure. Shade pulled his collar up as he headed inside holding tight to Sue Ann's hand. She was surprised when he did not remove his sunglasses, but said nothing.

The first floor was filled with Alaska Native art from every indigenous culture in the state.

"So? Are you going to keep me in suspense?" Sue Ann put her hands on her hips and stared at Shade, waiting for an answer. It was then she saw a beautiful woman dressed in a fashionable black silk pantsuit, her elegant stilettos tall, expensive, and impractical. Her nametag read Dr. Hattie Baird, Museum Curator, and Sue Ann started toward her. Shade stayed back, and Sue Ann felt sure he was only feigning interest in a large canvas of historical Siberian Yupik artwork depicting a whale hunt.

"Excuse me, but could you tell me if you have any pieces by Shade Dubois?"

"Shade Dubois? I don't recognize the name. Does he possibly paint under a pseudonym?" The woman never acknowledged Shade or even cast him a glance.

"I really don't know, but he paints huge canvases of the Aurora Borealis," Sue Ann added, looking around for Shade, who had disappeared.

"Ah! That helps. The Northern Lights is a favorite subject of artists in Alaska. If you will go down the third wing, all the way to the end, you'll find a room filled with our magnificent lights."

"Thank you, Dr. Baird."

"Glad I could help you. I don't believe I got your

name. Is that a lovely southern accent I detect?"

"Sue Ann Parish. Dr. Sue Ann Parish. I live at Moose Springs and am totally intrigued by the lights and Alaska in general. I'm from Mississippi originally but moved up to take the job of principal of the school."

"Well, it's good to meet you, Dr. Parish. Enjoy the exhibit." The elegant lady walked over toward another group of art admirers but turned back before reaching them. "Please bring your students on a field trip some time."

Sue Ann still could not find Shade. She shrugged her shoulders and headed for the third wing.

The Northern Lights gallery was by far the most popular section of the museum and displayed works for sale as well as for exhibit only, but it was Suite C where there was standing room only. Native American flute music played softly in the background, as the same slow, external strobe lights used by Shade in his studio worked their magic, making the paintings come alive on the walls. Squeezing through the crowd, she stood looking up at the huge canvas, just a little smaller than the one in Shade's studio. The price tag on it was a staggering $350,000. Across it was stamped the word SOLD in bold red print. All but one of his paintings were sold. But it was the name sketched in the bottom corner in small, sweeping script that caught her eye.

"Raven!" screamed at her, and she reached out, wanting to touch it, but withdrew her hand when the Do Not Touch sign caught her eye.

"It's awesome, isn't it?" A sweet voice sneaked up on her as a petite teenage girl with a slight Asian-doll look stood next to her, gazing upward, following the bright colors of the Aurora Borealis from the base of the log cabin in its forefront to the highest point where the lights reflected off the mountains behind. Sue Ann recognized the setting, but the cabin was more like hers than Shade's.

"Old Sawyer's cabin," she said under her breath.

"What did you say?" the girl asked.

"I was just saying how I love the old cabin. It's a perfect contrast, with its rustic simplicity, and showcases the lights, the dominant feature."

"Yes, it is." The girl folded her arms. "You have a good eye for art and an excellent way with words." The girl held out her hand to Sue Ann. "My name is Tulen. I work here part-time. My mother is the curator."

Sue Ann turned to face the girl and was met by sapphire blue eyes. Blue eyes were rare among Asian children, and Sue Ann knew the girl's Caucasian ancestry must date back prior to the French war in Indochina that ended in 1954, an ancestry that allowed her recessive blue genes to prevail.

Sue Ann left the museum a few minutes later after searching for Shade but not finding him. She checked the parking lot and saw him standing by the truck. Once Sue Ann was in the truck, he started it up without making any comment or asking any questions.

Shade was moody and silent most of the ride back to his cabin, and Sue Ann wished she had not requested the visit to the museum. She'd had no idea it would affect him this way, especially after seeing the money he made off his art.

"The man's a genius, or he's got more money than he can spend. Either way, can we keep him, Mom?"

Betsy's words had proved true, but the most disconcerting discovery was the beautiful part-Asian pixie princess, Tulen, with eyes identical to Shade's.

A few hours later, they turned in to the road that led to Shade's cabin. When Shade stopped the truck, he propped his hands on the steering wheel and laid his head on top of his hands, making no effort to get out. Several seconds cut through the silence until he lifted his head and turned his eyes to Sue Ann. His glare was a cold, cold glacier, and Sue Ann felt uncomfortable, like an intruder in her lover's world of secrets.

"You saw her, didn't you?"

"Which one? Dr. Baird—or your daughter, Tulen?"

Shade said nothing as he opened the truck door and came around to Sue Ann's side to help her out and to take her overnight bag.

After entering the cabin, Shade put on coffee and headed into the studio, closing the door behind him. A few minutes later, Sue Ann knocked on the door, her hands full of coffee mugs.

"Come in," Shade announced as if talking to a visitor.

Shade was sitting in his chair in silence, watching his masterpiece perform the ballet of Aurora but without music. A folded letter sat on his lap, and Sue Ann felt she was intruding upon his silent misery.

She handed the cup of coffee to Shade, who did not leave the chair. He took it and, in return, handed Sue Ann a photograph. After taking a sip, his eyes met hers, and he began to talk as she stared at the picture of the girl in the museum.

"Seventeen years ago, I took an assignment in North Vietnam, behind enemy lines. The job required stealth, invisibility, and the propensity to kill, a job I could only accomplish alone, except for a translator, assuming I could find one.

"The translator's name was Lam, which means 'jungle,' an appropriate name since Lam was left at the edge of the jungle as an infant. The Catholic sisters found her near the orphanage and saw the baby's mother run away through the jungle. They knew whose child she was and who the father was. They also knew Lam would not stand a chance if they didn't take her in. Her eyes alone would make her a hot item in the sex market.

"Lam's father was an American mercenary hired as an operative through a private American company to fight with the French in Indochina before they were defeated at Dien Bien Phu. He was said to have very light blue eyes, probably like mine, white hair, and was very fair complexioned, almost albino. Even though brown is a dominant eye color, Lam got the recessive gene from her father and had dark blue eyes with the addition of flecks of gold—she looked like she was mothered by an Indochinese tiger.

"Growing up in the Catholic orphanage in Saigon, one of the last ones allowed, Lam was taught to speak English. But the main thing Lam learned was never to trust any man, especially American soldiers, who raped her repeatedly in the jungles whenever she tried to run away from the orphanage.

"I found Lam just before going across into North Vietnam. She was a petite, tiger-eyed beauty, and only seventeen at the time. Lam agreed to help me by translating what was being said in the VC camps we stalked at night. I had no idea what the outcome of this partnership would be.

"Having the craftiness of a tiger and the soft step of

a fawn, Lam led me right into the middle of the Viet Cong central unit and to the man I had been paid to kill. It was an easy shot, but I chose to sneak up on him while he showered and cut his throat with my knife, much quieter but also more dangerous. Within seconds, I was threading my way back through leech-infested water, rice paddies, and jungles filled with real tiger eyes watching and ready to grab me for their next meal. I clutched my knife, ready for a tiger attack since I could not risk firing my rifle. Fortunately, the tigers did not attack, although I sensed one's presence. Perhaps, he felt the same camaraderie I did with him and knew we were soul mates, both with the natural instinct to kill."

Shade dropped his eyes and sipped coffee before continuing.

"When I reached our rendezvous spot, Lam had disappeared, and I did not have time to look for her, knowing the general's body would soon be discovered. His company, about fifteen hundred strong, would be searching for the assassin responsible. Two years passed, and my memories of Lam faded." Shade looked at Sue Ann, not wanting to finish the story but knowing he had to in order for her to understand.

"Yes, we had sex. She teased me, constantly flaunting her nude body in front of me and begging for it. I never raped her, Sue Ann, but I certainly felt nothing for her except satisfaction in relieving my young, pent-up sexual craving.

"Again, I took an assignment, but this time it was to kill a dignitary in the South Vietnamese government, someone who might become a political leader but was a known VC sympathizer. I was to track him as he secretly made contact across enemy lines. Again, I needed Lam's help. I went to the orphanage looking for information of her whereabouts. The Catholic sister who had directed me to Lam two years earlier saw me and asked me to wait in her private quarters. Soon, she brought a baby girl, a little over a year old, and placed her in my arms.

" She told me, 'This is your daughter, Tulen. It means Angel,' and she began the questions that turned my world around and started to change the way I looked at everything.

" 'What will you do with her?' Sister Agnes asked me. 'Allow her to live on the streets of Saigon and be the target of every man who wants to rape a blue-eyed Amerasian girl? If I did not hide Tulen, she would be stolen and sold for use on the slave sex market, even as a toddler, until her little womb is torn to pieces, resulting in her death. You must help. Find a way. Your genes fill her soul, and her eyes, your eyes, plead with you.'

"I sat in a chair and looked down at the baby in my lap. The little doll stretched her light blue eyes wide open, as if knowing she needed to prove she was my daughter. Her eye shape only hinted at the slant of her mother's ancestry, and she had the most beautiful smile I'd ever seen. I held her close to my face, and she reached her tiny hand out, first touching my lips and then my eyes. It was like she recognized me, Sue Ann, but we'd never met."

Shade grew quiet.

"So how did you save Tulen? And what part did Hattie Baird play in this?" Sue Ann leaned forward and placed her hand on Shade's leg, still stretched out on the ottoman beside her.

"I can't tell you about Hattie; that's hers to tell, but she adopted Tulen and brought her to the U.S. as a favor to me. Other than seeing her as a baby, I've only seen my daughter one other time until today. I couldn't stay in the museum, Sue Ann. It isn't safe for me to be around my daughter. I send her typed letters with no return address, and I use a false postmark, and I never send a photo. She doesn't know me, and it has to stay that way."

"And what happened to her mother in South Vietnam? Where is Lam today?" Sue Ann sat with her hands folded, waiting. Again Shade grew quiet and introspective.

"I completed that job without Lam, but later, I saw her in a bar in Saigon. She was drunk and hanging all over a bunch of GIs, letting them do anything and everything to her. I was repulsed, but she was my daughter's birth mother. I took Lam away and paid for a bungalow for her in a small village. She never once asked about Tulen."

"And you slept with her again." Sue Ann's voice was filled with disgust as she moved away from Shade and stood, her eyes focused on the painting with her back to him.

"Yes, but only because she got me drunk on snake wine."

"Eve and the apple, huh?" Sue Ann turned and stared at Shade, letting him see her disappointment.

"Snake wine is a mixture of snake venom and alcohol. It's highly potent. I meant to have one drink with her, but before I knew it—well, I don't have to tell you what happened. After we had sex, I passed out. It was like being in a coma, until I felt her knife plunge deep into my back the next morning. I rolled off the cot, grabbed the knife out of my back, ripping my own skin in the process, and went after her even though she had a pistol pointed at me. She had a VC flag draped around her lower body, taunting me about how they took care of her, and she would kill me for them." Shade rubbed his hands through his hair, and Sue Ann could see his hands shaking.

"I killed her, Sue Ann. I killed Tulen's mother with my bare hands around her throat."

"My God! How horrible, Shade!" Sue Ann returned to the ottoman and sat with her eyes focused on Shade before changing the subject.

"So you are the phantom father in your daughter's life?"

"Yes. I make sure she is educated in the most prestigious private girls' schools, and she and Hattie want for nothing. I'll always take care of my daughter financially, but I have to stay away from her to protect her. She can never know me, Sue Ann."

"Protect her from what, or should I say from whom?" Sue Ann's eyes took on a look of both disbelief and fear.

"That's enough." Shade shook his head. "I'm not free to tell you more, not now, and I pray to God I never have to."

"Just one question, and I'll leave it for now. Were you hired by the CIA or the U.S. military?"

"Sometimes both, but I wore no uniform, and if I killed for them, there was no record of it. I was a hired gun, a sniper with an eye as keen as a raven and the strength and prowess of a tiger. Call it a soldier of fortune, a mercenary, an operative, whatever in the hell anyone with money chose to call me is what I became, but the truth is I was a hired gun, a sniper, a hit man. The last job I did like that was in 1969, and that was where I made a mistake, one that cost me. The price is never being able to be around my little girl, but that's all I'm going to tell you, at least for now."

Shade pushed the remote, closing the doors to the painting, and left the chair. He stopped at the door and turned back.

"I need you, Sue Ann. God knows, I need you right now." Shade held out his hand, and Sue Ann took it and followed him to the bedroom.

****

Later in the night, Sue Ann was awakened by Shade's body jerking as he groaned in his sleep. His arm was no longer around her, and he was lying on his stomach with his legs spread apart and his arms spread upward holding his head. Again his body shook. She raised herself on one elbow and watched him for a few seconds to see if he was waking from his nightmare, but his groans and whines continued. Shade trembled again. His whole body quaked as if in distress, and Sue Ann moved close to him, spreading her leg over his hips and rubbing his back, especially where the long raised scar stood, the scar Lam had given him.

Without warning, Shade leapt to all fours, like a wild beast, and growled like he was in attack mode. He had become a tiger ready for the kill, and Sue Ann was his prey. Jumping astride Sue Ann, he pinned her arms to the bed and hooked his feet under her legs; she could not move under the weight of his body. His eyes pierced the darkness in a crazed, nonhuman glare as he gave another loud guttural sound, an adrenaline release that knew only one escape.

"Lam, you mother-fucking whore!" He screamed at Sue Ann, not recognizing her in the darkness or in his insanity.

Sue Ann tried to move, but Shade had gone mad. He put both hands around her throat and began squeezing, watching her through pale, disturbed eyes. She grabbed his hands and tried to pull them off her throat, but he had the strength of a grizzly, and she was no match. She was going to die at the hands of the man she loved, and there was nothing she could do to stop him.

As the room began to spin, she wheezed out a soft "Shade." Coughing and sputtering, she felt his hands relax.

Rolling out from under him, she tried to stand but couldn't. All she could do was fall to the floor and sob while holding her throat.

Shade sat on the bed, staring down at Sue Ann, his eyes even paler than usual and his face as white as the Alaskan snow, as if the deep crease of disbelief across his brow had turned a switch on and then off. His mouth gaped in horror, and tears flowed down his cheeks.

"Oh, God! No!" he yelled as he left the bed and ran out of the room.

Sue Ann heard the back door sling open with a loud bang and realized he had run naked into the cold with nothing to protect his feet from frostbite or his body from hypothermia.

She held her throat and went after him, stopping at the door to look for him. Shade was on his knees heaving, beating the ground with his fists. Sue Ann pulled her snow boots on and grabbed her parka and Shade's.

"Shade!" She approached him with caution and put his parka around his shoulders. He threw it off as he continued to heave.

"Go back inside," Shade mumbled between retches.

"Not without you! Come on, Shade. Let's go inside." Again she stretched his parka around him, and this time he kept it on his shoulders.

"Please! Just go back inside. I'll be in..." He hurled again.

"If I go in, will you come in soon?" Sue Ann spoke through chattering teeth.

"Yes. Leave me." Shade pulled back on his haunches and buried his head in his hands.

Sue Ann walked back into the cabin but watched from the window to make sure Shade didn't run away. In a few minutes, he headed back toward the cabin.

Sue Ann met him at the door with a down comforter warmed by the stove.

"Here! You'll get hypothermia."

Shade pushed the comforter aside and headed for the kitchen. He stopped and put his elbows on the kitchen counter, leaning down, rubbing his hands through his hair again. With one more rush of adrenaline and a cry of self-hatred for what he had done, he drew back his fist and plunged it through the cabinet above him. Wood splintered and flew inward. Shade reached through the torn wood and took down a large medicine bottle. He opened it and took several of the pills out and popped them into his mouth. As he turned back to face her, she saw his tears frozen against his eyelids, now forming thin paths of melting ice down his face.

"I'm so sorry, Sue Ann. God help me, I would never harm you, in my right mind. I should never have talked about Lam." Shade approached her but stopped, keeping his distance. He did not take her in his arms, thinking she must be terrified of him. Sue Ann hesitated and then went to him and wrapped her arms around his waist.

Shade hugged her tight and cried into her hair, big emotional man-sobs of agony and disbelief at what he had done.

"It was a nightmare, Shade, a very bad nightmare."

"No, Sue Ann. I had a recurrence, an episode—something I thought would never happen again. I haven't had to take those pills in years." Shade held her out so he could see her throat. He rubbed his fingers over the red marks and began sobbing again as he pulled her to him, holding tight as if afraid she would run away from him.

"God, I can't believe I did that to you—the only woman I've ever loved, and I tried to kill you." He held her out and looked down into her face. "You need to get away from me, as far away from me as you can. Do you hear me, Sue Ann?"

"You thought I was Lam. You hallucinated, Shade. My throat does not hurt. You stopped, sweetheart. You stopped yourself from hurting me."

Shade wrapped himself in the down comforter and headed into the studio. He was not about to risk sleeping with Sue Ann, not tonight.

Within a few minutes, he was curled in front of the

soapstone fireplace, sound asleep from the effect of the strong medication he had taken to prevent recurrences like this one.

Sue Ann pulled another down comforter out of the closet, grabbed a pillow, and stretched out on the floor in the studio. With the curtains open, she stared out into the snowy scene she loved so much. The Northern Lights faded in, overwhelming the Milky Way, and began their drama just for her. Perhaps it was a sign, like Noah's rainbow of old, a promise of no more recurrences or episodes of insanity. Perhaps it was a sign of forever love.

"Perhaps," she whispered to the lights.

Chapter Fourteen
The Nugget

Christmas was magnificent in Shade's cabin in the wilderness, topped off by a huge spruce tree cut by Shade. With Sue Ann's help, he dragged it inside to the studio, where the cathedral ceiling could house the monstrosity. Shade had boxes and boxes of ornaments, most hand-painted by him, and it took hours to decorate the tree, with his demand for balance and perfection.

"You really like big, don't you, sweetheart?" Sue Ann looked up as he stretched to put the sparkling star on the top branch. The only thing missing was Betsy, but Sue Ann had heard the excitement in her voice when she called her, and she knew sending her back to Annie was the right thing to do.

"I do like big. Don't you?" Shade raised his eyebrows at Sue Ann. "You want 'big' right here under the tree?"

"Later. You promised you'd show me Old Sawyer's little cabin he used at the gold mine. Who knows? I might find another one of his fishing baskets."

****

Sue Ann held tight as she rode on the back of Shade's snow machine. After about fifteen minutes of riding through woods and hollows, they reached what was left of Sawyer's mining operation.

"This is it." Shade waited for her to get off and

took her hand, leading her down into the trees.

Old Sawyer's rustic cabin was a mini replica of Sue Ann's, with the sourdough's craftsmanship, or lack of it, shining through. It was also the cabin perpetuated in the painting in the museum. Shade knocked the snow off the steps and cut a pathway to the door with his snow boots.

"Can we go inside?" Sue Ann was careful as she walked up the steps onto what was left of the porch.

"Old Sawyer wouldn't have it any other way, Darling. He was a recluse but enjoyed occasional company. He liked going into town, too, where he'd drink himself into oblivion in the Roadhouse."

She walked around the room and noticed a few pieces of elegant porcelain stacked in a homemade cabinet. "Old Sawyer had pretty good taste for a recluse." She picked up a cup and looked under the bottom. "Limoges—very expensive."

As she placed the cup back in the cabinet, she noticed a tarnished silver picture frame lying face down on the shelf. She picked it up, wiped it on her coat sleeve, and held it out to Shade.

"So who is this handsome man with the handlebar mustache? And look at this sophisticated woman, with her long brown hair draped over her shoulder."

"That's Old Sawyer's wife, Victoria. She was a mail order bride from back east. Believe it or not, she loved Old Sawyer, or so the story goes, and he adored her. She died in childbirth with their baby boy only two years after they married."

"How sad!" Sue Ann replaced the picture on the shelf but left it standing.

"I found Sawyer's journal when I was building the

cabin. It's an amazing piece of history, so I gave it to Jake for the museum. There's one story in it that concerns his giving Victoria an engagement ring when she first arrived."

Sue Ann leaned against the primitive table listening to Shade. Her mind was reeling with a pioneer love story she knew she would write, maybe as her first romance novel.

"Old Sawyer found a huge gold nugget in one of the streams on his place, and he put it away, hoping to get him a wife at some point. When he brought Victoria out, he showed her the gold nugget and told her he was having her a band made out of it for her wedding ring. She was thrilled, knowing the value of the huge nugget, and held it in her hand, turning it over and over, admiring it.

Old Sawyer was quite the joker, and he grabbed the nugget and put it in his mouth like he was going to swallow it, dancing around the room, taunting his fiancée. Victoria lunged at Sawyer, trying to get the nugget out of his mouth, and Sawyer backed up, tripped over a rough spot in the floor, and…"

"Tell me he didn't swallow it!" Sue Ann laughed, imagining the scene in the old cabin.

"Yep, he swallowed it, all right. Victoria was heartbroken, thinking she would never see the valuable nugget ring she had been promised, but two days later, Sawyer showed up at the Roadhouse where she was staying while they waited for the circuit preacher to come around and marry them, something Victoria required, being from the East, but not necessary in Alaska, where anybody can perform a marriage ceremony. Sawyer was all spiffed up, wearing a dress shirt and bowtie, probably the one in the picture, and carrying a brass bucket. Right there on the front steps of the Roadhouse, Sawyer dropped to one knee and asked Victoria for her hand in marriage, something pretty ridiculous since he'd paid for her to come to Alaska for just that purpose."

"What was in the bucket?" Sue Ann watched as a big grin covered Shade's face as if he were waiting for this question.

"Shit! Sawyer's shit, and right in the middle of it was the huge gold nugget."

Sue Ann laughed until her sides hurt.

****

On Christmas Eve, Sue Ann cooked a turkey with all the trimmings, the southern delicacies she had learned to cook from her mother, plus fried chicken, Shade's favorite, as a bonus. Later, as they sat drinking wine, cuddled in the big easy chair by the Christmas tree, he pulled a small box out of his pocket and handed it to her.

"Merry Christmas, Sweetheart!" He smiled as he held out the box.

"No, Shade!" She drew back, giving him a disapproving shake of her head. "We agreed not to give each other gifts, knowing what it cost for Betsy's plane ticket. This is not fair. I don't have anything for you."

"You always have what I want, Darling, and it doesn't cost a penny. Open it."

Sue Ann held the box, staring at it. Seeing the smile on his face, she pulled the ribbon off and opened the top. Inside was a jewelry box, and in it she found a ring made from a huge gold nugget. In the middle, protruding from inside the shadow box of an intricate rope design, was a very large light-blue gem the exact color of Shade's eyes.

Her mouth flew open as she removed the ring and held it up to the light.

"It's beautiful, Shade! But it's too much. No telling what the nugget alone is worth, and this huge stone must have cost a fortune. It has to be at least four carats."

"It's a natural blue diamond, and you are worth far more than this gem to me, Darling. It's seven-point-three carats and can finance a wonderful, luxurious life for you and Betsy for the rest of your life if you ever need to sell it. I'm rich, Sue Ann, and I'm a keeper. Just ask Betsy." He took the ring and placed it on her ring finger. "No more empty heart, Darling. You, my love, have made me far richer than this diamond ever could."

She stared at the beautiful ring on her finger, and it hit her.

"This is not Sawyer's gold nugget ring he gave Victoria, is it?"

"Yes, it is, but don't worry. The jeweler cleaned it thoroughly." Shade cut his eyes at Sue Ann, who smiled as she looked down at the beautiful shiny ring.

"The diamond is beautiful. I've never seen a blue one." She could not stop looking at the ring.

"I gained the diamond as partial pay for a job I did for a client in South Africa a long time ago. This is one of the rare blue diamonds from the Cullinan Mine there. The stone was originally commissioned by an Arabian sultan, but because of a coup, the diamond was never claimed and was sold to the man I got it from."

"A sultan? You're kidding, right? You're talking—I can't say it."

"At least a million, Sue Ann. It's insurance for you and Betsy, but it is also my way of expressing how much I love you. As long as you don't tell anyone what it is, they will never know its worth and will probably think it's gaudy costume jewelry. Wear it, baby, for me. When you look at the blue, you'll see my eyes looking at you with more love than I ever knew possible, and it doesn't matter where I am."

She took his face in her hands and kissed him as tears of happiness filled her eyes.

"All I want is you with me, Shade. I want your eyes more than this million-dollar diamond. Remember that, if you ever decide to disappear again."

Later, Shade took the mattress off the bed and dragged it into the studio so they could make endless love with the Northern Lights shining above them and reflecting off every ornament on the tree and from the star on top. Beacons of light illuminated the room, dancing and bouncing from the tree to the skylight and even off Sue Ann's ring as magic, an invisible sensual aura, surrounded the couple.

After the first time they made love, he held her in his arms, rubbing his chin over the top of her head as it lay on his chest. Once again he let her long blonde curls run through the fingers of his free hand and moaned with the satisfaction of having his only love so tight against his body.

Sue Ann held her ring finger up so the Sky Dwellers could reflect off Old Sawyer's gold and highlight Shade's eyes mirrored in the blue diamond.

"Other than 'Big,' your eyes are my favorite of your attributes, my darling. But I do love your thick dark hair—'raven wings' I once called it." She lifted her head and ran her fingers through his hair and kissed him with sweet passion.

"But then, I also love your muscles, the way they ripple down the entire length of your body from your tight chest with its soft manly down, my favorite place to rest my head, and down the arms that hold me and make me feel more secure than I've ever felt." Her hand followed her words as she let her ring finger outline each ridge of muscle, with Shade flexing to add to her pleasure.

"Then the ripples skip to your legs, where I love to fit my body in between and feel you lock me in, squeezing tight before passion overcomes our desire for play. The ripples cascade over your body, reminding me of my favorite stream where I fly-fished in the Beartooth Mountains of Montana, searching for the prize, a huge rainbow trout perfectly named, with his greens and reds glistening in the sunlight, undulating ever so gracefully against the current like our bodies entwined, perfectly synchronized as we make love."

"You do know you're killing me, Darling, but please don't stop. It seems like every time we make love, you come up with something new, something I've never experienced before. And your way with words spoken through that sexy southern accent is the best foreplay imaginable, especially when you tease me."

She moved down again to finish her monologue for her audience of one, who lay back, locking his hands under his head and closing his eyes.

"Torso and legs meet in my favorite forest so lush and fertile, feeding and enriching my pleasure and culminating in the masterpiece." Sue Ann ran her fingers gently through his manly stand of black hair, stopping to massage his testicles, enjoying the loud groans of pleasure she created.

Sue Ann let her hand trail to Shade's best feature and ran her finger lightly the full length of it. He lifted his head to watch her in action. After a few long seconds, she leaned down, giving him the ultimate pleasure. She stopped, sensing he was ready for the finale, and smiled at him. His eyes met hers, and his mouth widened in a big grin as if wondering what she could possibly add to her dramatic foreplay.

"The masterpiece, your jewel, was sculpted for me alone and slides into place, a perfect fit, like the last piece to the passionate puzzle that is Sue Ann and Shade loving, giving each other absolute unadulterated pleasure." She climbed on top of him, resting on her knees as she lowered herself on him, moving up and down, teasing as he stretched, trying to capture her. She wrapped her feet under the backs of his thighs and held tight. His hands reached around her, grabbing her cheeks and pulling her tighter and tighter as he thrust so deep she felt he would tickle the back of her throat, and she moaned loudly.

Shade raised himself to his knees as she locked her legs and arms around him. Standing, he walked with her to the table beside the easels. With one swoop of his hand, brushes and palettes flew to the floor as he propped Sue Ann's hips on the edge of the table. He never withdrew from her as she leaned back, her lover attacking her breasts, sucking, fondling, as he continued to drive into her, going deeper and deeper to the unfathomable depths of her pleasure. He rubbed her magic spot with his fingertips, adding to her pleasure and bringing her to the tip of the biggest orgasm she had ever experienced.

"Keep your eyes open, baby. I want to see you enjoying what I do to you."

Leaning on her elbows, she locked her eyes on his as he drove into her and waves of pleasure swept through. She whimpered, containing the scream she wanted to let loose as he thrust one last time and held it, overflowing her chamber and adding his own moan to hers. With his manhood still pulsating, he picked her up, holding tight to her hips, and carried her back to the pallet on the floor, where he lay down, keeping her on top. He kissed her deeply, letting his tongue play with hers like two rainbow trout teasing each other in a fast ripple as his masterpiece, her masterpiece, shrank back to normal. She rolled off him but snuggled close as he held her, winding her curls around his finger.

Sue Ann became quiet, enjoying the brilliance of the lights moving over them and reveling in the greatest gift of love in her life. She knew there would not, could not, be another love as passionate as what she felt for Shade and thought he felt the same about her. After moments of holding each other as the lights cast colorful shadows over them, he spoke.

"I wish I could express the way I see you, all that I love about you, Sweetheart, but my feelings can only be expressed in the way I make love to you, and, even more so, through my paintbrush. When the portrait is finished and hanging in our cabin, our home where I pray we will always be together, look at yourself in the portrait, at the way your green eyes dance under Northern Lights, and you'll know what I loved the most about you." He held her hand up where the lights again reflected off the ring.

"I'm not the kind of man who will ever walk you down an aisle or pledge my undying love to you in a public ceremony, but this is my vow, my commitment to you, Sue Ann Parish. I will cherish you, honor you, and, most of all, protect you as long as I have breath in my body." Shade laced his fingers through her hair and raised his body so he could direct his eyes to hers.

"I will love you forever—and then some."

Chapter Fifteen
"Boots by the Bed!"

Everyone in town asked Shade and Sue Ann when they were getting married, after seeing the ring he gave her, but neither would give an answer. While winter raged on, Shade took some time off from his painting to add a room onto Sue Ann's cabin, a nice big bedroom downstairs on the opposite end of the cabin from Betsy's room.

One day, Sue Ann came in from school to discover a water-holding tank being installed, complete with a shower. But the biggest surprise was a stainless steel electric toilet, an Incinolet, sitting in the middle of the living room ready to be hooked up.

Sue Ann and Betsy took turns sitting on the shiny toilet while Shade laughed. At one point, Betsy stretched her sweater sleeve over her hand and polished away smudge marks.

"So, Shade. When are you planning on marrying my mama and making her an honest woman?" Betsy sat on the toilet, one leg crossed over the other, swinging her foot.

"Betsy, I told you not to ask Shade that. It's not important to me or to Shade. I just want him with me, and he feels the same about me. We've said our vows to each other, and that is better than a public ceremony."

"That's right. We're putting it on the back burner."

Shade had a hammer in his hand, and as soon as he made the remark he stuck the hammer in his tool belt, frowned, and shook his head. "Damn. I hate clichés. Can't believe I said that."

Sue Ann remembered the first time he had made the statement and laughed.

The next week, she moved her things into the new bedroom. As she placed her jewelry box on the dresser, in her mind she saw her dad when he gave her the box, his last gift, a "no occasion" present, letting her know in the only way he could how much he loved her.

Opening the drawer where she kept his keepsakes, memories of the father she had loved and lost swept over her. She emptied the contents into her hand, and his wedding band called to her. Her parents were not affectionate to each other, but many times her father expressed to Sue Ann how her mother's green eyes, just like Sue Ann's, were what "snagged him" as he put it. Sue Ann's mother knew how much her husband loved the color of her eyes, and after they secured a healthy bank account and moved to the coast, she gave her husband his first and only wedding band, a wide gold band inlaid with one huge emerald, the color of her eyes, deep in the center, with many smaller emeralds completely encircling the band. Sue Ann held the ring up, the sunlight casting beams on the emeralds and making them glisten and twinkle—a dazzling effect. Her father's hands had been big like Shade's, and she knew what she would do with this ring.

Daddy, you would be so proud I finally found a man to love me and want to protect me like you always did. Now I just need to find the right time to say my vows to Shade.

****

"March rolls in like a lion and out like a lamb."

Helen read the old idiom to the primary students on the first day of March and asked each one what they thought this meant. The answers were typical young children answers, with everything from "The circus is coming to Fairbanks" to "It gets warm by the end of March so you don't need no wool long johns anymore."

But March brought in bad weather warnings for Shade, making him watch the skies, watch the horizon, watch the roads, and watch the backs of not only himself but his loved ones.

It was mid March, and he had spent the day working on Sue Ann and Betsy's portrait. He was getting close to finishing, but this had to be perfect. After cleaning his paintbrushes, he covered the portrait and was about to grab a cup of coffee when there was a knock at the door.

He opened the door to discover Jake standing there, someone who never visited, least of all late in the day. Jake had a serious look on his face, and Shade moved out of the way so he could enter.

"What's wrong? Nothing happened to Sue Ann or Betsy, did it?" Shade watched as Jake removed his boots but not his coat, letting Shade know his visit would be short.

"No. They were fine when I picked my grandson up after school, but I have something you need to know about Ben."

"We don't talk about Ben." Shade's voice had an edge of anger. "We made an agreement."

"To hell with the agreement! You and I know what you did in Nam, and my family will always be grateful.

You did what no other man alive could do, going into that hellhole and pulling my crazy-ass little brother out of that POW camp. Hell, he'd been in there three years, forgotten by the Marine Corps and our sorry-ass government. I know we both agreed never to mention it, not even to each other, but something has come up."

"Do I have to hear this, Jake?"

"No, but you have more considerations than yourself now, Shade, so listen for Sue Ann and Betsy."

"You want coffee?" Shade tried to tone down the drama.

"No. I don't want coffee. I want you to listen to what I've got to say, and then we go back to never speaking about any of it again. Is that a deal?"

"That was the deal, but you're not abiding by it." Shade could tell Jake was not going to leave without telling him what he needed to, so he sat on the sofa and put his eyes on the floor, refusing to acknowledge the importance of the conversation.

"Some guy claiming to be with the CIA went to visit my brother in the vets' home yesterday in Palmer and happened to catch him on one of the rare days he was actually sane. My sister was there and couldn't believe what Ben told the guy." Jake took Shade's place by the stove, looking down at his friend, who still refused to make eye contact.

"He told this complete stranger how he ended up walking out of the jungle that day. Described you to a T, right down to those crazy eyes of yours. He told how you set the guard stations on fire and blew up some jeeps and equipment to divert attention. Then you crawled up covered in mud—a swamp creature, Ben called you—and cut the wires to free Ben and all the other poor bastards in the camp, although the VC recaptured the other POWs later. Ben said you carried him on your back, with all your other gear, through what he called the snake pit, a swamp area of the jungle where even the VC wouldn't go. Said you carried him four nights and hid him during the daytime. You took him right to the edge of a Marine camp, where you left him. Ben said when he turned around, you were gone, poof, disappeared like some kind of freak shadow."

"I know the story, and I didn't particularly want to hear it again. What's your point, Jake?"

"This supposed CIA agent wanted the names and addresses of all our family, thinking we might be hiding you out in Alaska, since it's kind of an escape hole for criminals. He already knew the family had raised the money to pay you or that company you worked for. He tried to convince my brother, and my sister, that you've turned against your country and the CIA wants to arrest you as a spy. Hell, he even called you by your real name, if Jon Shockey is who you are."

Shade gave no indication of surprise, denial, or concern. "Is that all?" he said.

"Is that all? Is that all? Shade, if what my brother told is true, and you went through the hell he described to bring him out of that prison camp after three years when nobody else could get through, why in the hell did you give the money back to my father? I'd say you earned it."

"Is that what this is about? The money?" Shade stood and glared at Jake.

"No, but I never knew you did all that. The reason I came was not to discuss your insane heroism but to let you know somebody is asking questions about you, and my sister says she does not believe he was with the CIA. I can get a description of him, if you want."

"It's not necessary. I know who he is. Is that all?" Shade looked at his watch. "Sue Ann will be worried if I don't show up pretty soon." Shade stood and walked to the door, indicating the conversation was over. Jake threw his hands up in the air in disbelief and headed for the arctic entry, where he put his boots on.

"One thing, Jake."

"Yeah, Shade. Anything." Jake stopped after opening the door.

"Don't mention any of this to anybody, especially not the name Shockey, and please make sure your sister doesn't, either. Convince her none of it is true. She doesn't know my name or that you know me, right?"

"No. That was the deal we made when you moved here. Nobody in my family knows about you. I can keep my word. Hell, Shade, Sis already thinks Ben was hallucinating. Said Ben has been watching too many Vietnam War movies."

Shade closed the door behind Jake, leaning against it.

"Damn!" he said aloud.

****

Shade was unusually affectionate to Sue Ann when he entered the cabin. He grabbed her and kissed her hard, a forewarning of a long night of lovemaking ahead, except for the fact that Betsy was home. It was a school night.

"I don't know the occasion, but I'm willing to celebrate anyway, if you want to keep it up." Sue Ann pulled him to her for another kiss.

"Have I told you recently how much I love you,

Sue Ann?"

"Not since this morning, so I think you're probably due." He led her to the old brown couch and held her in his lap.

Betsy came bounding down the stairs and stopped when she saw them cuddled on the couch.

"Good grief! You two have no shame." She turned to the kitchen, grabbed something out of the refrigerator, and headed back upstairs. "Let me know when you're done. I might want to watch TV later."

Sue Ann and Shade laughed.

"Are you hungry, Shade? There's chicken left from last night, and I can fix you a sandwich to go with it."

"You don't have to wait on me, Sue Ann. I keep telling you that. Do all southern women really do these things for their men?"

"That's how I was brought up."

"I'm good. Not really hungry. I've been snacking all day while I worked."

"So how are we coming? And when will it be finished?"

"I don't know. It will probably be on hold for a while."

She pulled away and looked at him. He refused to make eye contact with her.

"When do you leave, and how long will you be gone?"

"How do you do that?"

"Do what?"

"Read me like that." Shade saw the hurt in Sue Ann's eyes and pulled her back to him.

"I don't know if I will be leaving, but I just wanted you to know the possibility is there."

"And you won't tell me why you're leaving?" She rubbed his leg, not looking up.

"Business. Just business." Shade left the couch and opened the pie safe. "Let's listen to Northern Voices tonight." As he opened the doors to the cabinet, he ran his fingers over the tin cutouts in the door panels and secretly hoped he would have many years of being with Sue Ann under these Northern Lights.

Sue Ann watched him, and his nostalgia grew contagious. After he turned the station on, he headed back to the sofa to find she had scooted to the end, wanting him to lie down and put his head in her lap.

As the broadcast started, she began playing with his hair as he moaned with pleasure.

"That feels so good. I love you, Sweetheart."

"So you've told me two other times today, but who's counting."

"Going out to Marvin at Coldfoot from Sis. Mama's not doing good. Come home ASAP."

"Roger to Hope at Crossbriar. Shutting down trapline. Be home in a week. Love to you and the kids."

"Going out to Raven from Wolfman. Mama Bear moving. Bad eye infection. Not see at all. Boots by the bed."

Sue Ann tensed when the message came on, but she sensed no reaction from Shade. Maybe her ideas of these messages being for him were all wrong. Then again, maybe he was trained not to react to anything. When Northern Voices was over, she eased his head out of her lap, walked to the pie safe, and flipped the radio off.

"I hope you're coming back," Shade said in a low, dreamy voice. "I love it when you play with my—raven wings."

She sat back down and put his head back in her lap.

"Let's don't turn the TV on tonight. I just want to hold you and pretend you'll never leave me for longer than a day." Her voice was low and full of emotion.

"I don't want to leave you, Darling, but sometimes things come up, and I have to."

"For business, right?" She was easing into taking the plunge.

"Uh-huh." He sounded as if he was dozing off. "But I might be gone for a couple of weeks. Will you and Betsy be all right without me?"

"Does this business involve Wolfman and Mama Bear?" Sue Ann decided it was time to find out who Shade Dubois really was.

He sat up and stared at her. His whole demeanor had changed.

"How do you know this, Sue Ann?" His voice lowered, he glanced toward the other room as if waiting for Betsy to stomp in. "Nobody should know." Anger in his look, he continued, "Promise me you haven't told anyone else, not even Betsy." He held tight to her arm.

"You're hurting me, Shade." She pulled away from him and walked to the window.

Shade moved to stand beside her and faced her, putting his hands on her shoulders gently.

"I'm sorry, Sue Ann. I didn't mean to hurt you, but it scares the hell out of me for you to know so much." He looked out without seeing. "How did you find out? This could be dangerous for you and Betsy."

"Northern Voices. You should stop using the name Raven if you don't want people who know you to figure it out, or at least take the tag off your Harley." Sue Ann folded her arms. "I think you're okay to use it on your paintings, since no one knows you're an artist." She paused for a few seconds. "I think I broke your code, too, or at least some of it. Tell me if I'm wrong."

He leaned against the wall of the cabin and crossed his arms, giving her his full attention.

"Shoot."

"In the first message you sent to Wolfman and Mama Bear, you said, 'Been ill in GS.' This made no sense at all to me until I realized you were sending a code for something happening in Billings. That very day, Don told me about a conversation he had with you about a murder in Billings, some banker. He said you always get a Billings newspaper. 'Bad,' one of your favorite one-word sentences, told me whatever happened was, and I quote, 'bad.' 'Eye on the sky' could mean you're watching, or someone is watching you. How am I doing so far?"

"You're ready to star in a James Bond movie." He looked not the least bit amused but kept his position beside her. "Is that all you have?"

"Well, let's see. You use the same closing in almost all of your messages. Either it's 'Boots by the door' or 'Boots by the bed.' I would think 'Boots by the door' means be prepared but maybe not ready to dart out into the cold just yet. You have time to get to your 'boots by the door.' 'Boots by the bed,' on the other hand, would indicate something dire is about to happen. You're on red alert and must be ready to slide out of bed, into your boots, and go after—whatever, or whomever."

"Okay. So you've figured out some of it. For God's sake, and ours, please stop playing detective, Sue Ann, and don't go spreading this around—to anyone." He went back to the sofa and sat on the edge with his hands folded, elbows propped on knees. He kept his eyes on her but offered no smile or back pat for her genius.

"I have some questions." Sue Ann moved to sit beside Shade. "I have no idea who Wolfman is, but I suspect Mama Bear is Hattie Baird. So why does she have to move? And I take it she isn't moving back to Seattle, since you say, 'Not see at all.' Now that was clever!"

"Obviously not clever enough." This time he gave her a quirky grin.

"And while we're on the subject of Mama Bear, alias Dr. Hattie Baird, alias whoever, why was she in Fairbanks in the first place? Are you in love with Hattie?"

Shade turned to face Sue Ann and put a hand on each of her arms and rubbed up and down.

"I am in love with you, Sue Ann, only you. Now that makes four times I've told you today. But Hattie is important to me since she takes care of Tulen. That's all I can tell you right now."

Sue Ann left him and walked into the bedroom. When she came back, she was holding scissors. Pulling her braid around in front of her, she snipped off the bottom two-inch section wrapped in the green leather strip she always used as a tie.

"What are you doing, Sweetheart?" Shade stood beside her looking bewildered and a little upset.

"Don't worry. There's plenty left." She untied the leather and retied it, wrapping it several times, pulling it tighter, and then tying it in a double knot.

"Take this with you, honey, so you'll always

remember there is a woman waiting on you, a woman who loves you unconditionally, no matter what. And, please, Shade—always come back to me."

****

Pussywillow buds were the hot topic of conversation at show-and-tell on April Fool's Day, except for first-grader Abigail, who told all about how her daddy dug them a new outhouse over the weekend. Both topics were reminders of spring's coming. Not only had the first pussywillow bloom been spotted, the Tekooni River had too much slush water on it for snow machines to travel over its winding, rough pathway in order to reach other villages on winter's shorter route.

"Spring breakup is on its way, but I think it might be a little later, probably not until May," Rose told the kids in the class meeting. "But it is time for us to make our predictions for the Ice Classic." The younger children put their names beside a date on the calendar showing the frozen river this year. The older kids chose time as well as date for their best guess.

****

Shade had been gone for three weeks, and Sue Ann was miserable without him. She had no idea what business took him away from her, but she sensed it was surrounded by danger. Every night she retired to their new bedroom to listen to Northern Voices, hoping Shade would send her a message.

"Telephones can have many ears you don't know about," he'd told Sue Ann, so she watched the radio as if it were a telephone, knowing he would not call. But her first report of trouble that might involve Shade did not come from Northern Voices.

Sue Ann was spending another late evening at

school, trying to catch up on her principal reports, and had the school's television playing while she worked. As she walked across from the library to her desk, her arms laden with books, she was alerted to a special report out of Fairbanks.

Early this morning, the body of Dr. Hattie Baird was found shot to death in the vault at the Fairbanks Museum of Art, where she had served as curator for the past two years. Dr. Baird was on sabbatical for the last month, but had returned to the museum to locate some documents she had left. Interim Curator Rochelle Cauthern had opened the vault at Dr. Baird's request yesterday afternoon. Miss Cauthern said when she saw the door had been closed and the lock turned, just before closing, she assumed Dr. Baird had found her documents and left. No suspects are in custody at this time.

Books tumbled from Sue Ann's hands as she fell to her knees. All she could see in her mind was the beautiful girl Tulen, who was orphaned again. Her next thought was Shade. She knew he'd had nothing to do with Hattie's murder, but Sue Ann also knew he would search out and find the person responsible and blow him away or kill him with a knife.

"What am I doing falling in love with a man with this kind of a past?"

She knew what her friend Elizabeth in Mississippi would tell her: "Run for your life and drag Betsy with you. Forget about this man and come home to people who love you and won't put you in harm's way!"

Harm's way! Was that where she was living right now with her daughter? Sue Ann needed time to think, and it seemed Shade was giving her plenty of that.

The time seemed to drag that night as she waited for 9:20 and the chatter to bounce between radio towers, but there was no message from Shade. Perhaps she should not have told him what she had figured out from his messages to and from Wolfman and Hattie. Maybe he would never message again.

Shade did not show for the next few days. Sue Ann took work home with her now, afraid for Betsy to come into an empty house after going to work at Jake's kennel. That weekend, another news bulletin popped on the screen, and Sue Ann froze as the reporter began.

"Fairbanks has another murder crime scene today, but this one is more lurid than that of Dr. Hattie Baird a week ago. The body of a male looking to be in his forties was found in a wooded location outside Fairbanks. The witness who found the body described the murder scene as "gruesome." The victim has not been identified at this time. For more details, watch tonight's late news at ten.

Sue Ann was grateful Shade had installed the huge satellite dish, even though she had complained at the time about it taking up half her back yard, not to mention displacing several of her trees. With the questionable life she was living with Shade, Sue Ann needed to become an addicted news watcher but prayed she would never see him handcuffed and wearing an orange jumpsuit.

The horrific scene of the second murder in a week in the Fairbanks area was the dominant story on the ten o'clock news. The witness, an older man who lived in a cabin outside Fox, had found the body and went into great detail describing "what he seen." His speculation was that the man's body was stripped of clothing and left covered in blood, with some private parts cut off, just to attract wild animals like bears coming out of hibernation.

"It was the most god-awful sight I ever seen. His (bleeped) were cut off, and he died all bowed up, holding hisself, naked as birth. Don't know how anybody could do such a thing to another man."

The reporter asked for help from the public in identifying the victim but only gave a description and did not show a picture.

"The victim's head is shaved, and he has a large scar on his right shoulder where it looks as if a tattoo was removed a good while ago. A touch of black and gold body art can still be deciphered at one edge of the scar. If you have any idea who the deceased might be, or have any information concerning this crime, contact the Fairbanks Police Department or Alaska State Troopers at once. Law Enforcement is investigating the murder for a possible connection to the murder of Dr. Hattie Baird. More news as it develops."

Pacing, pacing, looking at the radio, praying for Shade's safety. Sue Ann repeated the cycle time after time as she waited for 9:20. Surely Shade knew she was worried and would send her a message.

At 9:15, Sue Ann turned the radio on and listened to gospel music until the chatter started. The first two messages were birthday greetings, followed by a warning about slush ice on the Yukon River. Then she heard it.

"Raven to Nugget. Mining gold beats trapping animals. Need a real hot fire."

"He's at his cabin!" Sue Ann ran to the phone and called Betsy, who was staying at Jake's watching old videos of the Iditarod that had Joe Redington, Sr., the Father of the Iditarod, and Susan Butcher, Betsy's idol, in them. Betsy just knew Susan would be the winner of many Iditarods in the near future.

"Shade is home! I'm heading out there, Betsy. I'll be home tomorrow. Stay with Jake and Bernice until I get back."

Sue Ann threw on her snow boots, grabbed her parka and mittens, and jumped into her truck, heading out of Moose Springs. She had never driven to Shade's cabin at night, but the days were getting longer, and with luck, she'd make it before it got too dark. Besides, fresh snow had fallen, lighting up the road.

Sue Ann pulled her truck into the shed at the foot of the trail and was disappointed not to see Shade's truck already parked there. She pulled her hat over her ears, put on her mittens, and began the trudge upward. As she climbed, she looked up to see the Northern Lights waving at her, and she smiled.

Just as she got almost to the top of the hill, where she'd hit the path to the cabin, lights illuminated her. An inkling of fear caused her to tremble, thinking it could be a trap. She waited, not knowing whether to descend the hill to greet whomever, or to run for the cabin and hope she could find Shade's gun.

"Sue Ann!" Shade yelled as he slammed the truck door and started toward her.

Sue Ann started back down the hill at a run, stumbled, and caused a small avalanche. Quickly, she got her balance again and headed for him. Shade moved at a slower speed than usual, but as she got close he picked up speed, scooping her into his arms and squeezing her so tight she couldn't breathe.

"Oh, baby, how I've missed you!" He held her face and kissed her hard.

Something felt different about his mouth, and she could tell he had not shaved today, but she didn't have time to worry about it right now. Shade was home, and he was safe. They held their arms around each other and ascended the rest of the hill.

Shade picked Sue Ann up a few feet from the cabin and hurried to the door, kicking it open once it was unlocked, letting it bounce against the wall in the entry. Reaching behind her, he closed the door and double bolted it, pulling the wooden latch across it, something she'd never seen him do before.

Shade didn't bother with lights as snow gear began flying in every direction, followed by his jeans, shirt, and underwear. He stood naked in the arctic entry and began pulling at Sue Ann's clothing, and before either could catch their breath, he swooped her up and carried her to the bedroom.

The cabin was warm, and Sue Ann knew Jake had built fires in the woodstoves for Shade's homecoming, probably the real reason Betsy had been invited to watch videos.

"Jake knew you were coming home and didn't tell me. I had to wait for your message on Voices."

"I told him not to tell you." He put her on the bed and grabbed her mouth in his, moved down her neck, stopped to feast on her breasts, and inhaled every inch of her. "Thought I'd test your 007 decoding skills a little. You're a clever, beautiful lady, and the one I'm ready to taste."

He moved down, kissing, teasing, probing, while she gasped. She had waited for this for weeks, too. He stopped and pulled himself up to face her.

"No more foreplay tonight, baby! I've had a hard on for the last sixty miles. I need relief."

He moved on top of her, entering her moist folds as she massaged his testicles. He groaned aloud as if in pain, and plunged deep, pulling her legs around him, pushing, grinding, until she joined him, crying aloud. He held tight, not wanting it to end but feeling surges of pain not associated with hard lovemaking.

Shade moved onto his back and pulled her on top of him, his erection still in her, pulsing, overflowing in her. Sue Ann lay still, enjoying the feel of him shrinking inside her until the last drop settled in her. She rolled off him, wanting his sweet kisses always given after making love, but when she moved her face to his, she got no reaction. He was asleep. She kissed him gently and realized his bottom lip was swollen. She sat up and examined his body in the dim light given off by the woodstove. Not believing what she thought she was seeing, she turned on the dim bedside light. His body was covered in knots, bruises, and cuts.

****

The next morning, Sue Ann left the bed, being as quiet as possible, not wanting to disturb her tired and injured lover. She pulled the covers back to check his body and saw more proof that the ecstasy of the moment last night was actually his crying out in pain. Only Shade Dubois could make love when he looked like he'd been in a battle.

She tucked the covers around him, kissing him gently before leaving the bedroom and going into the kitchen to make coffee. At ten o'clock, she heard him groaning as he moved.

"Well, you were a sore sight for loving eyes this morning." Sue Ann stood by the bed looking down at him, her hands propped on her hips in what he called her "principal" stance. She turned and walked to the other side of the room, where she opened the French doors to the mineral bath and stopped to check the temperature in the huge rock tub already filled with hot water from the springs.

When everything was ready for his much-needed soak, she stood at the doorway, looking at Shade.

Making no effort to leave the bed, he crooked his finger and beckoned to her.

"Come here, you." His voice was low and gravelly.

She sat on the bed beside him but kept her robe tied in front, making no effort to crawl in with him.

"Why didn't you tell me you were hurt last night? I could have killed you with what I did to you—and with what you did to me."

"Physical pain makes loving better. It's like when you scratch my back and bring blood with your fingernails when we have really, really good sex. Besides, I couldn't have waited." Shade ran his hand down her arm and stopped at her robe sash.

"Take it off. Lie with me a little while, baby." He began untying the sash.

"Shade, sweetheart, you're in no shape, and I'm afraid I'll hurt you."

"That's my decision. Get naked and come to me." He pushed the robe off her shoulder with one hand, groaning as he reached.

She stood and let the robe fall to the floor, then stood with her weight on one leg and her hands on her hips.

"No, Shade! We're not making love until you've had a soak in the tub. I need to rub ointment on your injuries." She put her hands up. "You have no say-so about this, so get your gorgeous ass up and into the tub."

"Is my ass gorgeous, Darling?"

"Every inch of you is gorgeous, as if you didn't know."

"Okay, but you don't need to help me. I can do this on my own." He threw back the covers and yelped. "I can do this," he grunted as he propped on one arm and threw his leg off the side.

"This is like *déjà vu*, huh, except it's me this time?" He spoke in a deep but soft whisper as if speaking hurt.

After sitting up on the side of the bed, he stood and cracked his back, twisted sideways several times, grimacing with each movement, and took a step forward.

"That hurts like a son-of-a-bitch!" Hurrying his steps to the big tub, he sat on the edge of the curved end, swung his legs over, and slid in, letting his whole body submerge, including his head.

"Shade!" Sue Ann raced to the tub and pulled his head up, thinking he had passed out. He came up laughing, spitting water.

She took the washcloth and soap and began bathing him just as he had bathed her after her wreck.

"Get in."

"No. We need to clean you up before I put the ointment on your cuts and bruises."

"I showered before I left Fairbanks. I just didn't take time to shave—for two days, actually. Get in!" He did not give her time to answer as he pulled her in on top of him, letting out a volley of swear words as her body hit his.

Sue Ann eased herself around to the other end of the tub and watched as his grimace spread.

"I know you won't tell me what happened, but at least tell me if the other guy got it worse."

"Yeah." He squeaked the word out. "He got it a lot worse."

"Hmm." Her mind raced to the interview of the witness who discovered the "gruesome" scene in the woods. She sat up and continued washing Shade. "Was it necessary to cut his balls off?"

This got a rise out of him, and he sat up, forgetting pain as he defended his actions.

"He killed Hattie, or at least helped kill her." Shade raised himself to get out of the tub and then fell back in. "Damn, that hurts!"

"Can you go to prison for this?"

"No. It's unfinished business from my mercenary days, and part of the deal I made when I turned state's evidence was that I'm immune. Besides—it was self-defense."

"Shade, you do know I have no idea what you're talking about, don't you? I know you were a mercenary, a hit man as you called it, but when did you turn state's evidence, and who was it against?"

Shade put his head back and closed his eyes. He began self-stimulation with his legs wide open and grabbed Sue Ann, pulling her in to him.

"Stop asking questions, Sue Ann, and make love to me. It's the best part of a bath."

Chapter Sixteen
Angel

It was Sue Ann's turn to pamper, and pamper she did, until her patient became serious and quiet. She left the kitchen and sat by Shade on the sofa. He laid his head in her lap, and she began massaging his neck after giving him a quick kiss.

"Are you okay, honey?" she asked in her best teacher voice.

"She's coming to live with me, Sue Ann. She has no one else now."

"Tulen?" Sue Ann looked surprised and then broke into a big smile. "That's wonderful, Shade. It's about time, but I hate the reason for it. Hattie was a lovely woman."

Shade frowned, taking on an angry look, and sat up.

"Hattie was a hard-ass mercenary who could kill and never flinch. Her brain was on overload when it came to technology and finding information, but she had no sense when it came to taking orders and avoiding danger. She was told not to go back to the museum, and she went anyway." Shade leaned forward, resting his elbows on his knees.

"So when is Tulen coming?" Sue Ann massaged the back of his stiff neck.

"Late this afternoon. Wolfman is bringing her."

"So I finally get to meet the illusive Wolfman, huh?"

"Don't expect a big greeting. Wolfman is kind of quiet—like a wolf."

Shade went outside and listened many times that afternoon, waiting for Wolfman to bring Tulen. Finally, he heard sled dogs in the distance.

"Sue Ann, I'm going to Old Sawyer's cabin for a while. When Tulen gets here, tell her I'll be here shortly." With that, he headed out the door and got on his snow machine.

She heard the dog team coming and knew it was Wolfman. How else would a loner called Wolfman travel in Alaska in the snow? Before they could knock on the door, she opened it, and Tulen stepped inside. She pulled the hood of her parka back and stood staring at Sue Ann. Sue Ann smiled and opened her arms, and Tulen ran into her embrace and sobbed. Sue Ann held her and let her cry while Wolfman took her things out of the basket of the sled and put them inside the arctic entry.

"Going now. You'll be okay here, girl." Wolfman never turned his face toward them. His voice sounded robotic as he spoke through a mechanical voice box like people who have had throat cancer. He never came inside or said "goodbye." He just released his brake and took off up the hill through the woods, giving commands to his dogs through the eerie-sounding voice box.

****

Sue Ann made cocoa for Tulen and sat by her on the sofa.

"I'm so sorry about your mother, Tulen. She was a

beautiful lady, and obviously very smart." Sue Ann put her arm around the girl again.

"Will my dad love me, Sue Ann? He doesn't know me, and I know he doesn't want me. He never sent me pictures or told me he loved me in his letters."

"He was protecting you, sweetie. Yes, your father will love you. He already does." Sue Ann hugged the girl again.

"I knew you were a kind lady the day I talked to you in the museum. I'm glad you're here."

****

Shade waited in the woods for Wolfman's dog team to come by, and ten minutes later he was standing talking to his old friend and fellow commando.

"Did he talk?" Wolfman asked.

"No. I tried everything, but he wouldn't squeal. I don't think he was the one who killed Hattie. Even after I cut his balls off, he just grabbed his bloody crotch, rolled around on the ground and laughed. Hell, I knew he wouldn't tell me where ONE was when I heard the fool laugh. You'd think he would have carried an L pill, but he didn't. Brave fucker. I can say that for him."

"Looks like he got a lick or two in on you. You slipping?" The voice box squealed and echoed off the aspens.

"Out of practice. But it'll come back to me if I need it," Shade answered, ignoring the malfunction.

"How many?" Wolfman asked, holding to the speaking device.

"Probably just ONE now, but I can't be sure. Hattie fucked up, Wolfe. She didn't need to go back for those receipts. If he knows those are my paintings, he'll find me sooner or later."

"Of course she had to go back. You should have expected that from her." Wolfe paused and then eased his sled around. "Gotta go. Eyes to the sky." Wolfe headed up the trail.

"Boots by your bed!" Shade called.

"Too late. See you in hell, Raven!"

Shade watched as his old friend, a mercenary who could never forgive himself for the killings he'd committed, headed over the hill and out of sight. To Wolfman, cancer was a sign from God that he would be punished for eternity, and he accepted it with dignity and courage. Shade sensed he would never see Wolfman again.

****

Shade opened the door and stopped to pull his snow gear off. Tulen stood and watched him. When he finished, Shade headed toward Tulen and Sue Ann.

"I saw you—in Seattle in the Space Needle. You looked over my shoulder and watched me sketch." Tulen kept her eyes on her father as he walked closer. When he got directly in front of her, he looked up, his eyes meeting hers, and pieces of two blue skies merged as pale blue met pale blue, each being absorbed by the other.

"I knew it was you. I sketched you while you pretended to be looking in another direction." Tulen reached into her pocket and pulled out a folded piece of paper and handed it to him.

Shade unfolded the paper and stared at it. Even with a pencil sketch, his eyes looked blue in their paleness against the dark coat he was wearing that day.

"I wanted to know you, Tulen, but it was too dangerous for you. I hope you can understand that and forgive me." His eyes remained on the drawing.

"I used to picture you holding me in your lap and telling me bedtime stories. Your arms were always around me tight." Tulen hugged herself in demonstration. "And you'd tell me you loved me, but you called me Angel, not Tulen. It was like on TV. But it never was to be." Tulen continued to stare.

Shade locked his eyes on his daughter's, thinking how much like him she was, and moisture filled his eyes. He took two steps toward her and opened his arms, and Tulen, his Angel, fell into his embrace.

"I love you, Angel. I have ever since I held you in my arms when you were just a baby in the orphanage in Saigon. I've never forgotten that moment, or you."

Chapter Seventeen
Leaving on a Jet Plane

"Through the week, Shade and Angel will be with us in town so we three can get to school. But on weekends, you and Angel will go with us to Shade's cabin." Sue Ann threw up her hands as Betsy started to complain. "This is nonnegotiable, Betsy. You will be with me from now until school is out. We will probably go back to Mississippi for the summer."

"Mom, I should have some say-so in this, and Angel likes it in town, too. Don't you, Angel?" Betsy turned to Tulen, known only as Angel in Moose Springs, and nodded her head as if urging Angel to take her side.

"Betsy, I love Moose Springs, and having you and Lena as friends is more fun than I've had in my whole life, but you have to understand something. I just found my dad, and I don't want to be away from him, not even for a weekend." Angel put her arm around Betsy's shoulder. "Please don't be mad at me. What if you had just found your mom after a lifetime of wondering who she was and if she ever thought about you?"

Betsy pulled her bottom lip to one side and rolled her eyes, tapping her foot to give herself time to think. "Okay. I get it, Angel. But can we at least take Lena with us to Shade's cabin some weekends, Mom?"

"Of course you can, but not every weekend."

Sue Ann was on edge as she stood at the window staring out past the satellite dish to the dark forest beyond. She had two girls to worry about now, and somewhere out there could be a crazed murderer out to get Shade and whoever else might get in the way. Shade had been quiet, not offering any additional information after killing the man in Fairbanks.

"Mom, is it okay if we run out to Jake's?" Betsy interrupted her mother's thoughts. "He has a new litter of puppies I want Angel to see." Betsy picked up the truck keys, expecting approval as usual.

"Not now, honey. I'd rather you two stay here until Shade gets home. He's running late, probably finishing a painting. I bet if you ask him, he'll take you out there tomorrow."

Betsy huffed and stomped her way up the stairs, with Angel trailing behind her. "I don't see why Shade has to chaperone us everywhere. I'm seventeen, for gosh sake. I've been driving since I was twelve—well, in the pasture at Parrish Oaks, at least." Sue Ann jumped as the door to Betsy's room slammed.

When lights reflected on the small front window in the kitchen, she left her watch post and headed for the door, hoping it was Shade.

As soon as the latch lifted, Sue Ann jerked the door open in a rage.

"Why are you late? You know I worry." She stood with arms folded, glaring at Shade.

"What happened to 'Hi, honey, how was your day?'" Shade grinned and gave Sue Ann a quick peck on the cheek before hanging up his jacket in the entry.

The pounding of steps on the stairs brought Angel to grab her dad around the middle in a bear hug. He wrapped his arms around her and kissed the top of her head. As he looked up, he saw Betsy descending slowly, arms folded, bottom lip out.

Shade glanced from mother to daughter and laughed.

"Well, if you two don't look just alike—blonde braids, tantalizing eyes, enormous IQs, and killer dispositions." He continued to laugh as he brushed past both and headed in to take his seat in Old Green. As always, he had stopped by the trading post and picked up a *Fairbanks Daily News-Miner*.

Betsy followed him and started in on her problem.

"Mom won't let me drive Angel out to Jake's to see the new litter. What's wrong with her, Shade?"

He reached for her hand and pulled her to the arm of his chair, putting his arm around her.

"Mom's a little bushy right now, Betsy." He cast a glance at Angel. "Because of what happened. She is being overprotective, and to be honest, I feel the same way. Eventually, Hattie's murderer will be caught, and things can go back to normal. Be patient, Betsy Boop."

Hearing this from him seemed to make everything okay again, and the girls retired to the upstairs with Noname at their heels.

"Thank you, Shade. I needed your support." Sue Ann took Betsy's place on his chair arm and put her arm around him, laying her head on top of his.

"That greeting I got at the door wasn't very loving, you know." He sat still, waiting for his usual kiss.

She reached over and kissed him, putting her hand under his chin for leverage. When she withdrew, she kept her face close, looking directly in his eyes.

"You're worried, too. I can see it in your eyes."

"Of course I'm worried, Sue Ann. I've put you, Betsy, and now Angel in a position of imminent danger. Truth is, I'd like to pack all of you up and take you into Fairbanks, rent a Leer, and fly our family somewhere far away where I can protect you."

"Our family—I like the sound of that." Sue Ann smiled and then realized what he had said. "Did you say 'fly'? You fly, too?"

"I fly. Actually, I own a Leer, but it isn't in Fairbanks. I'd just have to get us to where the plane is." He watched to see what her reaction would be, but she said nothing as she left his chair and headed for the kitchen.

"We saved you some stew. Do you want it now?"

"Not yet, but thank you, baby. I need to check the paper." He began turning pages, scanning for bad news.

"Nothing on the front page." He seemed relieved as he turned the page, but his relief was premature.

"Damn!" Shade threw the paper on the floor and headed outside.

Sue Ann let him go but picked up the newspaper to see what he had found, and there it was on page two in the obituaries.

The body of trapper Henry Wolfe was found today in his cabin sixty miles north of Moose Springs in an isolated area. Hikers trying to get to the upper Tekooni River ran across the cabin while on their way to find and film the river during breakup. The deceased appears to have died from natural causes and had been diagnosed with terminal cancer a year ago according to doctors in Fairbanks. An autopsy will be performed since the immediate cause of death is not known for sure. No signs of foul play were found.

Sue Ann rushed outside and found Shade kicking at the ground and rubbing his hands through his hair in his usual gesture of anguish.

"I'm sorry, Shade, but you knew he was going to die. The paper said 'natural causes.' "

"Natural causes, my ass! He was good the other day, and besides, his doctors had given him six months to a year."

"You think he was murdered?"

"Either that, or he knew he was about to be tortured, and he killed himself."

"Killed himself? How? The paper said there was no sign of foul play." She moved closer beside Shade.

"L pill." He said it low intentionally.

"What?"

"L means lethal. Cyanide. We all carried it either in pill form or crystals, in our former lives, but it doesn't matter. Wolfe is dead, and that means one thing." Shade's bright eyes cut through the night like a searchlight, or a distress signal. "He's getting too close."

Sue Ann shivered at the words, and Shade took her in his arms and held her.

"I don't know who is getting too close, but I'm scared, Shade. What do we do?"

"Not we. You. You are leaving tomorrow and taking Betsy and Angel with you. Go to Mississippi and stay with Elizabeth until I come up with a better plan." He turned his eyes on her as she remained quiet. "You do hear what I'm saying, don't you, Sue Ann?"

"This can't be happening. It's a nightmare! Surely I'll wake up tomorrow and find a man lying beside me who is not being trailed like an animal, or trailing someone else like an animal." Her voice cracked.

"I have your plane tickets already. I've had them for a week, just in case. All we have to do is call and confirm." He ignored her comment about trailing someone.

"First thing in the morning, you need to turn in your resignation. I don't care what you tell them, but you have to take the girls and leave."

"No! I won't leave you." Her voice broke.

"I can take care of myself, but not if I'm worried about him, or them, getting to you and the girls."

"What if something happens to you, Shade? I finally find someone to love, and…"

He cut her off, placing his fingers over her lips. Hands on her arms, he pulled her close so she could hear him speaking in a low voice.

"You picked the wrong man to fall in love with, Sue Ann. I was never good for you, but I let myself love you, knowing it was wrong. I couldn't stay away, and now you have to pay the price for my past. You're in the middle of this, and it's up to me to make sure you're safe. You don't have a choice. You're leaving tomorrow." He turned and headed back toward the cabin.

"Stop! Don't turn your back on me after giving me an ultimatum!" Sue Ann yelled at Shade. "We aren't through discussing this!"

He headed back, stopping in front of her.

"Shade, I can't just leave my job, and I can't leave you." She lowered her voice. "We can send the girls to Elizabeth, but I'm staying."

He grabbed her by both arms again, tightly.

"This is not a fucking spy board game you play

around the table after dinner, Sue Ann. I'm sorry for using that kind of language, but you have to understand this is real!"

He walked to the edge of the yard and sat on a stump, putting his head in his hands. She followed him and put her cheek to his, whispering in his ear.

"If you leave with us tomorrow, I'll go. Otherwise, I'm sending the girls."

"You have no idea who you are dealing with, Sweetheart."

"Then tell me. Maybe it will change my mind." She stood staring at him, waiting for his explanation.

Chapter Eighteen
Tiger's Eye ONE

"Let me grab our coats. We need to stay outside to talk, so the girls won't hear, and this will take a while. I don't want to do this, but it's the only way I can convince you of the gravity of the situation."

When he came back out, Shade handed Sue Ann her jacket, took her by the hand, and led her to the porch on the other end of the cabin. As they sat on the edge, she thought about the day she and Betsy had seen Old Sawyer's town cabin for the first time.

"It seems just like yesterday when Betsy darted away from Jake and me, and the next thing I knew she was on her knees, her little butt scooting backwards from under this porch as she retrieved Old Sawyer's fishing basket. 'It's a sign, Mom,' she told me, and we bought this cabin. I love it here, Shade, but I love you more. I'm willing to leave if you can get us some place where we can change identities or do whatever we need to do to beat this, but you have to come with us."

"It's only taken him two years to find me in Alaska, and this is the Last Frontier, Sue Ann. He's left his marks everywhere he knows I'll find them, starting with William in Billings. William has managed my money all these years, made sure Hattie and Angel were taken care of, and found me buyers for my paintings. When I read how Bill was castrated, I knew who killed him. It was his favorite method of torture, his attempt to get information. I doubt it worked with Bill, but his killer wanted to leave his calling card, knowing I'd find out.

"Even the two missing people in Fox are signs of the man who wants me dead. The address of Fielder was the first cabin I built in Alaska. He purchased it from me ten years ago when I moved to Moose Springs. When the paper stated he had rented the small cabin behind to a drifter, I knew who that was. This guy is a master of disguise, and the smartest man I've ever known.

"There's no other place to run to unless you're prepared to leave the country, Sue Ann. I don't think that is feasible for Betsy. She's such a strong-willed little devil, like her mama. She won't be one to hide away from life, but we'll damn sure take her with us kicking and screaming, if that's what it takes. Angel won't be a problem. She's used to moving, and right now she is enamored with her old man, as I am with her."

"Who do you mean by 'him' and 'us'? You said it took 'him' two years to find 'us.' It's time you let me in on your past, Shade. At least I'll know what we're up against."

He sat silent, looking up at the sky. The days were longer now; winter was coming to a close. He wished the Sky Dwellers would come out and give him the support he needed to open up his life to the woman he loved, but that was possible only in the night skies. He was on his own, and it was time to resurrect the past he had tried to hide.

"I finished Yale when I was twenty-two. My father

was disappointed in me, because my degree was in art and I was not going to be a lawyer and join his prestigious firm as a partner. Being an only child, I was a spoiled smart aleck who thought I knew more than just about anybody. I was an athlete—strong, fast, muscle bound, and disciplined from working out hours every day—and I was out to conquer the world. My best friend at Yale joined the Marines when we finished school and was sent to Vietnam during the 'advisor' era." Shade made quotation marks with his fingers.

"During Jamison's first tour of duty, he was killed by a VC sniper. That set my mind in motion for what I'd become, pretending I was seeking revenge for my friend's death. I read every *Soldier of Fortune* magazine and book I could find and got myself so hyped up on hero worship I could not stand being around myself. I'm sure I disgusted everyone in the elite community where I lived in Philadelphia, as well. I practiced constantly at the gun range with assault rifles and every kind of gun imaginable, and while showing off one day at the range, I caught the eye of a man who said he owned a security company that operated overseas in the hot spots. Of course I was pleased when he told me I was the best shot he'd ever seen and he wanted to see what else I could do. I met him two days later at a temporary recruitment facility he had set up in the Poconos. Before I had time to think about what I was doing, I had become part of Tiger's Eye, a company of hired killers who operated mostly in Indochina."

"Tiger's Eye!" Sue Ann repeated under her breath. "Was that the tattoo you had removed, on your shoulder?"

"Yes. The tiger's eye symbolized our sharp-shooting skills and the stealth we used to get close to the target, kill, and slip away without detection. Hattie, Wolfman, William Donovan who was the banker murdered in Billings, and the man I killed outside Fox—we all had the same tattoo. I'm not sure how many others are still in existence, but I think most have put it in the past like we tried to do. Most of our jobs were in Indochina—Cambodia, Laos, North Vietnam. The Indochinese tiger is one of the stealthiest creatures alive; thus the name of our special group. Each operative was called by a number written in all caps, never a name, to keep each of us anonymous; the lower the number, the more advanced in skills and the higher paid."

"So what number were you?"

Shade was hesitant to answer.

"TWO, first behind the owner of the company known only as ONE. We were notorious, and sometimes we'd don uniforms and infiltrate U.S. military units to get into the areas where we had a hit scheduled. I never knew if we were approved by the military, but it didn't matter to me. I was in it for glory, money, and the thrill of the kill."

"That sounds so barbaric, so unlike who you are, Shade." Sue Ann shook her head in disbelief. "I'm sorry, but this is all so hard for me to comprehend—but continue with your story."

"I wish it were a 'story,' Sweetheart. Then at some point we could turn to the last page and declare, 'The End.' But the book is too thick, and I'm afraid there will be many sequels. And yes, it is barbaric, but it is who I was then, and you need to know all of it now."

"I know I do, Shade, but it is so terrifying." She hooked her fingers in his and held to his arm with her other hand. "Please—tell me what I need to know."

"FOUR, the man I killed the other day, was sent as a decoy to Fairbanks, but he knew where ONE was. There was no way to get FOUR to talk. I hate now I did what I did, but I was upset with what they did to William and to Hattie, especially Hattie. They hit too close to my little girl. In my mind, I was torturing ONE, and God help me, but I felt no regrets for what I did. At least, we don't have to worry about him anymore.

"Tiger's Eye ONE is the man who started Tiger's Eye as a so-called security company. ONE is the man who recruited me and the man who now wants me dead. Fifteen years ago, I killed his younger brother during a job. SEVEN, as in Tiger's Eye SEVEN, hated me and kept sabotaging my jobs, hoping to replace me in his brother's ranking system. I was better than he was at everything, something he could not tolerate. It was kill or be killed, but ONE couldn't see it, even though I warned him about what would happen if his brother continued to be a threat to me.

"I was assigned to a job in Cambodia, and ONE sent his brother with me, saying he wanted SEVEN to watch and learn. That just deepened his brother's resentment. I was on one side of a compound, and SEVEN was supposed to cover me from the other side. With my shooting ability, I was always the triggerman. I got within shooting range, and SEVEN, using a silencer on his rifle, shot down a branch above me; it hit right beside me. The crashing noise was like an alarm to the VC guards, and they headed in my direction. I lay still, and fortunately a tiger walked out right beside me, and the VC took off, thinking that was what had made the noise. I completed the job, but not from the location intended. I sneaked around to SEVEN's position and killed the target, but not until I had knocked that son-of-a-bitch SEVEN in the head with the barrel of my gun. Then I cut him, letting his blood soak the soil, an appetizer for my tiger friend. I left him there to die, either from the tiger or from the VC. I exchanged my rifle for Seven's, proof he had killed the target.

When I got back to our base, ONE asked where his brother was, and I told him what happened. I was never a person to lie. Besides, I was young and invincible, so I told him straight up. ONE turned and walked away, but I knew that was the end of my career as a Tiger's Eye. Seeing the look in his eyes, I knew he would seek revenge; it was time for me to end my war games. Another reason I wanted out was that our leader had started taking jobs I wanted nothing to do with, like killing women and children in villages and making it look like the VC did it. It was war propaganda. Our fearless and amoral leader was paid millions by some old rich fart from back east who wanted to sell weapons to the military and needed the war to escalate into a full-fledged declared war.

One night soon after, I went into Saigon, and the CIA caught up with me. They knew everything but needed confirmation of what ONE was doing. Tired of playing the bad guy, I gave them everything they needed and led him right into their trap. The CIA captured him and took him stateside for trial. He was in military prison for almost fourteen years, counting the two while he awaited trial, and then he escaped. For the last two years he's been hiding out, wreaking havoc on those who called themselves my friends, all with one goal in mind."

"Killing you." Sue Ann moved closer to Shade and put her arms around his waist and her head on his shoulder, demanding he surround her with the comfort only his embrace could offer her. "You said 'they.' Does he have others helping him?"

"Yes, some of the old operatives rejoined him, but I have no idea how many. At the highest point of Tiger's Eye, I know there were twenty-seven operatives, but not all were in Indochina. Truth is, Sue Ann, it will never really be over until..." He did not finish his sentence.

She left the porch and faced him.

"No! You're not going to let yourself be killed for us. Please, Shade! Tell me you'll fight for your life!" She was hysterical and buried her face in her hands. He held her tight in his arms as she sobbed.

"I will fight to live, Sue Ann. I want to be with you for a long time. We may not have the piece of paper, but I promised to cherish you and protect you forever, however long that may be. I said my vows, and you have my ring as proof." He kissed her as if it were a replay of a beautiful wedding scene with both renewing vows to love each other forever. But the only veil lifted was the veil of secrecy and horror surrounding Shade's past.

"Now put this out of your mind, Sweetheart." He needed to get her off the subject. "We have to make every minute count. You and the girls will leave tomorrow. When it's all over, I'll find you. I have a place in the jungles of Costa Rica where we'll be safe. I'm not sure how we'll convince Betsy to go along with it, but we'll give it our best shot. I'm sorry I had to tell you all this, but I needed you to see why it is necessary for you to leave." He held her chin in his hand and pulled her eyes up to meet his. "I love you, Darling. I want to live to be with you and will fight for that honor, but I will defend you and our girls with my life if that is what it takes."

****

Lovemaking was strained that night, with Sue Ann an emotional wreck. She held on to Shade as if there were no tomorrow. As she lay in his arms, she knew what she wanted to do. Reaching into the drawer in her bedside table, she pulled out the velvet bag. It was time to take her vows.

"Shade, there's something I've been waiting to do until the time was perfect, but I'm afraid to wait any longer." She sat up and looked down at him.

"What is it, Sweetheart?" He sat up also and scooted to put his back against the headboard, but before he could pull her close to him, she turned to face him.

"You are the man I have loved more than any, the man with whom I want to spend the rest of my life, and now is the time for me to take my vows just as you did when you gave me my ring." Sue Ann took Shade's left hand and flattened it against her bare leg. After slipping her dad's wedding band on his finger, she took his face in her hands.

"I promise to cherish you, to honor you, and to protect all that we have together for as long as I live. I love you unconditionally, Shade Dubois. I will love you forever—and then some." She kissed him, a deep, passionate kiss that lingered as she hoped their life together would, but deep down she knew it was unlikely. As they kissed, their tears joined and flooded their faces, dripping on to their bodies held tight in an embrace as if afraid to part.

After they made love for the last time, Shade held Sue Ann and looked at the ring, a perfect fit, and smiled.

"So this belonged to the other man in your life, your dad Zeke. I'm honored, Sue Ann, and will wear it with pride. My little piece of those tantalizing eyes that trapped me not nearly long enough ago will always be with me, no matter where I am. Thank you, Sweetheart, for giving me the happiest months of my life and for loving me unconditionally."

Shade held Sue Ann all night, refusing to let go. They slept with the curtains open, their bodies and hearts enraptured as the Sky Dwellers watched over them. Neither suspected it would be their last time to make love under Northern Lights.

Chapter Nineteen
Breakup

Betsy was upset when Sue Ann told her she and Angel were being sent to Mississippi for safety until Hattie's killer was arrested. In her typical rebellious teenage fashion, Betsy fought it, but in the end Shade asked her to please do it for him and for Angel. As always, she listened to him.

After arguing relentlessly, Sue Ann compromised with Shade. She would put the girls on the plane in Fairbanks and would follow them the next weekend. She pleaded with the school board for a short sabbatical necessary to "take care of personal business," and they acquiesced, even offering her a contract for the next school year, a decision to be made later in the summer.

Sue Ann spent the day helping the girls pack and assuring Angel she would love Elizabeth and her family. Explaining to Elizabeth what was happening was not so easy. Elizabeth read right through Sue Ann on the phone and told her to get her butt home immediately. The friend sensed danger where Sue Ann and Betsy were concerned, but assured her Angel would, of course, be welcome. Elizabeth and Annie took turns talking to Betsy and Angel, and Angel felt reassured. With sad eyes and a heavy heart, she made her father promise to come to Mississippi as soon as possible.

The next day their bags were packed and waiting by the door, ready for the trip to the airport. Sue Ann tried not to appear worried but was distraught over having to send the girls away.

"Mom, Angel and I are going to look at breakup one more time. I need some pictures to show Annie. She won't believe the monster icebergs pushed up on the banks." Betsy started to pick up the truck keys but decided to wait for her mother's okay.

Sue Ann bounded down the stairs, carrying a suitcase.

"No, Betsy. Shade told you he did not want the two of you leaving the house. Remember?" Sue Ann dreaded what was coming next.

"This is getting ridiculous, Mom. We've been down there a million times with you and Shade."

"Exactly! You don't need to go any more, and definitely not by yourselves." Sue Ann knew Betsy was going stir crazy inside and reconsidered. "I thought you were meeting Lena at the Roadhouse for a farewell cinnamon roll."

"You mean we can do that? I figured that was a 'no,' so I didn't bother to ask."

"You can go to the Roadhouse since it's so close, but don't be gone more than forty-five minutes. Shade should be back soon. He said he was just going to pick up a few things at the cabin. It's best to head into Fairbanks tonight, so we don't have to get up so early tomorrow to get you two to the airport."

Betsy grabbed the truck keys before her mother changed her mind, and she and Angel bounded out the door.

****

Shade hated the feeling he had. It was the same as the old days, and he couldn't shake it. He needed to get his family out of town tonight, but he needed to be prepared for what he knew was coming, too. Grabbing the three-wheeler keys, he headed out of his cabin soon after getting there. There must be no delay in getting back to Sue Ann and the girls; he could no longer risk being away from them. When he reached Sawyer's mine, he stopped and turned his eyes and ears in a complete circle, making sure he heard and saw nothing out of the ordinary. After unlocking the heavy wood door behind the Danger! No Trespassing sign, Shade turned on his spotlight and headed down into the mineshaft, found where the tunnel forked, and headed left, stopping when he saw his cache of emergency equipment—special commando clothing he had designed and had custom made to match the foliage of the Interior's wilderness in every season, just in case he needed it. He slung the large camouflaged bags over his shoulders and headed back out of the shaft. When he got back to his cabin, he threw the bags into the back of his truck, took one more look at his cabin, and drove away, back to his family, all that he cared about in the world.

****

Betsy and Angel ate their cinnamon rolls slowly, waiting for Lena, who seemed to be a no-show.

"I can't believe she didn't come to say goodbye. Guess she's on Indian time, as she calls it."

Betsy picked up Lena's cinnamon roll and headed back to the kitchen with it to get Sally to box it. As she walked back to her table, she noticed a straggly-looking guy sitting in the corner eating. Worn camo that looked like it had not been washed, ever, covered him from head to toe. His long dark hair and beard were unkempt, and seeing the food droppings in his beard almost made Betsy gag. When she passed by his table, she glanced at him, and he smiled and winked, causing her to hurry by.

"Look at that creepy guy in the corner, Angel." Betsy whispered, cutting her eyes back at the man.

Angel turned her head in the direction Betsy nodded but turned back quickly when she caught him staring at them.

"He is so disgusting. If Mom knew he was here, she'd make us come straight home."

"What do you mean 'she'd make us come straight home'? I thought that was what we were doing."

Sally came out with the box and handed it to Betsy.

"Thanks, Sally. How much do we owe you?"

"Boss says it's on the house, seeing as it's your last cinnamon roll for a while. I hear you're going to Mississippi for the summer. Now, that's going to be hot and muggy."

"Yeah, but we'll be back at the end of the summer. Moose Springs is home now." Betsy and Angel got up to leave, and Betsy picked up the box. "Tell Jack thanks for the cinnamon rolls."

"You bet. Where are you girls off to now? Little last minute sightseeing before you leave town?"

"Just down to the landing. I want to take some pictures of breakup, what's left of it. Now, that's something you don't see in the South." The girls headed for the door. "See you in August, Sally."

As the girls headed out the door, Angel noticed the guy putting money on the table. "Let's hurry and get out of here before that creep comes out."

The girls jumped into the truck and sped out of the parking lot. Betsy looked in the mirror and saw the man reach under the steps and pull out a guitar case and a pack.

"Oh, my gosh, he's a musician!" Betsy said, and they both laughed.

"We aren't really going to the landing are we, Betsy?"

"I know, Angel. I promise we'll go really fast, snap a couple of pictures, and then get back home. Mom will never know." Betsy looked down the road toward Lena's house and threw on the brakes when she saw Lena walking slowly toward them. Rolling down the window, Betsy yelled, "Hurry up, Lena. We've just got twenty-five minutes, and we need to go to the landing to take some pictures."

Lena ran to the truck and then made a sharp turn, running back toward her house. Angel had already moved to the middle of the seat. Betsy pulled in at Lena's front yard just as Lena bounded up carrying a cassette tape.

"You're late," Betsy chided as she handed Lena the cinnamon roll.

"You know—Indian time," Lena answered.

Angel and Betsy looked at each other and burst out laughing.

"What?" Lena asked through a mouthful of cinnamon roll. "Put the cassette in. Mom got it for me. It's Michael Jackson's new one, 'Thriller.' Wait 'til you hear 'Beat It.' "

Before they could get back down the road, two of the boys from school stopped them, wanting to tell

Betsy and Angel goodbye. Betsy kept looking at her watch but hated to be rude, so they talked a while.

****

The drifter walked down the road at a fast pace and held out his thumb to the old truck approaching.

"Need a ride?" the teenage boy asked, looking across his pretty redheaded girlfriend already scooting over next to him.

The drifter laid his gear in the back and hopped in.

"How far you going?" the girl asked.

"Oh, close to the river, I reckon. I'm camping. Wanta see this breakup I hear so much about."

"It's a good one this year," she added.

"When you due?" The man asked the girl, noticing how she rubbed her basketball belly.

"Any time now," the boy answered, smiling big. "It's gonna be a boy, or I'm sending the little shit back. He's gonna be named Bo, Junior, after me." The boy yelled as his girl punched him in the side. They rode the next few minutes in silence.

"Thanks for the ride. This is close enough." The drifter jumped out and grabbed his gear, hitting the side of the truck to let the boy know he could drive off. The boy shifted gears and floorboarded it, trying to play like a racecar driver in an old truck barely able to do thirty miles per hour. Still, Bo hooted as loud as he could.

The hitchhiker headed off through the woods to pick the perfect spot overlooking the landing; he wanted to see what the onlookers saw as they gazed upon their last breakup, their last anything.

He shot the pregnant girl first, one deadly shot with a low-caliber bullet between the eyes as she sat on a log looking toward the river. Her head was back, laughing, a good belly laugh shared with her unborn child.

Spring breakup was almost over, but the townspeople still came every day to the landing on the Tekooni River. Children came to play on the mountains of ice pushed to shore by the river torrent breaking free after months of captivity in the frozen north. But this day, the outing turned deadly. Four more would follow the girl; enough to spread terror and trepidation throughout bush Alaska for decades to come.

"A mad man, a drifter, who leaves macabre scenes of death and brutality hanging in his wake!"

"A demented marksman who thrives on watching blood and life flow from his victims, especially women, the younger the better."

"A demon hell-bent on destroying anyone, or everyone, who crosses his path."

And his all time favorite:

"A masochistic monster, a huntsman of human beings for thrill kills, getting his kicks through spreading pandemonium and terror among locals."

The shooter chuckled, thinking of the names and descriptions he had been given by the media. In reality, none fit.

Mad man, drifter, demented marksman, monster, demon; all kill for the sake of killing without any aspiration or purpose.

He had laughed loudest when he heard the news commentator refer to him as a "drifter," implying someone of low intelligence, perhaps insane, down on his luck, wandering from place to place with thoughts of comforts and luxuries overshadowed by his attempt just to survive.

"If only they knew how many degrees I have from

prestigious universities; and if they could see my beach house in the Caymans or my villa in Tuscany! All is not as it seems." He had talked to the television set that day while in his hotel room in Billings, one of the many cities where he had left his mark.

No. Drifter was certainly not what he was, but it was his favorite disguise.

In his "exercises," as he chose to call them, he was purposeful, driven, and passionate, with one main objective. Fourteen years had been wasted; time checked off while morphing from hired executioner to "model prisoner," all to secure his transfer to a low-security prison. The deal was he was to turn informant for the CIA, an agreement he made without hesitation but with no intention of keeping.

His escape was easily maneuvered while en route to his new prison home—he killed the two guards who escorted him. And now, two years later, he was still free to move from place to place, even state to state or country to country, always incognito, and always leaving his warning signs for the one man he would trap using the two teenage girls he had just seen in the Roadhouse. He had done his homework and knew both girls were important to his target. He would succeed in the accomplishment of his primary purpose for living: "Retribution!"

Hiding in the clump of trees overlooking the landing, he looked through high-powered binoculars and smiled. The bullet hit dead center on the pretty redhead's forehead, but the shot could not be heard over the loud pops and cracks of the remaining ice floes in the river. The girl's body slumped, caught in a distorted angle between the log she was sitting on and the tree behind her. One hand dangled, lifeless, to the ground, and the other lay across her protruding stomach as if, while taking her last breath, she tried to protect the life inside her, like a mother reaching for a child when hitting the brakes. The red hole oozed little blood, and she looked as if her head was nailed to the tree. Her eyes were wide open and peeked through the long curly red hair framing her pretty, pale, dead face. After dismantling the .22 caliber rifle, something he used every once in a while just for fun and extra practice, he put it in his guitar case and pulled out a high-powered weapon and put it together in moves so fast his hands appeared bionic.

"Beth!" A voice echoed from the river, and the shooter turned his head sharply to the right, chasing the voice.

"Watch this, Beth!"

The young man who called himself Bo looked to be no more than a high school student, maybe a dropout, and wore a camouflage jacket and no cap. He leapt from the bank of the river fifty yards or so away from the young woman and landed on a large flat piece of ice that wobbled under his weight at the edge of the water. The ice floe bumped into smaller chunks of ice and sent them spinning in the opposite direction. Loud cracking sounds erupted like a thunderstorm pushed by rushing water. He jumped to another floe, balancing himself like a circus performer, as the Alaskan breakup brought him closer to his girl. But Beth's eyes and body didn't react to his antics this time. As his nature-made raft brought him closer, he realized something was wrong. His leaps became hurried and careless as panic overtook him.

"Beth! Baby! What's wrong?" He landed on the ice floe closest to her and moved his feet back and forth, balancing his weight to keep from being dumped into the river, and got ready to jump back to land and to Beth.

The shot resounded like a BB from a Red Ryder, its noise cancelled by the thunderous roars and crackles of the river ice. The young man clutched his chest and dropped to his knees, never taking his gaze off Beth.

"Beth!" He mouthed her name, but no sound left his lips as his ghostly gaze froze across the short span between him and the girl he would never cuddle again; between him and the child he would never cradle in his arms or give his name.

Blood spurted between his fingers as he fell onto his side near the edge of the ice; the snow on the ice floe melted, forming a warm red pool around him. No longer able to perform his balancing act, the small chunk of ice dumped what remained of the young man into the frigid water, taking him away from all that he had known as life.

****

More came to marvel at the rebirth of the Tekooni River, main character in the great Alaskan spring thaw. Hundreds waited with eager anticipation each year to see who came closest to guessing the date and time of breakup. This year the pot had been worth thousands, but it was over, the pot claimed, and yet still they came, as if seeing breakup for the first time.

The third victim was a man in his fifties, who got out of a new truck. He glanced back at the shiny metallic blue Dodge, noticeably proud of his rig. After limping from his parking spot, he stood at the edge of the river, looking up and down as he lit up a Camel. The shooter might have thought twice had he known he was killing a fellow veteran, this one from World War II. Then again, it probably would not have mattered at all. A round circle of blood filled the back of the veteran's head as he was propelled forward to land between two ice floes that swept him down river.

The shooter looked at his Rolex, kept hidden under his long camouflage sleeve. Time was too important in his business not to be exact and was never trusted to cheap mechanisms. This was one especially made for men like him and could be used at a water depth of 4000 feet. The ordinary person would just think he had stolen it off some poor bastard who happened to be in his path, never thinking a drifter could have paid for it—or the many others he owned.

Thirty minutes had gone by, but he was a patient man and would wait for the real reason he was here. He had overheard the two girls talking at the Roadhouse and knew they were coming to river gaze. He recognized the one with the short hair, mostly from her blue eyes, *his* eyes.

The man's thoughts were interrupted when an older couple drove up.

Damn! This has to be quick. It's almost four, the time they had to leave the river. I can't let these two get in my way!

He ducked behind his barrier and readied his rifle, his sights following the couple to the landing.

A big round man and a short frail woman got out of their car and parked a good piece from the river, like they were afraid their old Buick might somehow slide into the icy torrent. They walked hand in hand to the riverbank, stopping every few feet as the man snapped picture after picture with his wife pointing, directing the next shot.

The fat man was picked to go first, and the rifleman hit his mark as the bullet entered the old man's heart. The woman screamed and bent over him, frantically pulling on his big head, trying to wake him from endless sleep. She cried and yelled for help that would not come, and watched as red covered the front of his shirt. Her hysteria was quickly diverted to fear for self as the marksman walked toward her, aiming the rifle at her face at close range.

Before she had time to beg for her life, he shot her full in the face as her eyes grew large with the horror of what was about to happen. Her body fell on top of her husband's, and their hearts joined for one last fling as their blood flowed together out of their bodies.

The murderer propped his rifle against a tree and began dragging the woman toward the river. He dreaded breaking a sweat with the fat guy, but he would not get to complete the deed.

As he returned for the huge man, a red truck pulled up and parked in the trees away from the river. He grabbed up his rifle and headed into the woods. Three teenage girls disembarked from the truck and danced and sang their way to the river. The shooter raised his binoculars from behind a stack of felled logs and focused on the girls. A smile covered his face as he recognized them from the Roadhouse, the pretty little blonde and the blue-eyed Amerasian girl, the main targets of this adventure.

"Bingo!" he said under his breath.

"Beat it! Beat it!"

The girls shook their butts, keeping time to their singing as the tall Indian girl moon-walked backwards toward the river. The man left his perch behind the clump of trees, preparing to come up from behind, knowing they would try to leave in a hurry when they saw the dead man. In his mind, he plotted.

You two get to live, for a while anyway. Bait for the son-of-a-bitch I've dreamed of killing for fourteen years. I'll shoot the Indian girl in front of you, and there's no way you'll run.

Jon Shockey, get ready! Your ass is about to be mine!

The blonde girl was the first to see the old man lying on the ground and rush to him. The other two followed at a run and knelt beside their friend. The tall girl felt for a pulse but found none.

"He's dead!" the girl announced. "And we need to get out of here! The blood isn't even dried, and that means whoever shot him is still close by." All three girls jerked their heads around as they heard twigs snap behind them. Their eyes grew large, but they did not move as the shooter, the drifter clad head to toe in worn camouflage, approached, aiming a rifle at them. His long matted hair and straggly beard covered his face but not his black eyes that bored holes through them, warning them not to move.

"Please! Please don't shoot us, mister. We'll give you time to get away before we leave." The Indian girl took the lead in what seemed to be her role.

"Afraid not, girls. Two of you are coming with me."

"Two of us?" The blonde asked, as her friends moved in closer beside her. The shorthaired girl began to cry, and the Indian girl put her arm around her.

"Thata girl!" He walked closer and, with his rifle barrel, motioned for the consoler to move away from the other two.

"You! Indian! I'm going to count to three and give you time to get to the truck, but if you're not there by the time I yell three, one of your friends is getting a bullet right between the eyes like that pregnant redhead got earlier. Do you understand?" He smiled as the girl got to her feet and glanced at where the truck was parked.

"You killed Beth?" The girl stood defiant, opening and closing her fists, but the shooter ignored the question and began to count.

"One…"

"Run!" The blonde girl screamed and put her arm around her other friend, who had her hands over her ears and her eyes closed. The Indian girl sprinted toward the truck without turning. But when she got halfway, a bullet hit her in the back, knocking her face down onto the ground.

"No!" The blonde yelled as she stepped over the man's body, going to the aid of her friend. She stopped when she heard the murderer's voice.

"You want your little friend to die, too?"

The blonde retraced her steps to where her dark-haired friend cowered on the ground, on her knees with her hands over her head like she was about to be executed.

A few minutes later, the two girls, prodded by the murderer's gun barrel in their backs, disappeared into the wilderness with their abductor.

Chapter Twenty
The Bait

Sue Ann watched out the window, but Betsy and Angel did not come home. They were thirty minutes late, and she was terrified. She had started out the door to walk to the Roadhouse looking for them when Shade drove up. He was about to take two big camouflage duffels out of the back, but Sue Ann came running.

"Shade, we've got to look for the girls. They didn't come back." Sue Ann was wringing her hands, and Shade grabbed her and held her to him.

"Where did they go, Sue Ann? I thought we agreed they'd stay at the house today."

"I let them go to the Roadhouse to have a last cinnamon roll with Lena, but they should have been back thirty minutes ago. What if somebody…"

"Don't, honey! They probably just stopped to talk to some of their friends. We'll go to the Roadhouse and see if they're there."

Shade sped to the Roadhouse, trying not to show the alarm he was feeling. He jerked to a stop, and he and Sue Ann threw the doors open and ran up the steps to the Roadhouse.

"Sally, have you seen Sue Ann and Angel?" Shade yelled as soon as they stepped inside.

"Yep. They left here a good forty-five minutes ago, heading to pick up Lena and then going to the landing to take pictures of breakup."

Sue Ann looked at Shade. "I told them to come straight home and *not* to go to the landing."

"Let's go by Lena's house and then to the landing. They've probably just lost track of time, Darling. They are teenagers." Sue Ann was shaking, out of control, and he put his arm around her, holding onto her as he led her out of the Roadhouse.

"Thanks, Sally," he called over his shoulder as he closed the door.

Sally knew something was wrong and remembered the drifter in the corner. She dropped her pad on the table without taking an order from the couple seated there and hurried after Shade.

"Shade, wait up!" Sally was tall and took two steps at a time. "I don't know if it means anything, and I hope it don't, but there was a man, a real weirdo dressed all in camouflage, who got up and left when the girls did. I didn't think anything of it at the time, but he didn't look like the type to have much money, and he left without eating even half his food. That didn't seem quite right."

"Describe him, Sally, but be quick." Sally quickly described the drifter, giving his approximate height and weight and everything she could remember. Shade thanked her and started rolling the window up while backing up in a hurry.

When Sally got back inside, the man asked if they were going to be served or not, but Sally just walked on by without a word and headed for the phone, calling Jake first and then Helen and Rose and everybody in town with a phone.

Shade passed Lena's house and made the circle back to the road.

"The truck isn't here. I'm going to the river. Hold tight, Sue Ann!" Shade turned the curve fast and stomped the accelerator, not stopping when he got to the gravel road that would take them to the landing.

"There's the truck!" Sue Ann screamed as they approached the landing.

"Two other vehicles here. Maybe they're all right, baby."

She stared ahead, sitting on the edge of her seat, and opened the door before their truck stopped. She took off running to the landing, not waiting for Shade, and screamed as she saw Lena lying in the path ahead.

"God, no!" Shade yelled as he ran, passing Sue Ann in order to reach Lena. She was lying on her stomach and not moving. Blood circled the back of her shirt.

Shade bent down to see if she was breathing as Sue Ann rushed up and dropped to her knees beside the girl. Sue Ann began wiping Lena's hair from her face.

"Lena, sweetheart, where are Betsy and Angel?" She continued to talk to the girl while all the time her gaze searched the landing.

"I need to turn her on her side, Sue Ann, and see if I can get a heartbeat."

Shade gently turned the girl over, and heard a soft moan.

"Thank God! She's alive," he said, but Sue Ann had left Lena and was heading toward something big lying near the water. As she approached, she saw the body of King Turner, a man who had moved to Moose Springs when he retired from the post office in Ruby. He and his wife liked village life but had wanted to live on the road system so moved to Moose Springs. Sue

Ann fell to her knees beside him and began screaming for Shade.

Within minutes, Jake pulled up with Bernice, and then Helen and her husband, and Rose, and Don, and before long almost the entire town was there. Shade had started giving Lena mouth-to-mouth resuscitation as soon as he got her on her side but told Jake to get someone to take over. He needed to get to Sue Ann. Soon Bonnie arrived with bag in hand and set in to save Lena. She sent one of the high school boys who lived closest to the landing to his house to call the State Troopers and the Medevac with the message "Multiple shootings at Tekooni Landing at Moose Springs. Dispatch troopers and Medevac immediately." Rose came up next and ran to her daughter, screaming.

Shade left Lena as soon as Bonnie arrived and ran to Sue Ann, who seemed to be in shock, walking in circles with her arms folded, calling for Betsy and Angel as if they were just outside the cabin. When he approached her, she fell to her knees, hugging herself and sobbing.

"Sweetheart, you have to get control. I need you to be calm. I have to go after the girls. The sooner I get on his trail, the sooner I can bring our girls home safe." He took her face in his hands and pulled her to him. "Do you hear me, Sue Ann?"

"Yes." Sue Ann nodded her head. "Go, Shade. Bring them home."

He stood and waved to Helen and Bernice, beckoning them to come and help with Sue Ann. Jake came with them.

"What can I do, Shade?"

"He's got Betsy and Angel, Jake. I can't wait for

the Troopers. In fact, I wish Bonnie hadn't called them, but I know she had no choice. Only one person can save our girls, and you're looking at him. But it won't be quick or easy."

"So, what now?"

"Get my truck and drive it through the trees. Stop out of sight of the crowd. I don't want anyone to see what I'm doing."

Jake left at a trot, and within minutes Shade saw his truck heading through the woods upriver.

He stood beside Sue Ann, who seemed to be coming back to him. She held out her arms, and Shade lifted her, holding her tight.

"I love you, Sue Ann. Don't ever forget the vows we took. I'm going after the girls. Pray, Sweetheart. Can you do that for me?"

"Yes. Please be careful, Shade. Tell the girls I love them, and I'll be waiting on them and you. Come back to me, Shade. I love you."

He kissed her, a quick but deeply passionate kiss that promised only, "I love you." Taking one last look into her green eyes, he smiled, trying to give her reassurance, and headed into the woods in a smooth, perfect jog.

Shade was a commando again. He would think and act like a tiger, but his main mission was to save lives, with the exception of the murderer turned kidnapper. Shade became Raven, also known as TWO.

Chapter Twenty-One
Raven

"In practice we always base our preparations against an enemy on the assumption that his plans are good; indeed, it is right to rest our hopes not on a belief in his blunders, but on the soundness of our provisions. Nor ought we to believe that there is much difference between man and man, but to think that the superiority lies with him who is reared in the severest school."
—*Thucydides*

Jake waited at the truck for Shade.

"No time for speeches or explanations, Jake. The sooner I'm on his trail, the quicker I'll kill the bastard and get the girls back."

In seconds, Shade stood naked, his civilian clothes lying on the ground in a pile. He dug into the first duffle and pulled out thick pants, shirt, and socks made from a special material, breathable and waterproof, both needed for the fast-changing Alaskan weather. These were followed by combat boots laced tight. His clothing was designed to perfectly match the surroundings: greens that matched different shades of spruce, birch leaves, and low bushes; varying shades of gray both light and dark to match the bark of the trees; and all painted with the precision of a master artist—or a commando. He donned them quickly, and they fit snugly to his body, giving him the freedom to move with dexterity. He pulled out a tube of black paint and covered his face, neck, and hands, making sure his eyes were completely surrounded. Next he added green streaks over the black.

Jake thought of Ben's description of the Raven and saw just how fitting it was. He continued to watch as Shade opened the backpack and pulled out a disassembled assault rifle. In the fastest movement of hands Jake had ever seen, Shade assembled the rifle, threw in a magazine, and was ready, with three knives held around his waist on a canvas leather belt and a chest strap holding extra ammunition. Last, he slung a small pack, in the same camouflage pattern, over his back. He turned to head into the forest but stopped. Reaching for his jacket on the ground, he pulled out the piece of Sue Ann's braid and stuffed it inside his shirt, next to his heart. He balanced the weight of his gear and headed toward the trees on the most important mission of his life.

Jake said no trite goodbye or empty good luck slogan, knowing his friend would ignore both. As Shade took a few steps toward the woods, he stopped and turned back to face his friend.

"The mine; left turn; look for the ore bucket turned upside down; dig down and retrieve the packet. If I don't make it out, follow the directions. No questions; no arguments; no refusal."

With the same even-paced jog he had already used getting to the truck, Raven disappeared into the trees. Jake watched but was only able to discern the slightest movement as Raven blended in perfectly with the wild foliage.

****

Raven had been sprinting for two hours. He knew to follow the river, but he also knew ONE would have many tricks planned. No way was this his first time to the area, although he had given the locals that impression: stranger to the locals, yes; stranger to the wilderness area, no. Raven suspected ONE had hidden a boat ready for a fast getaway up the central channel of the Tekooni that was free of ice and flowing fast, and One's first move would be to get to the boat. As Raven headed over the next rise, he heard the sound he was hoping not to hear—a chopper, probably loaded with SERT, the State Troopers' Special Emergency Response Team, ready for action.

Raven did not want to be mistaken for the murderer; he dove behind a stack of felled logs, probably some trapper's future cabin. Stealth would be highly important, since the only darkness on what was to be a clear night would be from about midnight to 3:00 a.m. not counting civil twilight, dusk and dawn, where there was enough light for outdoor activities—meaning enough light to be detected by one trained to see in darkness. Raven knew he had to get close enough to see Betsy and Angel and know they were okay.

As he lay behind the barrier, he started trying to think like his old enemy, something necessary if this mission was to be successful.

"My main objective is the rescue of my girls; my second objective is to kill the miserable son-of-a-bitch and get him out of my life. But will he be out of my life? Hell, he probably has a barrage of former operatives— or new crazy kids like I was—ready to take over if I succeed and kill him."

Raven's thoughts were interrupted by the sound of rapid gunfire, like a battle. He left his hiding spot and ran toward the river, reaching the bluff just in time to hear the explosion of the chopper and to see the distant flames and smoke as the helicopter spiraled down to crash into the river. The exchange had taken place a couple of miles upriver, and he knew he could catch up with the killer before morning, but he could not rush it.

A couple of miles upriver. Not that far. Gotta think like a Tiger's Eye.

Then it hit him.

The murderer's objective is to draw me out and kill me. He'll use the girls to do that, and he won't kill them until I'm dead. But he will torture them and leave a trail for me to follow, a trail of body parts or clothing, objects to upset me and throw me off balance. I have to become a tiger—a stoic son-of-a-bitch who feels nothing and is affected by nothing.

He stood on the bluff looking upriver and saw helicopter debris washing toward him. The bodies of two men bobbed up and down in the water, but not for long. The thick silt of the Tekooni River covered the two men, creeping into the fibers of their clothing and dragging them under, out of sight, out of life. A third man clung to what looked like a seat and showed signs of life that would not last long in the icy water. Shade watched but could not run to the river's edge to try to save him. Then he heard it: A motorboat, throttle wide open, speeding upriver, away from where the helicopter was shot down.

Think like the murdering bastard! Why is he speeding upriver when he wants me and knows I'm behind on foot? The quicker he gets at me, the sooner he can run for good, but not until he sees me dead. Outthink him, Raven!

Raven sat behind a dark, wet stump where he knew he would blend in, not visible even from the air, and waited for midnight, when the little bit of darkness would begin, but he knew it would still be light enough to move around. He did not close his eyes. That would not happen for at least forty-eight hours. He reached in his pocket and pulled out one of the pills sealed in foil, a pill that would speed up his metabolism, keep him focused, and balance his thought processes. He had never done drugs as a young person, but he had learned to love them in Vietnam.

Putting the whole scenario out of his mind, Raven thought about his advantages. He knew this river, had killed a moose on it every fall since he'd been here. He'd killed many bears, as well, mostly for Jake and Bernice to tan into beautiful bearskin rugs to sell in the museum gift shop. And he was a trained tracker with the instinct of a tiger.

As the pill took effect, his thinking became sharper; he was able to put aside the people he loved and to focus on the man he would kill. Raven could see himself sitting beside the giant jet motor of the riverboat he shared with Jake every autumn, sitting high on the water, propelled against the current. In his mind, he followed the straight run of the river with its fall banks screaming in oranges, yellows, and reds, almost as vivid as the Sky Dwellers. He could see himself speeding several miles ahead to the spot where the river narrowed and curved again at the point where a slough connected to the river, the spot where he always bagged a moose. He could relax for miles as the Tekooni ran straight, never having to turn the handle to guide it or increase the throttle to go faster, since it was always wide open. This was the time to warm his hands in his pockets while the jet motor was on automatic pilot, or the closest thing to it. This was the time to…

The river runs straight for miles and miles! Automatic pilot! I know what he's doing. The bastard is not taking the girls and heading upstream away from anyone pursuing him. He's turned the throttle wide open and the boat is heading straight ahead without passengers. He's jumped into the frigid water and somehow swum to shore, where he left the girls bound and gagged. Hell, I taught him that trick on the Mekong River in Cambodia. I got the boat heading in the right direction, wide open and straight ahead, knowing the VC would head out after me. When out of sight, I jumped into the water and swam to shore, leaving the boat going forward without me. I hope his balls freeze and fall off.

Raven grinned at the thought of ONE, with shriveled-up testicles, shaking out of control as he reached shore.

Raven's grin faded as his thoughts took him to another scenario, a training exercise repeated many times between himself and ONE, a game of cat-and-mouse. Using rubber bullets, they would stalk each other, seeing who could hit the other one first. Every time, they were matched evenly, often shooting at the exact same time. One time, they each were shot in the head in the same split second as their scopes were aimed and the rifles shot with matched precision. Shade took the rifle from his shoulder and hid it beneath the limbs of a felled tree along with the chest strap of ammunition no longer needed. He could not risk a shot going wild and hitting one of the girls. The one part of the cat-and-mouse training in which ONE was no match for Raven was stealth, the art of getting close enough for hand-to-hand combat. Besides, ONE was at a disadvantage with two hostages making noise except for when they were bound and left in a spot.

And now he is backtracking by land, coming for a meet-and-greet and using my girls as a shield and as bait. I'll be ready for you, son-of-a-bitch! Come and get me.

Chapter Twenty-Two
The Bear Pit

Raven circled wide, making no sound as he stole toward the murderer. Sooner or later, he would fall into ONE's trap or, hopefully, get close enough to see the girls without being spotted. His raven eyes cut through the semi-darkness guiding him, casting beams of sight through scrub bushes, fallen trees, and thick spruce and aspen trees.

He stopped, casting his eyes in every direction, peering through trees so thick they looked like a green tunnel. He turned his head in every direction, like human radar, listening for any telltale signs of movement.

There!

After easing his knife out of the sheath, he clutched the handle, ready for hand-to-hand combat in the darkness. The sound of a twig breaking was heard again but in a different direction, and Raven knew ONE was here. Raven stood perfectly still, even forcing his heart to steady its beat as he heard another twig snap. ONE wanted him to follow or he would not be making even the slightest noise.

Raven took one clandestine step and stopped to listen again. He could hear twigs breaking in successive moves now, farther ahead, and knew the kidnapper had moved out of his path, going at a fast pace. Perhaps he was tiring of this game and was ready to go for the kill, but more likely, he was leading his pursuer to rendezvous with death.

Raven moved faster but took extra precautions with each step, knowing the killer's expertise in setting lethal traps. His eyes caught a glimpse of something up ahead, reflecting the quarter moon's slight glow. If he had not taken the pill, he would have charged ahead to reach her, but his impassivity kicked in, stopping him before getting to the murderer's first tease. Moonlight reflected off long, golden curls, and at first glance Raven thought Betsy had been scalped, or worse, and her beautiful head left to mock him. He held back, not rushing to see. When he was within reach, he saw Betsy's long curls tied together at one end, with the hair stretched over a rock and perched between low limbs on a spruce tree.

He breathed a sigh of relief, knowing Betsy would be devastated at having her long hair cut off, but at least she was alive. He thought of Angel, with her short pixie haircut, and prayed the murderer would not cut off an ear or a finger to lure him into a premature rescue attempt.

Now that he knew the trail he was to follow, Raven left it, circling around to the riverside, probably just as ONE expected him to do. Raven took a few quiet steps in that direction and again stopped to listen, repeating the maneuver several times until he could hear the current in the wide river moving fast. No more twigs were heard breaking; no sounds of any kind echoed through the spruce tree forest, but he still listened. Then he heard it, the soft moan of a girl's voice as if in a fitful sleep. Raven knew the girls would have been given a sedative to make them quiet and wondered if Betsy even knew her beautiful locks of hair had been cut off. He hoped she didn't.

Prolonging pain is a good thing.

He remembered Jake telling Ben's story of the mud creature stealing through the snake pit and cutting the wires surrounding the POW camp, but there was no snake pit in Alaska, and the vast wilderness of aspen, cottonwood, spruce, tamarack, and birch served as massive, spread-out prison walls for Betsy and Angel. He had to get closer and explore his options, reverting back to the stealth of his youth, with no thickness of dark night skies to conceal him.

As he crouched, looking through a stand of treelike shrubs of alder and willow, trying to decide what to do, things suddenly got brighter. He looked up, and Ursa Major, the Great Bear, sparkled against the black sky brighter than Raven had ever seen the constellation, as if it were being chased by evil. Something moved to Raven's right, something big, and he prepared himself for battle, gripping his knife by its handle.

The grizzly slung its head from side to side, sloshing drool from its giant cheeks.

Raven remained motionless, not making a sound as the bear growled and moved in another direction. Before it was even twenty feet away, a click echoed through the trees, and the bear began growling, slinging its body while dragging something with its front left paw.

A trap! The bear tripped the trap intended for me!

Raven heard another click and knew ONE had shot the bear using a silencer on his rifle. The bear growled louder, his angry head shaking as he tried to rise on his hind legs, ready to attack, but the trap kept him grounded. Another shot left in silent pursuit, and Raven took advantage of the distraction to get closer, hiding behind a bunch of stunted willows and alders. The second shot hit dead center, and the grizzly dropped to the ground. Raven could hear its death grunts and knew it would soon pass on to the next world.

In the light of the constellation and the moon, Raven could see Betsy's eyes, huge and terrified, staring at the huge furry carcass of the bear that had fallen only inches from her. Duct tape covered her mouth, and her hands and feet were bound with thin, tightly woven rope. Her body was secured to a tree with rope wound around and around so tightly there was no way she could escape. He scanned the grounds but could not find Angel, and, even with the pill, he felt an emptiness wash over him.

Raven flattened his body to the ground as twigs broke. ONE was coming toward the bear. He stopped on the other side of the huge bear and stuck the butt of his rifle into the fur. Betsy's whimpers caused him to swing around toward her and place the rifle barrel to her temple. She closed her eyes, holding them tightly shut, not wanting to see him pull the trigger.

He stood laughing at the fear on her face. With his back to the tree and his rifle pointed toward where Raven crouched, ONE picked up one of the bear's huge paws, stretched it over to Betsy, and pushed down, letting the sharp bear claw rip her jeans and the flesh beneath. She tried to pull away but couldn't. Her body shook as she watched her blood seep through torn denim. Tears flowed from her eyes, running down the duct tape and dropping onto her jacket.

Raven wanted to rush the maniac but knew he'd be shot before he could get two steps off. ONE walked to the other side of the tree, taking a seat on a hillock, his lookout. Raven watched but knew the murderer would not fall asleep. He had the same kind of pills Raven had taken and was just as alert. Another whine was heard, from trees a few yards over from the murderer, and Raven knew Angel was bound in that area. The avenger left his watchtower to go to Angel, and Raven seized the opportunity to crawl on his elbows and toes, holding himself off the ground by only a few inches, over to the bear and Betsy. He molded his body into the bear's embrace and caught Betsy's eye. Her eyes grew large, and he knew she didn't recognize him. Reaching to his side, he retrieved a small hunting knife and put it behind Betsy with the handle touching the palm of her bound hands. Putting his finger to his lips, Shade backed away, through the bear pit and back to where he could watch, now that he knew where the killer was.

Betsy held the handle of the knife and stretched her fingers along the blade, nipping her finger in the process, but she never flinched or whined. Raven thought Betsy had recognized him just before he left her, and he knew she would take the knife and begin cutting away the bindings. He hoped she would use discretion, knowing if the murderer caught her with the knife he would have no qualms about killing her.

It was late, and Raven could already see the first hints of sunlight hiding behind the distant mountains. He needed a plan, but for right now, he needed to hide himself better. Sunrise would bring more troopers, helicopters, and search teams, and it would bring the end to ONE, TWO, or both.

Chapter Twenty-Three
The Final Showdown

Ursa Major disappeared behind dark clouds that covered the sky before the sunlight could escape over the mountain, and Raven was relieved. As he lurked in the thick woods close enough to watch both Betsy and Angel, he heard movement in the woods behind Angel. He didn't move as ONE left his watchtower and crouched, sneaking toward the sound.

Raven knew this was his chance, probably his only chance. He pulled off the pack and opened a side pocket. Quickly, he unlaced his combat boots and set them aside, pulled rock climber's shoes on, and removed his small pack to lessen his weight, leaving only his remaining two knives on his belt. Furtive, like a tiger, or perhaps a mountain lion, he made his way closer, knowing he had to do something totally unexpected, and he knew what it would be.

The murderer took a different spot when he came out of the woods, closer to Angel, who was asleep. Propping his rifle on his lap with the barrel aimed at Angel, he took out a 357 Magnum, checked for ammunition, and re-holstered it.

"I know you're here, TWO—or should I call you by your Alaskan name, Raven? I'm gambling on you not having your rifle. Hand-to-hand was the only way you could ever beat me. I can almost smell your black face paint. Been a few years for both of us, but I've had two years to refresh my skills. Except for castrating poor FOUR, you've had no practice." Pulling his knife out of the sheath, he ran the blade down his arm, cutting the hairs. He held it in his hand and practiced a fast ripping action in the air.

"If it makes you feel any better, FOUR killed Hattie, for big bucks, of course, and he found the receipts with your name. The rest was easy. What a shame about Hattie. I enjoyed her so many times in the old days."

Raven never flinched at these words. This was old news to him.

"I've got my little castrator, my favorite knife, ready for you. Remember how quickly one can lose his manhood with this toy in my hands?" He put his head back and laughed, a raucous, devilish laugh that echoed off the spruce trees. Angel awoke, her eyes wide in terror as she watched her captor holding the knife.

"If you manage to live, which is highly unlikely, you will still be a pretty face that can charm any woman right out of her clothes like you did Lam, but that's all you'll be—a pretty face." Again he laughed. In one quick jerking action, he crouched beside Angel, his face against hers. His head was slick, free of the nasty beard and long, straggly hair. He rubbed his beardless face against Angel's soft pretty cheek, free of blemish.

"She's a pretty little thing, TWO—like her mother Lam."

Raven tried to shut out the words he knew were coming, but he couldn't.

"How does it feel to make mad passionate love to a woman one minute and put your hands around her tiny throat and squeeze the life out of her the next?" The kidnapper cast his eyes at Angel and saw her shake her head in disbelief. Her eyes filled with tears, but none escaped as she continued to watch the man and his knife.

"You like my toy, Tulen? Or do you prefer to be called Angel? Angel—exactly what you'll be in a few minutes if your daddy doesn't show himself." He crouched beside Angel and waved the knife before eyes that grew large with terror.

"Hmm. Perhaps I'll take off one of your ears. He held the knife to Angel's ear, nicking it, letting drops of blood fall onto her jacket.

Again he laughed, enjoying the torment he was heaping on the young girl and the father he knew was hiding and probably watching.

Raven remained still, trying not to be jostled into action before it was time. Remaining free of emotion was his best weapon to use in saving Angel and Betsy, and, no matter what, he had to wait for the right opportunity by tuning out ONE's merciless games of mental torture. Sensing movement, Raven looked toward Betsy. He watched the slight back-and-forth movement behind her and noticed how subtle she was as she cut through the ropes. He was proud of her and prayed Sue Ann would not be left childless.

Sue Ann!

The thought that he might never again hold her left him weak, and he knew he had to put her out of his mind. He turned his attention back to the murderer as he continued talking, trying to inject more fear into Raven's little girl and to scare her father enough to make him appear from wherever he was hiding.

"You always were the best at hiding, TWO, but that was in your younger days, before you discovered you had a daughter. Now I'm going to use your precious Angel to draw you out and make you do what you were not capable of doing as a young, strong, smart operative. You had real balls then—enough to kill my brother and tell me about it without so much as blinking an eye. And then you turned on me. The thought of watching you die has kept me going for almost fifteen years.

"You think you'll walk away this time, too, but it won't happen. I have operatives, old and new, lined up to take you down if you happen to get lucky and kill me first. Millions of dollars are waiting in a bank account for whoever takes your last breath—just in case I've gotten old and rusty at my trade. And they'll use Dr. Sue Ann Parish and these two girls, if they're still alive, to get to you, just as I'm about to do with your little Angel here." He grabbed her by the hair, pulled her head forward, and slammed it back against the tree. The delicate little pixie's eyes closed, and when he let go, her head hung forward as far as her bindings would allow.

Raven's blood boiled; rage rose from inside him, but he knew he couldn't give in to it. Timing was all he had in his favor, knowing the madman was now better trained and more adept at hand-to-hand combat than he was. Angel was unconscious, and that was a good thing. As long as what the masochistic bastard did to Angel or Betsy was not life threatening, he had to be patient in making his move.

As he waited, he thought the whole scenario through. What would be the purpose of his living if it meant his loved ones would relive this horror over and over until he was finally killed? He couldn't risk Sue Ann and the girls dying at the hands of some other monster. Raven turned his attention from the scene below and looked within his soul.

This is it—the final showdown. It's time to put an end to you, Son-of-a-Bitch, and it's time to let my family live without fear.

Raven looked up at the heavens so very close. Only a light dusting of darkness remained. Sue Ann, Betsy, Angel—they were who he lived for, and they were who he would die for.

"I know you've gotten rusty, Jon Shockey. You could no longer be number TWO in the shape you're in. You broke the most important rule of the Tiger's Eye. You let a woman win your heart. You know what I always told you and all the young operatives: 'Lose your heart—lose your balls!' "

ONE stood and, with one big slash of his knife, cut the ropes that kept Angel tethered to the tree. As she rolled to her side, he slashed through the bindings on her feet, allowing the knife to slice the inside of her tiny ankles in the process. Then he jerked the duct tape from her mouth and lifted her to her feet, holding her up with an arm around her waist and carrying her like a rag doll toward the bluff overlooking the Tekooni River. Angel was awake, but she did not cry out.

Shade heard movement and saw Betsy crawling into the trees away from the terrifying scene and out of ONE's sight.

Good girl! He spoke in his mind and turned his attention back to ONE, who was dragging Angel right to the spot where Shade wanted him.

"Come out, you son-of-a-bitch, or I'll throw her into the ice water. No matter if she can swim or not, the temperature alone will kill her in minutes, if the fifty-foot drop doesn't." He held the knife to Angel's throat as he continued to back up toward the big spruce trees that stood guard at the bluff's edge. The muddy waters of the Tekooni raged below, and Shade could see the terror in his daughter's eyes. In the distance, the sounds of choppers filled the air. Sunrise and the showdown were only minutes away.

"On the count of three, show yourself, or it's goodbye to your pretty little girl. "One…two…"

Before he could finish counting, a black-and-green phantom leapt from high in the tree closest to the murderer, landing on ONE, grabbing him, and slinging him to the ground away from Angel. Raven yelled, giving himself a needed dose of adrenaline as he pounced on the murderer, trying to pry the knife from his hand. The two men rolled down the incline, each holding firmly to the knife's handle and to each other. Raven was on top, twisting the knife still in the killer's hand, trying to force it down to his face. The men were evenly matched in strength until Raven was distracted for a split second as Betsy sprinted through the woods toward Angel. In that split second, ONE grabbed a knife from Raven's sheath with his left hand and plunged it into Raven's side.

Raven grabbed his side as he fell on top of ONE, who rolled him onto his back and smiled as he saw a circle of red forming across Raven's stomach. ONE looked up to where he had left Angel; she was gone. He glanced at where Betsy had been bound, and she, too, was no longer there.

"Shit!" The murderer yelled, grabbing the knife from Raven's hand and sprinting after the girls, who remained on his killing list. The choppers were coming closer, and he knew it was time to finish this and go deeper into the wilderness, where he had hidden a fast three-wheeler. This would take him to a tributary of the Tekooni where he had hidden a powerboat, and from there to another river and away from the Alaskan bush. His helicopter waited not far away, and once in it, ONE would escape to become another piece of Northern folklore, perhaps as notorious as Albert Johnson, the Mad Trapper of the Yukon, in neighboring Canada.

Just ahead he could see the legs of the two girls and knew they were as good as caught. With one giant lunge, he took Betsy down. Jerking her up by her now short curls, he held the knife to her throat and called to Angel.

"You, Angel, over here!" With his knife to their backs, he pushed the girls to the top of the hill overlooking the Tekooni. They hugged each other, knowing they were about to die, but neither of them cried or begged for their lives.

Raven waited in the bushes where he had dragged himself. He was weak from loss of blood, but he had managed to get himself back to the spot where he knew ONE would bring the girls to finish them off, the highest bluff overlooking the river, where the fall alone would assure their deaths if his rifle blast did not. The murderer stood in silhouette to the side and just below, looking up at the girls, his rifle aimed at them.

"Any farewell speeches, girls?" He raised the rifle, but as he clicked the safety off, Raven used his last ounce of adrenaline to rush him, yelling, plunging the knife he had pulled from his own body into ONE's groin and twisting, holding to ONE like a mad dog as the two men catapulted off the cliff and into the raging river below.

"Dad!" Angel screamed, moving to the edge, looking down with terror-filled eyes as the churning current took her father from her. Betsy put her arm around her friend as they watched Shade's and his murderer's bodies bob for a few seconds, only to disappear as the unforgiving Tekooni River took its latest victims downstream in its swift-flowing current.

Chapter Twenty-Four
The Painting

Sue Ann's heart was broken; she was having a hard time accepting Shade's death. Praying Shade had somehow survived, she kept hope alive for two weeks, until his body was found fifty miles downstream from where he and the murderer had gone into the river.

But it was not the State Troopers who came to bring her the bad news. A CIA agent from out of state came to tell her. As proof of his death, he handed her the ring Shade was wearing when he died, a gold wedding band inlaid with one huge emerald and many small ones. In offering his condolences, the agent told Sue Ann how Jon Shockey was considered a hero not only for saving the girls' lives but also for saving many POWs during the Vietnam War in his own one-man campaign to "right the wrongs of his youth."

Ironically, ONE's body had been recovered at the Moose Springs landing, lodged in a logjam at the water's edge shortly after he and Shade plummeted into the river. The troopers had to fight to get his body away from the locals who had found him and planned to hack him to pieces and "burn his remains right there at the landing."

"He deserves to burn just like his soul is burning in hell," one of Beth's and Bo's friends yelled at the troopers.

Shade, always fearful of having to leave his loved ones too early, had left a will leaving his family—Sue Ann and the girls—his assets, worth millions, including a company he owned named Raven Wear, a company that manufactured commando clothing like Shade was wearing when he died. But more importantly, he had left a set of instructions with Jake.

Sue Ann sat in Old Green, staring at the piece of paper Jake handed her.

"It's a deed to a place in Montana, a historic log cabin sitting on acreage in the Beartooth Mountains," she explained to Jake.

"Oh?" Jake left the couch and came to look at the paper she held out to him.

"Red Lodge, Montana. Bernice and I went there when we first married. Now, that is one beautiful little town. It's surrounded by mountains." Jake smiled, thinking of his friend. "Shade told me you and Betsy fished in Montana on the way up."

"Yes, we did. Do I have to tell you where we fished?" Sue Ann took the paper as Jake handed it back to her.

"Let me guess. Red Lodge." Jake smiled and shook his head. "Shade was a good guy, regardless of his past. You know he left Bernice and me his property here, Old Sawyer's mine and all the acreage."

"That sounds just like him." Sue Ann realized all of what Jake had said, and her mouth opened in mild shock. "You know about Shade?"

"Yes. He saved my brother Ben, who had been held in North Vietnam for three years as a POW—but don't mention it. No one in Moose Springs knows about it. Actually, my own brothers and sisters don't know I knew the commando responsible for saving Ben, but Shade would not like my talking about it." He handed the deed back to her.

"You should go and check this Montana cabin out, Sue Ann. It might be a place where you and Betsy can begin to heal, somewhere away from Moose Springs." Jake paused for a few seconds. "But I hope you'll come back eventually."

"Moose Springs is home, but I think you're right, Jake. We'll find this cabin in the Beartooths after we take Angel to meet her grandparents." Sue Ann put the deed back in the envelope. "I know it's selfish of me, but I hope Angel decides to stay with Betsy and me. They've become sisters in the few months we've had together, and they both went through so much. Betsy is grieving for Shade as much as Angel is."

She hugged Jake as he left and watched as he headed to his truck.

"Take time and heal, Sue Ann. We'll be waiting for you and Betsy when you get back, and Angel, too, if she decides to stay with you."

****

Sue Ann and Betsy escorted Angel to the home of her grandparents, Jonathan and Diane Shockey of Philadelphia. Shade had left instructions for Angel to be delivered to his parents after his letter was sent explaining who she was. In the letter, Shade pleaded with his parents to take Angel and raise her as their only grandchild, but only if they could love her unconditionally. If they refused, or if Angel did not choose to stay with them, Sue Ann was to take Angel and raise her with Betsy as her own daughter.

As the cab drove up to the mansion in an elite

section of Philadelphia, Sue Ann had to pry Betsy and Angel apart.

"It's time, girls. Let's go meet your grandparents, Angel."

A house servant met them at the door and escorted them into the front parlor, where Jonathan and Diane Shockey stood to greet them.

Angel looked at her grandparents and smiled. Diane returned the smile and moved to her granddaughter, putting her arms around her. Jonathan walked first to Sue Ann and held out his hand.

"I'm sorry for your loss, Sue Ann. I know what it's like to love Jon and lose him. We've lost him twice now." Then he turned to Betsy, extended his hand to her and offered her a smile but seemed unsure of what to say. But with Betsy, his words were not important.

"I loved him, too. Shade, that is. He was the closest thing to a father I've ever known."

"Yes, dear. Of course you did, and I'm sure he loved you."

Jonathan stepped over to where his wife and granddaughter stood getting to know each other. Sue Ann could not hear the conversation, but she could hear the pain in both their voices. Jonathan held out his arms to Angel, and she went to him, but Sue Ann could tell she did not feel secure yet.

"We should really go, and let you get to know each other. I told the cab driver to wait. We will be staying in town until tomorrow, to make sure Angel is all right. Whether Angel stays with you or not is her decision as well, Mr. and Mrs. Shockey, just as her father requested."

"I apologize, Sue Ann, but I sent the cab away after

having Angel's luggage removed. My driver will take you to your hotel, but there is something Diane and I want to share with you before you leave. Please, will you and Betsy come with us to the gallery?"

Jonathan led the group upstairs. Diane had Angel by the hand and would not let go. After turning down a long hallway, Jonathan opened the door on the end and asked them all to come inside. The room was large and dark. With a flashlight, he directed them each to a comfortable chair, the kind wealthy people put in their special media rooms.

As soon as they were all seated, music filled the room—Indian flute music setting the stage for the real show. Clear strobe lights moved slowly around the room like waves of soft moonlight, keeping time to the music. Then the Northern Lights filled every wall in massive paintings, Shade's masterpieces, circling around them just as the Aurora did in its natural setting in Alaska.

Angel left her seat and walked gingerly to the one she recognized as the painting from the Fairbanks Museum of Art. She dropped to her knees, looking up, tears running down her cheeks as the magic from her father's fingers swept across the wall, a panorama representing all that was the father she had only recently come to know, understand, and love.

Sue Ann and Betsy joined Angel, who stood with them, and together they held hands and swayed, soaking in Shade's Sky Walkers. Through their tears, they smiled, and soon smiles turned to laughter and joy. Shade had captured the excitement and happiness as only someone who loved the lights could do. Soon Shade's parents joined them, and Angel's grandparents held on to all that was left of their son, their granddaughter.

When the flute music faded and the paintings were again shrouded in darkness, Jonathan explained.

"I have been buying Jon's paintings for five years now, as soon as I was offered them by a friend of my son's, a banker named William Donovan. Jon, or I guess I need to get used to calling him Shade, never knew I was his main fan. Half of the paintings I bought from other lovers of his work and paid twice what I would have if I could have secured them first. But the painting Diane and I love most is not in the gallery, and I did not have to purchase it. It was delivered to us a week ago without our even knowing it existed. We have no idea who sent it."

Again Sue Ann found herself following the man to another room. Jonathan Shockey was accustomed to being in charge, and it showed. Jonathan stopped outside the door.

"This was Jon's room growing up, and we thought it should be yours now, Angel, if you decide to stay with us, or when you come to visit. We packed up all the sports memorabilia, and Diane decorated the room to what she thinks is more suitable for a beautiful young lady. Of course, you can make any changes you want." He opened the door and once they were inside, he turned on the overhead light.

It was a beautiful bedroom, huge, with its own sitting and studying areas, but the most outstanding thing about it was the portrait hanging over the mantel, a large painting but much smaller than the ones they had just experienced.

Shade had painted a self-portrait, all from his

imagination, or perhaps from his longing for such a scene. He was standing in a winter landscape, surrounded by snow-covered spruce trees and distant mountains, and was gazing up at the Northern Lights above and around him. Standing in front of him, wrapped in his arms, was Angel. Their identical sky-blue eyes danced with Aurora, who made father and daughter smile as they gazed upward.

Chapter Twenty-Five
Blessed in Love

Sue Ann and Betsy did not return to Moose Springs after their trip to Philadelphia with Angel but headed to Mississippi instead. Sue Ann needed time with Elizabeth, the only person she could talk to about losing Shade. Each night, Elizabeth and Sue Ann sat on the porch at Parrish Oaks, and Sue Ann told her friend stories of her time with Shade, leaving out most of his sordid past. Elizabeth cried with Sue Ann and told her, as she had many times before, she should be writing this in a book.

"No. It's too soon. I'm more concerned about trying to get on with my life right now. Do you think I'm jinxed when it comes to love, Elizabeth?" Sue Ann gave Elizabeth her full attention, knowing her friend would somehow ease her hurt.

"No, my sweet, dear friend. I do not think you are jinxed in love. In fact, I think you are blessed in love. I've never seen a woman give so much of herself in a relationship. And how your men love you! Even Tate loved you, Sue Ann. We used to talk about you all the time when we were together—which wasn't that much, but it was enough to see the stars in his eyes, and every star had your name on it."

"So what happened to Tate? Why did he leave me? Did you ever figure it out?" Sue Ann rocked, looking down through the giant oaks that gave her parents' Victorian home its name.

"No, I didn't. Don't think I haven't thought about hiring a detective just to see if they could find him and see if he had a good explanation, but I was afraid I might wring his neck in the process. Besides, you and Betsy have done just fine. Look at you, Dr. Parish. You've made something of yourself and established a new career and a new home in Alaska, even if I am still mad at you about that. You're an adventurer, Sue Ann. It just took you seventeen years to really get going at it. You, my friend, will find love again. I have no doubt about it."

****

Sue Ann bought an old Jeep in Red Lodge to leave at her cabin in the mountains. A forest ranger who knew the place well told her she could drive right to the cabin but only if she had something with four-wheel drive and could take a beating. What she purchased was actually an old forestry Jeep that the ranger assured her could get her in and out of there.

"We should be close." Sue Ann was enjoying the ride, and so was Betsy. Shade had indeed given them a piece of heaven, not only in the form of a cabin but also in the many acres that surrounded it. They wound around with the old forestry road trail, passing meadows full of wildflowers, all in the shadows of snowcapped mountains.

"There it is!" Betsy yelled, as they pulled up in front of the two-story cabin that attempted to hide in a grove of aspen. Betsy was standing, holding onto the rollbar. She had insisted they take the top down to be able to take in the full, heavenly landscape of mountains and lush forests, to breathe in the smell of evergreens and sage, and to listen to the welcoming symphony of streams cascading by with their ripples full of indigenous trout beckoning to the newcomers.

Betsy was already up the steps, to stand looking out at the panorama of their new second home. "This is far out!" Her "Woohoo!" echoed through the trees, loud enough to ricochet off the closest mountain peak. "I love you, Shade!" She cupped her hands and yelled to the mountaintop. Tears ran down her cheeks, and soon she and her mother stood arm in arm in tearful remembering.

Sue Ann unlocked the door and let Betsy inside while she went to retrieve their luggage, giving her heart time to revert to its slow, painful beat. As she headed back, she stopped and breathed in the sight of the weathered, chinked logs, thinking it was indeed a replica of Montana's pioneer history, a rich antiquity only Shade would think of for her and Betsy. She held her ring out and Shade's blue eyes appeared, looking up at her with a twinkle as they always did when sunlight was captured in the blue.

"Yes, my darling. This is where I can heal, but I'll never forget you, and I'll always love you."

"Mom, hurry! It's...it's amazing!" Betsy left the door and ran to her mom, taking the heaviest suitcase with one hand and pushing her mom forward with the other.

The cabin smelled of old logs and pioneer days, and Sue Ann knew this would be where she would write her first novel, a romance from the Victorian era; a story of homesteads and mail order brides; of women who could wear a fancy dress and twirl a parasol and yet could also straddle a horse, put up and tear down barbed wire fences, and herd cattle. She put the suitcase down and walked to the huge stone fireplace and ran her hand along the mantel hewn from one gigantic log, mounted with its flat side up.

"The fireplace is huge, Mom. I think we can put a barbecue grill in one side." Betsy circled the room. "And look! You don't have to go to the dump for furniture." Betsy plopped down on the overstuffed couch and sank in. "Now, this is a real sofa."

Sue Ann wandered over to a long, primitive, harvest table with six straight chairs and a long bench. Its rustic wood top reminded her of the one in her cabin in Moose Springs, and for just a second she was homesick. She noticed a new-looking switch on the wall and flipped it up. The great room flooded with light.

"We have electricity, but it looks like it was recently added. Hmmm! I think Shade planned this in the last few months. Maybe it was supposed to be ours to share with him."

Betsy went to the large window facing the front and pulled back the curtains. Dust flew from the fabric, reminiscent of Old Sawyer's town cabin when they'd first bought it.

"Oh, Mom, look!"

Mother and daughter stood arm in arm and gazed at the most magnificent piece of natural art they had ever seen—equal to the Canadian Rockies—or perhaps even better.

"And thanks to Shade, it's ours, Betsy. I just wish my love was standing here holding us as we view it."

"Shade is here, Mom. He's right here." Betsy

placed her hand over her heart.

Their somber moment was interrupted when they saw a man walking up to the cabin from the forest side, where there was no road. Sue Ann's heart rate sped up, thinking of the murderer who had taken Shade away from them. She felt Betsy tense in her arms.

"I'm sure he's harmless, Betsy. Don't be afraid."

Sue Ann left Betsy and headed out onto the porch, and as he approached she saw the man had a large package, wrapped in heavy rope to allow it to be carried on his back.

"Hello," he yelled as he came around the hitching post, another replica from an earlier age.

"Hi," Sue Ann answered, as Betsy came out to stand beside her, arms folded.

The man came up the steps. As he did so, he removed the package from his back and leaned it against the post, then extended his hand.

"I'm Custer Larson, your nearest neighbor. Well, that's a little misleading. Fact is, I'm your only neighbor. My cabin is about two miles down the trail through the aspens."

"I'm Sue Ann Parish." Sue Ann shook Custer's hand and smiled. Custer had dark eyes and complexion, with high cheekbones, but his long black braid intermixed with a few streaks of gray was what gave away his Native American heritage.

"What's in the package?" Betsy asked and then remembered her manners. "Oh, sorry. I'm Betsy." She extended her hand and gave Custer a good firm handshake.

"Well, I don't know. I was headed up the trail to where I leave my truck parked, and I met the delivery truck trying to bump its way out here. The guy asked me if I would drop it off. Said the new owners would be coming in a day or two. I couldn't just leave it on the porch, like I hear these guys do in town, so I took it to my cabin. I was out feeding my horses and heard this yell that sounded like it was backed by happiness, not distress, so I figured the new owners had arrived." Custer cut his eyes at Betsy and smiled.

Custer turned the package around. "Yep, it's yours. Says Dr. Sue Ann Parish right here on the front. Do you want me to carry it in for you? It's pretty heavy."

"Oh, please. Thank you, Custer." Sue Ann stood back for him to go in ahead of her, and he laid the package on the harvest table.

"Well, Betsy, let's see what it is, if I can figure out how to open the box, that is." Sue Ann headed for the kitchen to try to find a knife or something to pry off the heavy-duty staples holding the cardboard ends closed.

"Here. I'll help you with that." Custer pulled off the loose ropes he had put around the package for carrying it and took a hunting knife out of his sheath, prepared to open the ends of the box. When Betsy saw the blade, she gasped and ran to her mother. Sue Ann held Betsy as she trembled, and Custer looked confused and concerned. He quickly returned the knife to the sheath.

"I'm sorry, Little One. I didn't mean to frighten you."

He seemed to sense something terrible had happened to Betsy and set about to calm her. He took the sheath off his belt and laid it on top of the box, moving back away from it and away from Betsy.

"Now, Little One, you can go over to the table and

take the knife out of the sheath. You don't have to be afraid of me, ever, and you're a Montana mountain woman now, so you need to know how to use a hunting knife."

Betsy looked at her mother, and Sue Ann nodded her head, knowing this was something Betsy needed to do to begin her own healing process.

Betsy walked to the knife, her eyes glued to it, and pulled it out of the leather sheath. Her hand shook, and she held onto the handle with two hands.

"Good job. Now keep looking at the knife, but mostly look at the hand holding it. That hand controls everything the knife does, whether it's for good or for evil. Hold it with one hand and put the tip under each staple and pry them off on the end facing your mom." Custer watched but did not go near her. Soon, the staples were all loose. Betsy put the knife back in the sheath, picked it up, and walked to Custer. With moist eyes and a big smile, she placed the sheath and knife in his hands.

"Thank you, Custer." Betsy hugged the big man, and Sue Ann was surprised when he put his arms around her and hugged her tight, putting his head down on hers like Shade always did. Custer was tall like Shade, and was physically fit, although he was not musclebound.

"That's a brave little one. You and I are going to be good friends."

Sue Ann smiled, not knowing what had just happened but knowing it was a good thing.

"Custer, would you help me take it out of the box?" Sue Ann asked. "It appears to be a picture."

Custer grabbed hold of the picture as Sue Ann and

Betsy pulled the box away. He tore away the brown paper wrapping, turned the picture to face Sue Ann and Betsy, and watched as they held to each other with their hearts and eyes overflowing. Sue Ann had moved behind Betsy and put her arm around her with her face touching her daughter's, the same pose as in the painting Shade must have finished just before his death. Who had sent it to Red Lodge? She could only guess it had been Jake, following more of the directions left by Shade.

With Custer's help, they hung the painting of the lookalikes in their green fox-trimmed parkas over the stone fireplace. Sue Ann and Betsy's emerald green eyes perfectly matched the deepest green of the Northern Lights covering the sky over them and forming the perfect backdrop.

"It's a sign, Mama, from Shade, telling us we're gonna be all right."

****

Sue Ann had asked for a leave of absence until late in September, knowing sooner would be too early to return to Moose Springs. Betsy needed more time, and the Beartooth Mountains and their new friend Custer seemed to be just what mother and daughter needed.

The two months following their arrival in Montana were filled with hiking to high mountain lakes and fly fishing for indigenous cutthroat, rainbows, and brookies. To Sue Ann's surprise, Custer always used a fishing basket, a creel, to put the fish in so they would remain fresh in the water for cooking over a campfire that night. Many nights found them camping under the stars in the Beartooth Mountains, with stories told around the campfire, mostly Custer's stories of his ancestors, the Crows. He explained that he was a half-breed, his mother being full-blooded Crow. His white father had insisted his oldest son be named after the man whose death near the Little Bighorn River had made it into the history books.

Once again, Sue Ann and Betsy learned to laugh and enjoy life. Custer's voice was mesmerizing in its slow staccato, and Betsy never tired of his stories.

****

It was the end of September and Sue Ann and Betsy's last night before heading home to Alaska. The mountains were painted in fall colors, mostly yellows, and the highest peaks had already put on their snowcaps. It was a dark, cool night, so Sue Ann and Custer put on their jackets and sat on the porch in the rocking chairs Sue Ann had purchased when they first arrived. She had cooked trout almandine and wild blueberry pie for their friend this night, her way of thanking him for helping her and Betsy.

As they sat drinking their last cup of coffee before Custer headed back down the trail to his cabin, Sue Ann opened up her heart, telling him how much she had loved Shade and how he had died as Raven, saving Betsy and Angel. She explained this was why Betsy had been so fearful of the knife that first day.

Without hesitation, Custer reached out and took Sue Ann's hand, squeezing it and holding it tightly in his. In his deep, methodical Crow voice, Custer spoke of the raven.

"The raven in most Native American folklore is considered a trickster, a smart animal who takes advantage of his peer creatures and who can shape-shift into whatever is necessary to get what he wants and needs. I always felt the raven got a bad rap from my ancestors.

"I've observed this wonderful creature, the largest member of the crow family, and know him to be highly intelligent, like chimpanzees and dolphins. In the wild, I have seen the raven make his own toys out of pine cones and twigs, and I've seen him attempt to break open a dead animal carcass with his beak—and when not able to do so, make sounds like a dying animal to attract wolves. After the wolves broke the carcass open and ate all they wanted, the raven ate his fill.

"Ravens can mimic humans better than parrots, but here is the one fact, Sue Ann, that shows his great intelligence more than any other."

Custer looked Sue Ann in the eyes with a serious expression and held her hand even tighter.

"The raven mates for life, finding one love with which to share his life. I guess you could say the raven loves his mate forever—and then some."

Before Custer left that night, he left his hunting knife and sheath for Betsy.

"She can leave it here or take it with her," Custer said. "A mountain girl needs a good knife." Custer paused and looked Sue Ann in the eyes. "Like you, Sue Ann, need a good man to love you, but we'll talk about that when you come next time."

Sue Ann watched as Custer walked, in the moonlight, down the wooded path to his cabin.

****

Sue Ann and Betsy left for Alaska the next day, and even though Moose Springs was home, Sue Ann dreaded going back into the cabin without Shade. She knew she would sense him in every part of Old

Sawyer's town home and hoped that, with time, she would see the memories of him as a wonderful thing, without so much pain attached. As she drove across the pass, heading back to Moose Springs, she looked down at the ring on her left hand and felt like a widow even though she had not been through an actual ceremony. She held the ring up, and the moonlight reflected off the blue diamond, giving her the illusion of Shade looking at her with eyes that could send her into a spin with one twinkle.

As she passed by the spot where she'd had the wreck, she slowed, and in her mind she could hear him frantically calling her name. A little piece farther, she saw the turnoff to his cabin, or where his cabin had once stood, and her heart sank even deeper. More grief had been added to the disaster when Shade's cabin burned to the ground a few days after his death. No cause was ever determined for the fire. Sue Ann was glad Betsy was asleep and could not see her crying.

It was late when they arrived back at the cabin, and both were in somber moods when they entered. The cabin was too empty without Shade and Angel. Betsy went right to bed, not able to deal with reality right now, and Sue Ann set to unpacking not only her clothes but her grief. It was time to get on with life, but she did not know how this was going to be possible.

****

She and Betsy had been back several days, but Sue Ann would still not let herself go to where Shade's cabin had stood. As hard as she tried, she was unable to cope with her loss, even though it had been months since she lost him. But one night, a week after she and Betsy returned to the little cabin they loved, she found herself needing to go.

It was late, and Sue Ann couldn't sleep again, haunted by the emptiness of her bed. She pulled her sweats on and walked outside to sit on the edge of the porch, like she and Shade had done so many times. The Northern Lights were more brilliant than she had ever seen them, although the short days were just beginning.

Betsy was in Fairbanks with Helen, celebrating Lena's last therapy session and total recuperation from being shot. Before Sue Ann could stop herself, she was in the truck heading to Shade's cabin site. She was glad she had grabbed his leather jacket as she headed out the door. Sue Ann had meant to retire the jacket, to wrap it in plastic and tuck it away in a box just to preserve the wonderful scent of his aftershave, but she could not stand to see the hook empty when she entered and exited through the arctic entry.

"Maybe when his scent leaves, the hurt will leave," she had told herself. And now here she was walking through more good memories of Shade. She searched through the ashes and debris for something, anything, but in reality she needed no reminders. He would forever be in her heart. Shade had taught her to let go and to love again after seventeen years of holding onto the phantom Tate Douglas, Betsy's real father, but now Sue Ann found it even harder to let go of Shade.

As she walked to where his studio had stood, she found the remains of the soapstone stove that did not—could not—burn, and sank to her knees in the spot where Shade had held her in his arms in the easy chair after saving her from the wreck. She looked up, and Aurora was waltzing, holding the skirt of her iridescent ball gown as she danced, dipping and leaping across

Shade's heaven. It was the exact image of his masterpiece but with heavenly strobes fueling the goddess's graceful moves.

In her mind, Sue Ann could hear Shade's deep, dramatic voice.

"Do you hear it? The crackling noise? It's the voice of the spirit beings, the Sky Dwellers, trying to communicate with you. The Sky Dwellers only speak to those of us who believe. Always show respect, Sue Ann. Never shout at them, or shake your fists at them. Speak in a whisper, and sometimes, you will hear what the Sky Dwellers are telling you."

She bent her ear to the sky and heard Shade whisper, *"Sue Ann, I'll love you forever—and then some."*

A word about the author...

Dr. Sue Clifton is a retired principal, fly fisher, ghost hunter, and published author. Dr. Sue, as she is known, can't remember a time when she did not write, beginning with two plays published at sixteen. Her writing career was placed on hold while she traveled the world with her husband Woody in his career, as well as with her own career as a teacher and principal in Mississippi, Alaska, New Zealand, and on the Northern Cheyenne Reservation in Montana. The places Dr. Sue has lived provide rich background and settings for the novels she creates.

Dr. Sue now divides her time between Montana, Mississippi, and Arkansas and enjoys traveling with Woody as well as with her 5000-plus fly fishing group Sisters On the Fly. She loves all things vintage, including her 1950 camper and her 1951 Plymouth Savoy "Woodie 2."

Dr. Sue is the author of seven novels, four in her Daughters of Parrish Oaks series with The Wild Rose Press, Inc. and three paranormal mysteries elsewhere.

Visit Dr. Sue at:
        http://www.drsueclifton.com

Thank you for purchasing
this publication of The Wild Rose Press, Inc.

If you enjoyed the story, we would appreciate your
letting others know by leaving a review.

For other wonderful stories,
please visit our on-line bookstore at
www.thewildrosepress.com.

For questions or more information
contact us at
info@thewildrosepress.com.

The Wild Rose Press, Inc.
www.thewildrosepress.com

Stay current with The Wild Rose Press, Inc.

Like us on Facebook

https://www.facebook.com/TheWildRosePress

And Follow us on Twitter
https://twitter.com/WildRosePress